THE BEAR'S BROKEN OMEGA

A.J. CANE

CHAPTER

ONE

R*EID*

I dug my fingernails into my palms until they broke the skin, desperate to distract myself from the lonely ache in my chest that felt like it would swallow me whole if I let it.

My instincts screamed at me to seek out Trent, my mate, but I refused to give him the satisfaction. He might control me in all the ways that mattered, but I was determined to hold onto whatever shreds of dignity I could.

Flopping onto the ratty bed, I winced as a broken spring poked my back and I adjusted my position, pulling a threadbare blanket over myself. God, I wished they'd give me a better way of staying warm. They might be shifters, but I wasn't, and I didn't run as hot as them.

Curling into a ball, I breathed in slowly, trying to calm my nerves, but grimaced when my nose filled with the scent of mold from the stained walls. How could the pack stand it? Surely their sensitive noses should mean they'd make more of an effort to keep the place clean—or at least livable.

But no, it didn't seem to bother them.

Then again, not much did.

No one had protested when Trent violated me by mating me against my will. No one said a word about the omegas who were kept in the basement or the ones who'd been assimilated into the pack but were still little more than prisoners. The alphas under Trent's rule happily took advantage of their prisoners—in every possible way—without a second thought.

They were monsters who ought to be put down. Unfortunately, I hadn't figured out how to do that yet. I might be a powerful warlock, with more magic reserves than most, but between my lack of training and inability to do anything that might harm my mate, I'd never been able to bring myself to either escape or take down the pack.

I loathed the Pack Alpha with every fiber of my being, but a twisted part of me that was controlled by my magic loved him too. It fucking sucked.

If only I hadn't been stupid enough to fall for his charming lies, even temporarily. That had been all it took to condemn me to this life where the only choice I had was whether to give in and lose all sense of self or cling to the remnants of the person I used to be, even when it only seemed to cause more harm than good.

Voices filtered through the wall and a moment later, I sensed Trent tug on our bond. I'd heard mate bonds could be pleasant, but the warped thing between us only ever caused me pain. It wrapped around my ribs and made it difficult to breathe, the sensation tightening with each second. I knew it wouldn't let up until I did what he wanted.

I resisted for as long as I could, until my chest felt like it might explode, and then stumbled out of the pitiful room and into the living area. No one was there so I followed the sound of noise to the foyer just inside the front door, then came to an abrupt halt.

What the fuck?

The room was in absolute carnage, with the pack all in their wolf forms, facing off against an eclectic set of adversaries. Bears, a mountain lion, a big wolf, and several birds that flew above heads and dive-bombed Trent's wolves, pecking at their eyes.

My heart stuttered, then lifted.

Fucking finally.

Someone had come to help. Trent must have fucked with the wrong clan and they were going to make him pay.

But as quickly as my spirits rose, they dropped again as a bear lunged at me. Luckily for me, one of Trent's wolves intercepted it.

Terror flashed through me, freezing my blood in my veins as I realized that the interlopers wouldn't help me if they thought I was willingly on Trent's side. They'd kill me too.

A snout shoved me from behind and I stumbled.

Move, Trent said in my mind. *Do something.*

I lifted my hands and sent a shower of blue sparks into a space between two shifters, praying I wouldn't hurt anyone. I'd never been taught to use offensive magic—that was the last thing my coven would have wanted me to know—but I'd figured out how to throw sparks when I'd reacted instinctively to being hit by one of Trent's wolves, and I'd been practicing it since then.

Unfortunately, my aim was shit and the sparks struck one of the larger bears even though I'd meant to miss. He roared in pain and shied away.

I glanced at the door that led through to the kitchen, wondering if I could make a run for it through the kitchen window, but at that moment, the massive wolf fighting on the side of the interlopers leapt at Trent and they collided in a flurry of claws, teeth, and fur.

Attack, Trent barked, yanking on the bond once again.

Reluctantly, I sent out another shower of sparks, wishing I could vanish as they hit the enemy wolf and the smell of singed fur soured the air. I was just glad he hadn't thought to ask me to shield him. I hoped someone did what I couldn't and took him down.

Something smacked into me from the side, knocking the air from my lungs. I stared up into a snarling mouth full of razor-sharp teeth. Briefly, I considered trying to get the shifter off me, but Trent hadn't ordered me to and I wasn't going to do anything to help him if I didn't have to.

Agony tore through me. I looked around frantically, feeling like my insides were being ripped out through my belly button. The wolf that Trent had been fighting had gotten the upper hand.

An awful ringing filled my ears and I clutched at my chest, tears leaking from my eyes as a part of my very soul was destroyed. I screamed, the pain worse than anything I'd ever experienced, as if the skin was being peeled from my body and salt poured on the exposed tissue.

Trent was dead.

All of a sudden, the beast was off me, and I rushed across the room, throwing myself on Trent's body. He'd already returned to his human form and his throat was a pulpy mess of blood and bone.

Sobs wracked me and I grabbed his shoulders and shook him, that traitorous part of myself that considered him a true mate desperate to force him to open his eyes and blink up at me, even as the rest of me was horrified by the humiliating display of grief for a man who'd been no more than a captor and abuser.

Reality didn't seem to matter. He'd been a part of me, and now he was gone. My psyche was splitting in two.

I reared back and screamed, light blazing around me in a visible display of my sorrow that I had absolutely no control over. My magic reacted to strong emotions, but I'd never had much say in how it responded or what it did.

The same wolf that had taken out my mate pounced on me, bowling me onto my back. His green eyes stared into mine as he lowered his blood-covered muzzle to my throat.

So, this was how my life would end.

Gulping, I shut my eyes, preparing for the fatal blow.

"Stop!"

My eyes flew open. The wolf above me looked as startled as I was.

A naked man dropped to his knees beside us, bleeding from a shoulder wound. He was broad and muscular, with an immense build that made me think he was one of the bear shifters I'd seen earlier. His face was craggy and his eyes were a deep shade of brown, like chocolate melting in the sun.

The fractured pieces of my broken heart shifted, a couple of them knitting back together.

"He's my mate," the man said, his nostrils flaring as if he was inhaling my scent to confirm this ridiculous allegation. "I couldn't smell it before. The bond with Trent must have altered his scent, but now it's clear. Don't hurt him. Please."

The wolf growled, but a moment later he shifted into a muscular man with long, dark hair. "Keep him secured. He's dangerous."

The liar nodded, his gaze never wavering from my face. "Clay, get the cuffs that are spelled to bind magic."

Another man jogged over with a pair of cuffs. My breath caught in my throat and I thrashed but couldn't break free.

Use magic, idiot.

I only wished I knew how.

One of the cuffs was slapped onto my wrist and my muscles went slack. I stared at the ceiling, tears pricking in the backs of my eyes.

Trent had been killed, but I wasn't free. I was still a prisoner with no say over my own fate. Honestly, I should have known better than to hope for more. I was a tool that people used. Had been for my whole life.

Gods only knew what fresh hell would await me once these new shifters figured out how to control my magic.

R*EID*
My captors unloaded me outside a building that could have been mistaken for a house if not for the small plaque on the front door declaring it to be a medical clinic. I wondered idly if they intended to experiment on me somehow, but I couldn't bring myself to care as much as I should.

Later, I had no doubt my new situation would sink in properly, but for now, I'd mentally detached from my own body. It was the only way I knew how to survive the debilitating pain of Trent's death. I ached, and it wasn't fair, and I hated that I was grieving him.

He'd forced an unwanted mating bond on me. Yet despite the fact my feelings for him had been magically induced, I grieved him anyway.

My eyes stung and my cheeks were wet but I was scarcely aware of those sensations when a man with a silver mustache opened the door and waved us inside. The cuffs chafed like salt on an open wound, but the pain wasn't physical, only psychological, so I couldn't tune it out the same way I had everything else.

Once again, I found myself cuffed and at someone else's mercy. Once again, being untrained had meant that I wasn't able to protect myself. And now, I'd find out what price I was going to pay for that shortcoming.

We entered a reception area attached to a small waiting room. I jerked away from the man who'd escorted me to the door and made my way to the corner. I dropped to the floor with the wall at my back, brought my knees up to my chest, and rested my forehead on them. Tears immediately soaked the fabric of my jeans.

People crowded into the cramped space. Several unfamiliar voices all spoke over each other and I was too emotionally exhausted to pick up on the thread of the conversation. My fingertips were cold and I dug them into my shins in a fruitless attempt to defrost them. A heat pump whirred overhead, but I was chilled to my core. I didn't think I'd ever feel warm again.

"Hello." I sensed someone kneel in front of me but I didn't look up. "My name is Dr. Black. What's yours?"

I didn't reply. The voice was kind, but I knew a trick when I saw—heard?—one. This man with the gentle voice had been sent to lull me into complacency.

"Are you hurt anywhere?" he persisted.

I kept quiet. As if I would give them any information they could use against me. They already had me as defenseless as a kitten because of the damn cuffs. What more did they want?

A soft touch brushed my shoulder and I flinched. Dr. Black immediately withdrew. When he left, I let out a breath and sobbed quietly into my jeans until another person approached.

"Hi Reid, I'm Nurse Allison. I'd like to check you over and see if you need treatment. Is that okay?"

How did she know my name?

I drew my knees even closer to my chest and shook my head. I didn't want anything to do with these people. They'd murdered my mate.

Good, a voice whispered deep inside me. *He deserved to die.*

Guilt swamped me as soon as I had the thought. He'd been my *mate.* How could I even think such a thing?

He was your jailer, not your lover.

In truth, it didn't matter what he'd been. My soul hurt, regardless.

Someone grabbed my arm and I flailed, my heart racing and adrenaline spiking through me as I fought to protect myself. But then a blood pressure sleeve looped around my arm and I realized they weren't trying to hurt me. At least, not yet. I looked at the floor and let the doctor do as he wanted.

"Is it true?" a woman asked from somewhere else in the room. "Is he Zander's mate?"

Zander.

Was that the name of the enormous bear shifter with the chocolate brown eyes?

"That's what Zander said," a man replied, his tone dubious. "Is he here?"

My lungs constricted and I burrowed tighter into the corner, grateful when the doctor removed the sleeve so I could wrap my arms around myself again.

He couldn't be here already. If another alpha tried to claim me on the same night I lost my mate, I might die. I honestly wasn't sure I could survive going through something so traumatic when every part of me felt like an exposed nerve.

"Not yet." The woman tutted. "Poor dear."

There was a rustle of fabric and then a matronly lady

with a square face and kind brown eyes lowered herself to the floor in front of me.

"Hello, sweetheart. I'm Melinda Blackwood. I'm here to take care of you, okay?"

No. Not okay. I had no idea what "taking care of" meant. Was she going to get rid of me?

Surely not. If they were going to kill me, they'd have done it already, right?

They wanted me for more than that.

"First, let's get this blood off of you."

A hot cloth dabbed at my neck. I hadn't even realized that I'd had any blood on me, although I supposed it made sense considering how I'd thrown myself on Trent's body.

It was my mate's blood.

Bile rose up my throat and I gagged on it.

She shushed me and patted my back. "You're okay, sweetheart. I'm getting it off you. We're going to change you into something clean and warm, all right?"

I stiffened. They were going to strip me?

"Don't worry," she murmured as if reading my mind. "I'll clear the room. No one will see anything. You're safe here."

Safe. I almost laughed. I'd never been safe. I certainly wasn't now.

Somewhere behind me, I heard my name and tensed again. It was one of the omegas who'd been kept in the pack house with me. She was telling someone about how Trent had tricked me into going on a date with him six months ago only to assault me and force a mating bond.

I wanted to shout at her. To yell and scream until she stopped sharing what she had no right to. I didn't want these people to know my story. All they'd do was use it against me. But the last of my energy had deserted me and I couldn't summon enough strength to speak a word.

"Please leave me alone with Reid." Melinda's tone was completely calm and strangely soothing.

"Zander is outside," Dr. Black said. "He wants to see him."

I whimpered. Please, no. I couldn't... It was too soon. Maybe tomorrow I'd be strong enough to make it through whatever lay in store for me, but not yet, not now.

"Don't let him in," Melinda said. "He can be patient."

Thank the gods. Perhaps I was only delaying the inevitable, but I'd take what small wins I could get. After all, I may have exchanged one prison for another, but I was still a prisoner.

"He's determined," Dr. Black replied.

I bit my lip until I tasted blood. *Please don't let him touch me yet.*

CHAPTER

THREE

Z ANDER

"I'm afraid I can't allow you in to see him," Dr. Black said, his elegant mouth turned down at the corners.

"But I need to," I protested, my bear battering against my skin, desperate to break free.

Our mate was in pain. Our mate was scared. My bear wanted to comfort the young warlock and nuzzle away his distress.

"I need to know that he's all right."

My emotions had been in turmoil ever since I'd scented the warlock after his bond with that evil bastard Trent had been broken. I'd already been told that the poor omega had been forced into the arrangement and basically used as a tool and a weapon, but he'd still had a bond with Trent, whose death must be excruciating for him.

I needed to be with him.

I growled. "Doc, you know I respect you, but I have to see him with my own eyes."

Dr. Black's grimace deepened. "I'm sorry, but I must

insist. This comes directly from your mother. She's the only one the boy has allowed interaction with."

I gritted my teeth. Momma was the one keeping me from my mate? How could she? Didn't she know how much it hurt to have met him but be unable to see him or get close to him?

"The good news," he continued as if he couldn't see the murder in my eyes, "is that he seems to be the healthiest of the omegas that were rescued today, physically speaking. He doesn't appear malnourished or bruised, although we'll have to confirm that later. Of course, there are other types of assault than beating..."

A growl rumbled through me and I fought the urge to tear the door from its hinges, knock the doctor aside, and go to my mate.

The thought of Trent raping the beautiful little warlock with cherubic cheeks and soulful blue eyes made me wish I'd been the one to kill that son of a bitch. He hadn't been good enough to lick my mate's shoes let alone anything else.

I could only hope that Trent hadn't repeated the assault after mating him. Doing it once was horrific enough, but doing so continuously when there was no purpose behind it would be absolutely sickening. I had an awful feeling though. It was distinctly possible that the warlock's bond with Trent had made him long for sexual contact between them.

A magically forged connection didn't make it consensual.

All it meant was that *my* mate had been controlled and coerced using magic that he was unable to resist.

Claws burst through my fingertips and my teeth elongated.

"Zander," Dr. Black warned. "This is exactly why you

can't come in. He's been through enough without facing down an alpha bear shifter. He's already been mistreated by a mate. There's no need to terrify him further."

I deflated, my claws and teeth retracting. I knew he was right, but every part of me rebelled. How could I ensure my mate was safe if I couldn't even see him?

I closed my eyes and allowed my other senses to take over. When I concentrated, I could hear soft breathing coming from within the clinic, with faint hitches that made me think he was crying. I inhaled traces of salt and ozone—from his tears and the unique aroma of warlock magic.

A shudder ran through me.

"Fine," I said, then turned and stripped, leaving my clothes in a pile on the doorstep as I allowed a shift to roll through me.

My bear came to the fore and, as soon as I was steady on the ground, I took off across the street, around the residences separating the doctor's clinic from the surrounding national park, and into the woods.

Guilt tugged at the edge of my consciousness but I ignored it. Yes, people needed me, but there was no way I could be my usual unflappable self right now. All I'd do was make everything worse. It was for the best if I ran off all of my agitation.

I dodged around trees and sucked in cold, crisp mouthfuls of air until my legs burned and the jitters under my skin had eased, then I circled back around to collect my clothes. I shifted when the clinic came into sight.

Dad was leaning against the wall of the clinic, his hands in his jacket pockets, waiting for me. As I approached, he straightened, gathered my clothes and tossed them to me. I caught them and dressed quickly. Shifters had a higher body temperature than humans so we tended to stay warm for longer, but that didn't mean the chill air wouldn't get to me if I walked around naked outside in the middle of winter.

"I know this must be hard," Dad said, and all I could think was that he had no idea how I felt. He and Momma had been high school sweethearts. His mate hadn't been traumatized. They'd had it easy.

He raised his eyebrows and I wondered if every single one of my thoughts had played across my face. "You need to be patient with him. He's been through a lot and it could be weeks or months before he's recovered enough to even consider mating again."

"I know." I did. But I also couldn't deny it stung that my mate didn't seem to feel the same pull toward me that I felt for him. It was self-centered, but I'd always assumed that when I met my mate, they'd be eager to get to know me. I didn't know how to proceed with someone like my warlock. "I'll give him time and space to heal."

"Good." Dad nodded at me as if he'd expected nothing less. "Perhaps you can introduce yourself tomorrow and take it from there, but go slow."

Anything less than claiming him now felt glacial, but I didn't have a choice. I wasn't going to fail the first test of being a decent mate.

The question was, how the hell was I supposed to just go home and go to bed when I knew my mate was suffering?

CHAPTER
FOUR

R*EID*

The rich scent of coffee woke me, but I didn't trust it. I blinked quickly to clear my vision and took in my surroundings. The sun streamed through the window, blindingly bright, a floorboard creaked in the hall, and the walls seemed to close in around me.

Nothing was familiar, and every sound made me curl even more tightly into myself, desperate to hide from whatever threat would appear first.

I knew how these things went. Any perceived kindness was a trap. If they intended to offer me coffee or breakfast, it was because they wanted something from me in return.

Checking that I still wore the sweatpants and T-shirt I'd been given last night, I allowed myself to experience a kernel of relief that it didn't seem like anything was amiss. Sleeping in unfamiliar circumstances was risky but I'd been too tired to resist and the bed they'd given me was the most comfortable I'd been on in months.

"Good morning, sleepyhead." Melinda breezed into the room and came straight to the bedside, carrying a cup of coffee and a plate piled high with eggs, bacon, and toast. She set it on the nightstand. "Here's your breakfast."

I eyed the food warily. My stomach grumbled but I didn't reach for it. For all I knew, the meal could be poisoned.

"Go on," she urged. "I made it myself."

I narrowed my eyes at her, evaluating. She seemed genuine; so far she'd been kind to me, but perhaps that was just to make me amenable to their plans.

With a sigh, she picked up a strip of bacon and popped it into her mouth. "It's perfectly safe."

I didn't point out that she could have taken the antidote to the poison before coming in here, or that she might have a vial of it waiting outside the room to drink as soon as she left.

Melinda started to walk away and for a moment, I thought it would be that easy to get rid of her, but then she dragged a chair over and sat a few feet from me.

"Would you like to hear how the other omegas who were there with you are?" she asked, crossing her legs and smoothing the front of her neatly ironed pants.

I shrugged. I should care, but I was in survival mode. If something wasn't a direct threat, I couldn't summon the energy to feel much of anything about it.

I sat there, staring into space as she told me about how they'd gotten in touch with the families of two of the captive omegas and moved one into the local Omega House. She must have been paying a lot of attention to have picked up as much information as she had.

Hunger gnawed at my stomach. I hadn't eaten since yesterday morning. The pack hadn't treated me as badly as the other omegas, but I was still only given two basic meals per day and the attack had happened before anyone had brought me dinner.

My stomach gurgled again and Melinda broke off a piece of the toast on my plate and ate it, as if to demonstrate that it wouldn't kill me in horrifying and unusual ways.

"I'm just going to leave this here," she said, rising to her feet. "I need to check in on my family. My son, Danny, was one of the omegas kidnapped yesterday."

"I'm sorry for that," I murmured, keeping my head down as shame curled through me. I'd helped with the kidnappings. I hadn't wanted to, but with Trent twisting our bond to control me, there had been little I could do to resist.

She smiled. "It's not your fault, sweetheart. You take care while I'm gone."

With that, she swept out of the room. I glanced through the door as she left the small, single bedroom I'd been shut in. They'd locked the door last night and the window didn't open, so there had been no way for me to escape without shattering it. That would have immediately alerted the bear shifter doctor, who I'd been informed lived above the clinic. I didn't fancy being chased down by a bear, so I'd left it alone.

Now, however, I couldn't help but notice that she hadn't locked the door. If I tried to run, would I be able to sneak past the nurse and the doctor before they noticed?

There were footsteps in the hall and then the lock snicked into place.

Damn.

I lay back and stared at the ceiling, doing my best to ignore the fact that stomach acid was eating a hole in my gut. After a while, I grabbed a piece of bread and sniffed it. It smelled normal. Not that I knew if poison had a particular scent.

Hesitantly, I took a bite. I chewed, swallowed, and

waited. When nothing bad happened, I took another bite. Then all of a sudden I found myself wolfing down the toast, slowing only when my parched throat made it difficult to swallow. I sipped the glass of water on the nightstand, hoping it hadn't been drugged, and settled back against the pillows. I wasn't full, but at least I was no longer mentally foggy because my brain had no fuel.

I must have drifted off because a knock on the door woke me. I frowned. Who on earth would knock before entering? It wasn't as if I had any say in who came or went.

I stayed silent and a moment later the door eased open and a face peeked through. I relaxed slightly as I realized the intruder was an omega. For a moment, I'd worried it might be that alpha, returned to claim me.

The omega padded inside and closed the door. He was taller than average with brown hair, brown eyes, and a splash of freckles across his nose. There was something familiar about him.

It took me a moment to place him, but when I did, I shuffled up in bed, dragging my knees in close and reaching out as if to defend myself. Useless, since I didn't have access to my magic and this guy—omega or not—could easily beat me to a pulp.

"Hi, Reid." He gave me a bright smile. "Don't be scared. I didn't come here to hurt you. I just wanted to let you know how sorry I am that you lost your mate."

"I hated Trent," I spat, refusing to acknowledge the ache in my soul that said otherwise.

The omega shrugged. "You were still bonded. I've heard losing that connection can be very painful."

It was. Not that I'd admit as much. I'd been told about people who'd passed away soon after losing their mate because they simply lost the will to live. That wouldn't be me. I was going to live for decades purely to spite that fucking asshole who'd trapped me.

The omega edged closer until he was able to sit on the chair that Melinda had vacated. "I'm Danny."

Ah, Melinda's son.

I didn't speak. I owed him an apology, but first I wanted to know why he was here. Hopefully, if I waited long enough, he'd tell me.

Danny eyed the untouched egg and bacon and his nose wrinkled. "If you're more of a sweets person, I can bring you a pastry. I'm a baker."

I cocked my head. Why would he do that? I'd literally helped kidnap him.

"Or not." He shrugged again, as if it didn't matter. "Momma said you aren't very talkative."

"I don't trust her." I didn't trust any of them. Why would I?

He beamed, apparently pleased by my mistrust. What a strange omega. He snatched a piece of bacon from the plate and ate it. "No poison, I promise."

I narrowed my eyes. It was less likely he'd have been prepared with an antidote than Melinda, who'd made the food, so perhaps I could believe him. For now, at least.

Tentatively, I reached for the plate and ate a small piece of bacon. Nothing seemed amiss, so I tried a little more.

Danny continued smiling, as if I'd made his day. "I thought you might like to know a bit about Grizzly Ridge. That's where we are now."

I nodded, having already realized that, and continued slowly eating.

"We're a mixed clan. Our family are bear shifters, although my mate is a wolf." His expression became dreamy. "We only officially mated last night."

I scowled. He'd willingly let an alpha have control over him?

He shook himself. "Anyway, like I was saying, there are lots of different types of shifters here. We even have a vampire in town and a handful of witches. No warlocks yet though, so you'll be the first. I have three brothers. They're all alphas. One is the sheriff and the other two are on the local search and rescue team. You already know I'm a baker. What do you do?"

I didn't answer. Honestly, I didn't have an answer to give him. I'd never had the chance to do anything other than be used for my magic. I could have been an incredible warlock by now if anyone had ever allowed me to train, but both my clan and the pack had considered that too dangerous—apart from teaching me the basic spells that they wanted to use me for.

The pack didn't have any other warlocks, but they'd hired one to teach me basic scent and sound masking spells.

Perfect for kidnapping omegas.

"My mate is on the search and rescue team too," Danny continued, not put off by my silence. "Actually, you might have met him last night. He was part of the raid on the pack house."

My mind flicked to the image of the wolf bending over me, its teeth dripping with Trent's blood, its jaws ready to crush my throat.

I shivered. *That* was Danny's mate?

"Why would you let him steal your freedom?" I whispered, scared to ask but wanting to understand.

Danny's face fell. "I love him. The mating bond brings me comfort and joy. It makes me feel connected to him."

I shook my head. "Alphas just use omegas."

Perhaps he hadn't figured that out yet, but he soon would.

Danny sucked his lips into his mouth and his eyes shone with tears. "It shouldn't be like that. Most alphas don't treat their omega mates like Trent did. It isn't like that here. Alphas protect omegas. They cherish them."

Yeah, I didn't believe that for a minute. Danny had been brainwashed into thinking what they wanted him to.

"It's true." He spoke quietly but urgently. "The alpha who said he was your mate last night—you remember him?"

I gave him a look. How could I forget?

"Right." He nodded. "He's my brother. If you were to mate, he'd take such good care of you. He'd put his life on the line to make sure you were safe and happy."

A spark of anger ignited inside me as I finally realized why Danny was here. He'd been sent in by his brother to soften me up.

Well, it wouldn't work.

"Get out," I said bitterly. "Now."

CHAPTER

FIVE

ANDER

Z With a paper bag full of goodies from the bakery in hand, I entered the clinic, relieved when no one tried to stop me. I made my way to the private room where Reid was staying and reached for the door handle just as it swung open and flew toward me.

I stumbled backward and caught Danny before he tripped and went sprawling on the floor.

He looked up at me, his expression stricken. "I think I made it worse."

"Made what worse?" I asked, steadying him. The sour scent of distressed omega filled my nostrils. "What's wrong?"

He looked down, his cheeks turning pink. "I just wanted to help. I thought if I told him that we aren't like the Red Moon Pack, it would make him feel better. I tried to tell him that you aren't anything like that asshole Trent, but he took it the wrong way. I think he thought I was trying to trick him or something."

My heart sank as I listened and realized that the

distressed scent wasn't only coming from him but also from the room he'd left.

"You should probably give him some time to calm down," Danny said, looking anywhere but at me. "He didn't say much, but I think he was pretty upset."

Fucking hell.

My bear clawed at me, desperate to break through the fragile barrier between us and our mate. I didn't think he would accept it if I simply turned and left. He'd ride me until I at least satisfied him with a glimpse of our mate to prove he was safe, even if he wasn't happy with the current situation.

Safety trumped all else.

"I'll leave if he gets stressed," I said, circling around Danny to make sure he didn't try to block me from the door. "But I need to see him. Even if only for a few seconds."

"Don't scare him," Danny whispered. "He's been through enough."

"I won't," I promised. Gods knew that all I wanted to do was protect him.

Tentatively, I entered the room. My gaze went immediately to the bed, where the little warlock sat propped against a pillow. I drank him up, eager to spend time observing him properly without the distraction of a fight going on around me.

My breath caught. He truly was beautiful. Blond curls spilled around his shoulders. His hair was slightly stringy but I suspected he hadn't had a chance to wash it yet. Once he had, his mane would be stunning. His cheeks were plump, giving him a baby-faced appearance, and his eyes were the vivid shade of a mountain bluebird.

He was small. While I couldn't discern his height with him in bed as he was, I'd be surprised if he was more than five foot five or six.

When I noticed the gnarled scar on his shoulder with indentations from a set of teeth left by what must have been a ferocious bite, fury scorched my veins. A growl burst from me and my claws pricked the insides of my palms.

Reid recoiled, those bluebird eyes going wide with fear. His scent soured even further.

I took a deep breath and tried to calm myself. I already knew that he'd been mated against his will. It made sense that Trent hadn't cared to bite him cleanly or give him anything to help him heal. He probably liked seeing the signs of his violence on this sweet omega's body.

"I'm sorry." I inhaled again and closed my eyes so he wouldn't see my bear peeking through. "I didn't mean to frighten you. I just got angry seeing what Trent did to you. I'm Zander."

Once I was sure I had my bear under control, I opened my eyes again. Reid was looking away, his head turned to the side slightly, hiding the scar. He didn't make any move to talk.

Okay, I could do this.

I dithered, shifting from one foot to the other. It felt like I'd spent eternity waiting for my mate, but I'd never expected to find them in a situation as twisted as this. It was proving difficult to figure out how to approach him.

"I'm the, uh, sheriff," I continued, hoping that might settle him a little. "No one in Grizzly Ridge will harm you. I brought food. You must be hungry."

A brief glance at his breakfast plate showed that he'd eaten a little, although not much.

I extended the bag toward him. "I'm not sure what you like, so there's a donut, a fruit pastry, and a cupcake."

I wasn't one for sweet food but if he was, he might find comfort in the sugary offering. He turned toward me, his wary gaze shifting to one of longing as he looked at the bag.

He didn't make any move to take it though. In fact, the quick darting of his eyes made me wonder if he thought it was a trap and he'd be punished for reaching for the food.

My stomach clenched at the thought.

Reid turned away again. "Just do it."

I frowned. "Do what?"

He huffed, as if *I* were the one being cryptic. "You're here to claim me, right? You said yesterday that we're supposedly mates."

I stared at him for a long moment as the horror of what he was suggesting sank in. I tossed the bag onto the bed and backed away from him, my hands held up in surrender even as my bear whimpered for our poor, wounded mate.

He expected me to rape him. He thought I was here to replace Trent as his new alpha mate without any consideration for his well-being.

I tried not to take it personally. He'd been through a lot. But Gods, it hurt that he didn't expect anything better. I sank to the floor, hoping that doing so would make me appear less threatening.

"I would never force myself on anyone." I tried to keep my voice steady, but traces of anger threaded through it. Not at him. *Never* at him. But at all of the assholes who'd ever hurt him. "Especially not my fated mate. I know you're mourning and I hope we can eventually get to know each other, but I will respect your wishes."

He snorted, the sound bitter. "You say that now, but it's just a facade to control my magic. Everyone wants to control me. You're not any different."

My vision sharpened as my bear came to the surface again. It wanted to curl around our mate and protect him, and it didn't understand that being near him would only scare him further.

"I promise, I will never try to control you," I swore to him.

I caught sight of the disbelief on his face and my bear had finally had enough. It took over, clawing its way forward, and it was all I could do to back out of the room and tear off my clothes before the shift was upon me.

I bolted toward the woods, needing to get away from Reid before I frightened him further.

"Zander!" Danny shouted after me, but I ignored him.

CHAPTER
SIX

R^{EID}

Dr. Black looked at me like a disappointed parent. "Reid, you've been here for two days now and you've hardly eaten. You're weak. You need to get some fuel into your system."

I crossed my arms and raised my chin. I didn't think I needed to say that I didn't trust anyone here. My expression spoke volumes.

So far, they hadn't laced my meals with anything toxic, but that could be because they were lulling me into complacency.

He arched a salt-and-pepper eyebrow. "If we wanted to kill you, we wouldn't bother with poison. There's no point, when I could have one of the enforcers break your neck and bury you in the woods."

I stiffened.

His lips twisted in a grimace and his mustache twitched. "That wasn't a threat. I just want you to see reason and finish a meal before you pass out."

I gnawed on my lower lip. While I knew I could hold out for much longer, he had a point. If they'd wanted me dead, it would have been simpler to just kill me alongside Trent. Instead, they'd gone to the trouble of kidnapping me.

Reluctantly, I reached for the sandwich he'd brought me and took a bite. All I tasted was peanut butter and jelly. Even when I concentrated, I couldn't detect any strange undertones, so I finished it in only a few bites and put the plate on the nightstand.

"Good." His eyes twinkled. "Provided you eat, you're well enough to be discharged so we'll be moving you later today."

I froze, my senses on high alert and I cursed myself for relaxing for even a second. "Am I going to Zander's house to be claimed?"

Dr. Black's eyebrows furrowed. "No. You've been invited to stay at the Clan Alpha's house. Don't worry, they'll treat you well."

"I've heard that before," I muttered, dread churning in my gut and making me want to throw up the sandwich I'd just eaten.

Dr. Black leaned toward me, his forearms resting on his thighs. "I know you've had a rough time, but I swear to you, no one here wishes you harm."

I'd believe that when I saw it.

"I know it's hard to trust us considering what you've been through, and I'm sure you're still struggling with the loss of your mating bond, but if you're willing to take a tiny leap of faith, I think you'll find you could be very happy here."

I blinked rapidly, refusing to let my tears fall. "I used up my supply of faith a long time ago."

Even before I'd met Trent, I'd known not to expect kindness or good deeds. No one did anything without an ulterior motive, and meeting Trent and his pack had just reinforced that. I'd taken a leap of faith by going on a date with him, and look where it had gotten me.

I sure as hell wasn't lining up to do it again.

"I think you'll find that faith is infinite." Dr. Black stood. "You just need to look a little harder to find it within yourself."

I rolled my eyes. *Thank you, Yoda.*

"They'll be here to get you in a few hours."

He left.

I showered, brushed my teeth, and changed into a fresh pair of sweatpants and a T-shirt, relieved that at least I had clean clothes.

When someone arrived to collect me, I was surprised to find that it was Melinda, the kindly woman I'd met a few times now.

"My husband is the Clan Alpha," she explained as she escorted me to a large black car.

Oh. Well, maybe this wouldn't be so terrible. She seemed nice. Not that I trusted she'd stay that way, but the first few days might be bearable.

Perhaps I'd even get the chance to escape, although I wouldn't be getting far without help and I doubted I could convince anyone in this tiny town to lend a hand when it went against their Alpha's wishes.

She opened the door and held it while I got in, then circled around the other side. She sat, buckled, and pulled the door shut.

Smiling over her shoulder, she said, "We're going to take care of you."

I wished that didn't sound like a line from *The Godfather.*

The car started and she pulled out onto the road and turned left at the corner.

"If you really wanted to take care of me, you'd let me

use my magic," I muttered, glaring down at the cuffs that were still on my wrists. They looked like bracelets, but the truth was so much uglier.

With those cuffs in place, blocking me from my magic, I was defenseless.

And okay, fine, I didn't know how to do much with my magic, but at least I could use basic wards and throw sparks. That was a level of protection I didn't currently have.

I'd hardly dared to sleep last night in case someone came into the room while I was unconscious. Without magic, I had no way to defend myself and it wasn't as if I had any kind of muscle. Even Melinda could probably best me in a magicless fight.

Guilt flashed across her face. If I hadn't been watching her so closely, I might have missed it.

"You just lost your mate," she said softly, hesitantly. "We don't want anyone hurt, so we can't risk that yet."

Sighing, I went limp against the seat and looked out the side window. I hadn't expected any different, but disappointment rested heavy in the pit of my stomach anyway.

Melinda turned down a cul-de-sac that backed onto the forest and parked outside a two-story house—the largest in a row of similar homes. I waited for her to get out of the car before following her to the front door.

The interior was warm and welcoming. Homey in a way I wasn't used to. It reminded me of the houses I'd seen in the Hallmark movies I'd binged behind my parents' backs. They hadn't wanted me to watch TV or even to read books. Any of that might have given me hopes and dreams beyond what they had planned for me.

Gods forbid I want something for myself.

Melinda led me down a hall and into a cozy bedroom. The bed was piled with pillows and the bedspread was neatly turned down. The dresser was unadorned, as was the nightstand, so I assumed this was a guest room.

"You can stay in here," she said, gesturing at the bed. "If you need anything, please let us know. We want you to be comfortable."

I nodded even though I had no intention of doing any such thing. Letting them know what I desired would only give them something to use as leverage over me.

"I'm about to have lunch with Danny and Milo. Would you like to join us?"

I shook my head. "I'm tired."

I wasn't tired. Not even a little bit. But I didn't want to be stuck at a table with them while they studied me like a new exotic pet.

"We'll save you some in case you're hungry later," she said, retreating from the room and shutting the door to give me privacy.

"Thank you." I did need to eat more, and it didn't seem as if they intended to do anything untoward with my food.

I opened the dresser and went through each drawer, searching for a listening device, hidden camera, or evidence of spell craft. Then I checked underneath the bed and inside the nightstand. Finding nothing, I flopped onto the bed and closed my eyes. If only I wasn't too on edge to sleep. I could use the rest.

I waited until I really had to pee and then tiptoed out of the bedroom. I couldn't remember if she'd said where the bathroom was, but the sound of voices lured me in one direction. It was only when I reached the doorway that I realized I'd found the room where Melinda was sharing lunch with her sons.

Melinda and Danny both fell silent and, as one, they glanced toward me. I backed away, my heart in my throat.

Shit. Was I allowed out of the room? Would they think I'd been listening in on them?

My heart pounded so hard it was almost painful and I turned and sprinted for the guest bedroom, ignoring the discomfort in my bladder. I shut the door and leaned against it, debating whether to climb through the window to get away from them.

Only the thought that any of the supernatural beings here could track me in minutes stopped me from going through with it.

CHAPTER
SEVEN

I'd sunk to an all-new low.

Not content with taking my parents' word for it that Reid was safe and being well cared for, I'd snuck into their house hours after the last light had been switched off and I'd fallen asleep in the bedroom beside the one Reid was sleeping in.

I really had tried to sleep earlier, but the world of dreams had eluded me as I lay there, recalling Reid's expression when he'd believed that I'd come to claim him, willing or not.

My poor little warlock was so scarred. So traumatized.

Dr. Black had warned me that he was bitter too, but considering what he'd been through, who could blame him?

I climbed into the spare bed, shut my eyes, and focused all of my senses on him. His scent was like ozone and concrete during summer rain. Somehow refreshing and nostalgic all at once.

I breathed in the traces of his scent that lingered in the

air and allowed the rhythmic thud of his heart to lull me to sleep.

When I awoke, I lay in the dark, wondering what my mate needed from me—and what I could actually offer him that he wouldn't be too terrified to accept. Gradually, I noticed that there was a hint of another scent coming from him that I'd missed earlier. The faintest trace of honeysuckle.

At first I thought I was mistaken, but I crept to his bedroom door, my feet silent on the carpeted floor, and inhaled deeply through the crack beneath the door. The honeysuckle was definitely coming from him, but it was foreign too.

My stomach knotted. This could only mean one thing.

Reid was pregnant.

I pulled in a breath and slowly released it as a heaviness settled over my body.

My omega was pregnant with another alpha's baby. An alpha who'd terrorized him, taken him against his will, manipulated him, and twisted what should have been a pure and joyful bond so that he could force Reid to follow his orders.

Claws burst through the ends of my fingers and dug into the floor. I gritted my teeth because if I didn't, I might scream.

My poor, poor mate.

Alone and pregnant, in an unfamiliar place with people he didn't trust. He must be so scared.

I was tempted to smash through the door, rush inside, and curl around him. To hold him close and whisper reassurances and promise that everything would be all right.

But I didn't, for one very important reason. Doing that might make *me* feel better, but it was the last thing Reid needed. He hadn't been in control of his life for months.

Even now, he had to know that he wasn't being treated the same as the other omegas we'd rescued.

Because of his mate bond with Trent, we couldn't afford to overlook the risk he posed. We had to treat him as being potentially hostile. But in doing so, we were victimizing him further. He deserved softness and pampering, not mistrust and wariness.

As hard as I tried, I couldn't see a better way forward. All I could do was make it clear that whoever his pup's biological father was, I'd be their parent in the ways that mattered. I'd wanted children for years and that pup was innocent of their father's crimes. They deserved as much love and affection as any other baby.

"Zander?"

I turned, surprised to find Momma in the hall behind me. I must have been too distracted to hear her approach. I gestured for her to go the other direction and I followed her out and into the kitchen.

"What is it?" she asked, her face creased with concern.

I hesitated. This should be Reid's news to share, but if he hadn't done so already then there was a good chance he wouldn't. At least, not before someone else needed to know. We had to make sure he was getting enough nutrients and that the doctor was keeping an eye on him. Losing a mate while pregnant could endanger the baby.

"He's pregnant," I whispered, closing the door behind us. If Momma was awake, I had no doubt that Dad was too, but he must have decided that she was fully equipped to handle the situation.

"Who?" Her eyes widened. "Reid?"

I nodded.

"No." Her face fell. "He's pregnant from that... that..."

"Rapist," I growled. "Murderer. Fucking scum of the earth."

She eyed me. "Language, Z. Although I agree completely. Are you sure?"

"I smelled it. He obviously isn't ready to tell us, but we have to make sure he's healthy and has everything he needs."

"You're his mate," Momma said. "Of course we will."

"I'll be the pup's father," I promised her. "He or she doesn't deserve to pay for their father's sins. They'll be mine in every way that matters."

At least, as soon as I convinced Reid to give me a chance. I had a feeling that might take a while.

A sleepy Reid appeared in the doorway, rubbing his eyes. He stopped abruptly at the sight of us and his heart raced, but then he squared his shoulders and met my gaze.

"I know you were in the room beside me," he said, his voice wobbling. "What do you want from me?"

EIGHT

R*EID*

My heart was going crazy as I glared at Zander and Melinda. Zander took half a step toward me and I flinched, already anticipating a blow. It was stupid to make demands from an alpha, I knew that, but I was so not knowing what to expect.

Right now they were acting like I wasn't their prisoner. I might not be in chains, but I was captive all the same and them trying to make things seem different than they were just confused me. It would be easier if they used me like I was accustomed to without all of the prevarication.

Zander noticed my flinch and he stopped immediately, turning his palms outward as if to show me that he meant no harm.

I didn't know what to think. In my experience, Alphas *always* meant harm. The only time they showed kindness to someone was so they could manipulate them. But then, he'd brought me pastries the other day and had left when I'd told him to just get on with the mating.

I wanted to believe his pretty words, but I couldn't bear

the disappointment if I did and then found out I'd been wrong.

"All I want is for you to be happy and healthy. I said that nothing would happen to you against your will, and I meant it," Zander rumbled, a hint of emotion in his voice. "You won't be forced into anything."

I shook my head. "I don't believe you." No one ever gave me a choice. They just wanted to use me, either for my body or my magic. "It would be kinder to just be honest."

I hated waiting and wondering when everything would blow up.

Melinda backed away. "I think you two have some things to—"

"Please don't go," I cried, suddenly regretting everything I'd said and done in the last two minutes. Why had I thought it was a good idea to ask for answers when I wasn't ready for this temporary moment of peace to end? I'd been fed and given clothes and a nice bed. Why would I question that? It would only make them mad. "Please. I d-don't—"

Melinda froze in place. Her gaze slowly met Zander's and they exchanged a look that I didn't understand.

"Okay, Reid. I'm not going anywhere." She started to move toward me, her hand coming up as if to touch my face, but then she stopped. "I'm right here, okay? I'm right here and no one is going to hurt you. You're safe now."

A bitter sob wracked me. Could I ever truly feel safe again?

Zander frowned, the shadows hiding his dark eyes. "Jesus, sweetheart, you're holding onto so much pain."

I wrapped my arms around myself.

I won't fall apart. I won't fall apart.

I hadn't given in when my parents siphoned my magic from me and gave it to our coven's High Priest. Nor had I given in when I'd been kidnapped and violated. Now, every part of me wanted to finally crumple. To crack and shatter and not worry about picking up the pieces.

But I couldn't let go because no one else would protect me. If I didn't do it myself, I'd lose everything I had left.

"For as long as you're in Grizzly Ridge, I promise you'll be protected," Zander said, as if reading my mind. "I won't let anything happen to you."

I didn't believe him. Couldn't *allow* myself to believe him.

Despite that, it was nice to hear the words. Even if they were a lie. It was the first time anyone had said they'd protect me.

"I don't understand what you want from me," I whispered. It was exhausting trying to figure out what his next move would be and when it would happen. Being constantly on alert was draining on the best of days, but after having just lost a mate—consensual or not—it was almost debilitating.

Zander's expression gentled. "Right now, all I want is for you to heal and to make sure your baby is healthy."

Excuse me, what?

"What baby?" I demanded, looking down at my flat stomach.

I looked to Melinda, and she nodded as if to confirm that yes, I was growing a whole other life in there.

"Reid, sweetheart, you *are* pregnant." She said it as cautiously as if she were a doctor sharing a terminal diagnosis. "I assume the baby is Trent's."

No.

A piercing shrill filled my ears and I backed away from them.

"No, I'm not." I held out my hands defensively. "I'd know if I was. I'd sense it or something."

I couldn't be pregnant and not know. That was ridiculous. Especially since shifter pregnancies progressed so quickly. But then, human pregnancies didn't and perhaps my biology was slowing the baby's development.

"I can smell it." Zander sniffed as if to emphasize his words. "I'm sorry, but you're definitely pregnant."

I yanked at the cuffs, suddenly needing them off. If I had access to my magic, I might be able to sense a change in the well of magic inside me. I wasn't sure if I'd be able to tell that I was pregnant, per se, but surely if I paid close attention, something would feel different.

I dug my fingernails in and levered the edges, not caring that welts appeared on my skin and blood welled beneath my nails.

"Are you sure?" I asked Melinda, swatting at Zander when he tried to stop me. The cuffs tightened and bit deeper into my wrists, no doubt as a result of some kind of spell designed to prevent prisoners from escaping.

She shook her head. "Zander's sense of smell is more sensitive than mine, but I believe him."

"Then let me out of these so I can check. Please!" A tremor wracked me and heat burned behind my eyes, but I managed not to cry.

Her tone was apologetic as she said, "Dr. Black told us not to remove them."

"But you can?" I asked, getting straight to the salient point.

She bit her lip and glanced at Zander. "All magical cuffs in Grizzly Ridge are spelled to react to the Clan Alpha and his family."

"So get them off. I'm begging you."

I needed to know if I was pregnant with my rapist's child.

My mind was already spinning with the potential ramifications. But what if telling me this was just some way to control me? I couldn't let anyone manipulate me that way. Not again.

Melinda stepped closer. "Emotions are high right now and we're just worried you might do something you'll regret."

Like what?

What did I even have to lose?

The fight drained out of me and I slumped against the wall. My wrists stung and I couldn't bear to look at them. Tears dripped down my cheeks and I turned away so Zander and Melinda wouldn't see.

If they didn't want to free me, there was nothing I could do to change that. Once again, I was trapped with no access to my magic, no control over the situation, and I might be growing the spawn of a man I hated with every fiber of my being—but kind of loved a little too.

Zander heaved a sigh. "We'll remove the cuffs. *Temporarily.*"

Z ANDER

I hoped I wasn't making a terrible mistake.

"Zander," Momma began, but I cut her off with a wave of my hand.

"He needs this." It had just about killed me to see him claw at his wrists so desperately that he hadn't even noticed when he'd begun to bleed. I feared that if we didn't allow him this, he'd injure himself trying to get the cuffs off.

Not to mention the fact that I'd promised not to control him. The cuffs might be for everyone's protection, but that didn't mean they weren't controlling him. I couldn't make a liar of myself.

"Thank you." Reid sniffed, lifting his hands to his face—likely in an effort to dry his eyes—before turning back to us.

"Give me your hands." I held out mine, palms out, hoping that the position wouldn't intimidate him. I'd definitely gotten the impression that he didn't like alphas in his space, and he certainly didn't trust them.

The need to be free of the cuffs must have outweighed his fear because he placed his hands docilely in mine and I grasped the cuffs and gave the magic a few seconds to work before pulling them off him.

Reid brightened immediately. The scent of ozone filled the air and the shadows in his eyes lessened.

Guilt clogged my throat and I struggled to draw in a breath. I hated that we were doing this to him. I could only imagine how it would feel to be cut off from my bear the way the cuffs cut him off from his magic.

It wasn't fair. He'd been through so much already. I didn't want him to suffer for a second more, but we also couldn't take the risk that he'd decide to avenge his mate's death.

Yes, Trent had been his captor, but mate bonds were rarely logical.

A bluish-yellow glow surrounded Reid and he closed his eyes, his expression blissful as he reconnected with his magic. But within an instant, his face crumpled and he curled in on himself.

"I... I... something is different," he whispered. "I must not have sensed it earlier because of how my magic was being controlled. I can't tell what it is, but there's a new... flavor... of magic in the mix."

"I'll get you a pregnancy test." Momma hurried off before he could protest and returned a scant thirty seconds later. She thrust a pregnancy test into his hands. "Use this."

He nodded jerkily and brushed past us into the bathroom. The minutes he was gone passed by excruciatingly slowly. I knew what the result would be, and I hated to think of how it might affect him.

When he emerged, his face was pale and his hands were shaking. "It's true." His eyes filled with tears. "I'm pregnant by that... that *monster*."

His shoulders shook and he wrapped his arms around himself, lowering his head and biting his bottom lip so hard that I smelled blood.

My bear grumbled and Reid flinched away.

Shh, I warned my bear. *He doesn't know that you're unhappy he's hurt. He thinks you're threatening him.*

Mate, my bear sent back. *Comfort. Hold. Soothe.*

I started to reach for Reid but then froze, knowing he wouldn't welcome any comfort from me. Still, I had to try, right?

"Can I touch you?" I asked softly.

"No. I can't take it."

Reluctantly, I lowered my hand and started to back off but before I'd made it more than half a step, Reid swayed toward me. I stood locked in place, scarcely daring to breathe. While he might not consciously want me anywhere near him, subconsciously he knew that I could ease his pain.

I stayed right where I was, neither leaning into him nor moving farther away.

"It's going to be okay," I murmured, keeping my voice low and my tone gentle. "You're going to be all right. Whatever happens, I'm here for you. It's up to you what you do about this baby. Nothing is set in stone."

It would kill me if he wanted to abort the baby or arrange for them to be adopted, but I'd understand. He'd been through too much already.

"Do you want the baby?" I asked, forcing myself to go on. "If not, there are options."

Reid worried his torn lip and the metallic scent of blood intensified. "I don't want an abortion. That doesn't feel right for me. I need to think." He grabbed the sides of his head and groaned. "I hated Trent, but we were mates and then I lost him and now I'm pregnant with his baby.

It's a lot to process. I don't know what to do. I need time. I…"

"You have time," I said gently when he didn't continue. "At least a little. You don't have to make any decisions today. Whatever you need, we'll make sure you have it, so don't worry about that. But first, you should eat."

"I'll get started on breakfast," Momma said, her face wreathed with concern. "Is there anything in particular you'd like, Reid? Toast or pancakes or eggs?"

Reid rubbed his stomach. "I can't eat."

Momma made a soothing sound. "Sweetheart, you need to eat, for your baby's sake. I'll tell you what. I'll give you a while to gather your thoughts, but if you haven't come for breakfast within the next two hours then I'll bring you a plate."

Reid didn't argue. Momma retreated to the kitchen and I mentally debated what to do. I doubted that Reid would want me to accompany him to his room, but if I didn't then I'd have to cuff him again.

However much I might not want to believe it, Reid posed a threat to Grizzly Ridge. To my family. He'd said it himself: he had complicated feelings for his mate. He'd hated him, but the mate bond was there regardless—and we'd killed Trent. We simply couldn't risk the possibility of him retaliating.

But I refused to put the cuffs on without doing something for his sore wrists first.

"Come with me," I said.

His eyes narrowed with suspicion. "Why?"

"I want to treat your wrists."

He glanced at them in surprise, as if he hadn't noticed they were bleeding. "They're fine."

"Please." If he denied me this, my bear might mutiny.

He stared at me for a long moment, as if evaluating my sincerity, and then nodded.

I went to the bathroom and he trailed along behind me. I pulled supplies out of the vanity and spread them out.

"Can you sit on the edge of the tub?" I asked.

He perched there and held out his hands awkwardly.

I dabbed disinfectant onto a cotton swab. "This will sting a bit."

I wished I could take the pain away but unfortunately that wasn't within my power. We were lucky there were even medical supplies in the house. We didn't often need them, but since Milo had joined the family, Momma had made sure to stock the basics. We were all protective of the little human omega.

I swiped the cotton swab over his tender skin, dabbing away the blood and making sure that any areas where the skin was broken were cleaned thoroughly, then I tossed the swab in the bin and measured off two segments of adhesive dressing. I wrapped one around each wrist and secured them in place.

"Thank you," Reid murmured. "I... I appreciate it."

"You're welcome." I wished we could leave it there. "Unfortunately, the cuffs need to go back on now."

His eyes flew to mine and they widened. "No! Please, I'll do anything. Don't put those back on me."

I grimaced. "It isn't my decision. It's for the safety of the clan."

"I won't hurt anyone!"

"You might not mean to, but anything could happen."

His gaze darted to the door as if he was considering making a run for it, but then he slumped and held his wrists out for me to clamp the cuffs back into place.

"You say I should trust you," Reid said as he stood,

keeping his distance from me, and edged toward the door. "But how am I supposed to do that when you won't trust me?"

He slunk away, leaving me feeling like I'd been speared through the heart.

CHAPTER

TEN

R*EID*
A timid knock on the bedroom door came about an hour after I'd shut myself inside. I frowned, caught off guard. With how she'd spoken to me, I'd expected Melinda to just walk right in, and Zander certainly wouldn't knock so hesitantly.

Nevertheless, I ignored the knock. I didn't want to talk to whoever was on the other side. I was too busy trying to figure out what the hell to do.

I was pregnant.

With Trent's baby.

I'd always wanted children but not like this. That said, I couldn't punish a child because of who their father was or how they'd been created. The tiny being inside me was as much mine as they were Trent's and they deserved to be cared for.

I was conflicted.

There was another knock and then the door opened slightly.

"Hello?" a soft voice called.

I didn't respond. I didn't recognize the voice which

49

meant I hadn't met this person yet. If they were in this house then they knew I was being held against my will and they hadn't made any effort to help me, so I wasn't interested in talking to them.

"Reid?"

I kept my mouth shut.

A figure eased through the doorway. His frame was petite except for the bulge at his stomach, and he had ice blue eyes and tousled brown hair.

"Hi." He smiled, and there was a sense of gentleness about him that made me want to like him, but I was determined not to let my guard down too early, even if no one here had hurt me so far. They were still keeping me cuffed and helpless. "I'm Milo."

"You're not a shifter like them, are you?" I asked.

He seemed too petite for that. Unless he was, say, a rabbit or bird shifter.

"No, I'm just human." Milo padded to the bed and perched on the edge of it. "I heard you're pregnant."

A slightly hysterical laugh burst from me. "Has the gossip already got around town then?"

Milo's eyes widened and his hand came to rest protectively on his belly. "No. No one outside of the household knows, except for maybe Dr. Black if Momma called him. I'm mated to Zander's brother, so I heard it from him. I thought that talking to another pregnant omega might help."

I drew my knees to my chest and gazed down at them bleakly. "We have nothing in common."

"We're both pregnant omegas," he pointed out. "And neither of us are shifters."

I rolled my eyes. "You're pregnant by your mate. I'm pregnant by my former jailer. Unless..." I leaned forward, an awful possibility occurring to me. "You weren't... forced...

were you?”

There was every possibility that Milo hadn’t been allowed to choose his mate. I hadn’t, after all, and I was well aware that some magical communities abided by the old way of thinking, where omegas were considered property and their wishes were disregarded.

“Oh, Gods, no!” Milo cried, looking horrified.

Part of me was relieved, but another part twisted bitterly because he’d reacted as if he couldn’t fathom such a thing, whereas it had just been a fact of life for me.

“Then you have no idea how I feel,” I snapped, but regretted it when tears filled those pale blue eyes.

He sniffed and wiped his eyes on the back of his sleeve. “Sorry. You’re right, I can’t understand what you’re going through.”

“I’m sorry too.” I shouldn’t take my own hurt out on him. “Are you okay?”

“Fine.” His smile was brittle. “Just hormonal. You know how it is.”

“Not really.”

Perhaps my hormones were wonky thanks to pregnancy, but after the week I’d had, how the hell would I know? I could be crying because I was hormonal or it could be because my life was genuinely shit and I’d experienced the severing of a mate bond.

Nibbling on his lower lip, Milo seemed to summon his courage and scooted closer. “I might not have been assaulted like you, or forced into a mating bond, but I have been kidnapped.”

I frowned. That was the last thing I expected him to say. “What?”

He gave an awkward shrug. “There was this guy, Tomas. He was obsessed with me for some reason. He kidnapped me and was going to try to make me be his mate, although it wouldn't have worked because I'd already bonded with Everett. I was just lucky that my family saved me before anything bad happened."

I studied Milo with renewed interest. I'd met Tomas. He'd been a member of Trent's pack at one point. He'd been cruel even before his wolf had taken over.

"What would make you feel more comfortable?" Milo asked.

"Honestly?"

"Of course."

I gauged his sincerity and decided that he wasn't trying to manipulate me. He might be misguided, but he did want to help.

"I don't want to be a prisoner anymore." I doubted that would surprise anyone. I'd made my feelings on the matter clear enough. "I won't hurt anyone, I promise. I just want to be given my freedom and left alone so I can figure out what to do next."

Admitting so much to him made me feel raw and vulnerable, but he seemed like the kind of person who might actually do his best to get me what I wanted. And... Well, he was impossible to be intimidated by. If sending him in to see me was some kind of ploy, it was a smart one.

Milo's expression turned pitying and I looked down at my knees again, unable to stand it. "I'll do what I can." He started to reach for me but then stopped himself. "I'll be back soon."

I nodded but didn't look up as he rose from the bed, smoothed one hand over his baby bump, and crossed to the door. He closed it and the latch clicked into place, but I knew it wasn't locked. Right now, they didn't need to fear me escaping because with others awake in the household, I had no hope of getting away. A family of shifters could hunt me down blindfolded.

A while later, there was another knock, and when I called out for him to come in, assuming it was Milo, the door swung open.

But Milo wasn't alone.

Melinda and Zander stood behind him. Zander's muscles were coiled tight—he reminded me of a predator about to strike. He didn't move as Melinda moved to stand beside Milo.

"We've been discussing things," Melinda said, her motherly face full of empathy that I couldn't identify as real or false. "We can't set you free without any kind of support system in place because we don't know what will happen, but how about we call your family to come and get you?"

My stomach rolled nauseatingly. A whimper slipped from me and I plastered myself against the wall. My eyes darted from her to Zander to Milo, who smiled at me as if this might be exactly what I wanted to hear.

If that's what he thought, he was as wrong as it was possible to be. He might mean well, but this...

This was my worst nightmare.

"Please don't call them, I'm begging you." Spots appeared in my vision and I rocked back and forth. "Don't call them. They can't know... please, no."

Melinda approached me cautiously, like she might a skittish animal. "You have nothing to be ashamed of. Your family will understand. They'll want to help you heal. None of this was your fault."

"Don't call them," I pleaded, my vision going blurry. I wanted to explain that they'd gotten this all wrong and that my parents were the last people I wanted to see but I couldn't find the words.

"If it were my son, I'd—"

I thrust off the bed and leapt to my feet. "No!"

All my life, I'd been mistreated. I wouldn't let them return me to my original abusers.

Magic swelled within me, reacting to my terror, and tried to burst free. The cuffs on my wrists scorched my skin and the smell of burnt flesh filled my nostrils.

Then everything went black.

ELEVEN

*Z*ANDER

I caught Reid before he hit the ground. His eyelashes fanned over pale cheeks and he didn't stir as I carried him to the bed.

The scent of burning flesh filled my nostrils and I scanned his body, bile searing the back of my throat when I realized the cuffs had burned him. The skin around them was red and inflamed.

Oh, Gods.

I'd put those on him.

It was my fault he was hurt. I hadn't known this would happen, but it was clear he'd been afraid of them and I'd slapped them on regardless, more concerned about the rest of us than about his well-being.

What the hell kind of mate was I?

I touched the cuffs and carefully eased them off each wrist, revealing angry, weeping sores beneath. My gut twisted and I breathed through my mouth.

If I had to smell the damage I'd done to him, I'd puke.

"Is he okay?" Milo asked worriedly.

"He needs medical attention. Momma, can you call Dr. Black?" I arranged Reid so that he'd be more comfortable. "He needs to be healed."

Fuck, Reid wasn't a shifter. He didn't have shifter healing. His wrists might scar from this.

I'd never forgive myself if he was forced to endure a permanent sign that I'd let him down. Every time he looked at them, the scars would serve as a reminder that I hadn't protected him as a mate should.

I gazed intently at Reid's face as Momma stepped away. His eyes were still closed and he showed no signs of waking. I had to assume his magic had surged within him because he'd been upset and that was what had caused the cuffs to react so badly.

I'd heard that untrained warlocks could be dangerous because their magic responded instinctively to their emotions, but they were usually taught to manage it soon after their magic manifested. Had that not been the case with Reid, or had the stress of everything he'd endured overcome his training?

"He's not waking up," Milo said, echoing my own concern. "Why isn't he waking up?"

Dad appeared in the doorway and a growl tore from my throat. My eyes changed as my bear surfaced and fur rippled over my skin.

"Stay back," I rasped.

He held out his hands, placating. "I'm not going to hurt him. I just want to help."

I gritted my teeth. I couldn't handle any other alphas around my mate right now, not even Dad. "Can you get a drink for him? He might be thirsty when he wakes."

Because he *would* wake. I wouldn't accept any other option. We'd only just met. I wasn't about to lose him.

"Be right back."

Something else occurred to me. Or rather, some*one*.

The baby.

Could this have endangered them?

Terror gripped me but I shook it off. I refused to allow anything to happen to this baby. They would be fine and so would Reid.

"Zander." Dad was in the doorway again. "I have a glass of water and Dr. Black is here. Can he come in?"

"Yes," I ground out, even though my bear wanted to keep all alphas away from our mate and cradle him until all was well again. Reid needed medical attention, which meant I had to get over my misplaced possessive bullshit. "Milo, can you stay?"

Having another omega present might help soothe my ragged emotions.

"Of course." He scooted around Reid so that he was squished between my mate and the wall, out of the way of everyone else.

Dr. Black edged past Dad, taking the glass of water from him. He padded slowly into the room, giving me time to adjust to his presence. He was large and took up a lot of space, but he was doing his best to seem nonthreatening and that helped, as did Milo's calming presence.

"What happened?" he asked, setting the glass of water on the nightstand and keeping a distance of a few feet from my mate.

"Reid panicked about something. I think he felt threatened." Although I wasn't sure why. "My best guess is that his magic tried to protect him but it couldn't because of the cuffs, and when they reacted to his magic, they burned him and he passed out."

Dr. Black leaned toward Reid. "May I move closer?"

"Yes." I backed up, giving him access to Reid, but I didn't leave my mate. I didn't think I could let him go even if I wanted to.

Milo didn't move either. He took Reid's limp hand, providing silent support.

"Those are nasty wounds," Dr. Black said as he took one of Reid's wrists and carefully examined the damage. "I have a healing salve from Li that will speed recovery, but it will still take time."

"Will it scar?" I asked roughly.

"Most likely. Unless you mate him and he's able to access your internal healing magic. I'm not certain precisely how warlock-shifter mating bonds work."

I grimaced. I certainly wasn't about to suggest that option to Reid. I didn't want him to scar, but it would be worse to push him to do something he was absolutely terrified of.

Dr. Black smoothed his hand over Reid's forehead. "He's drained. Exhausted. I have a tonic that will wake him, but I want to bandage his wrists first."

"What about the baby?"

"Baby?" Dr. Black sniffed and one of his eyebrows flew up. "He's pregnant?"

"By that piece of trash."

The doctor ran his hand over Reid's abdomen and closed his eyes, his forehead furrowing as he concentrated. "As far as I can tell, the baby is unaffected. Its heartbeat is regular and I can't sense anything out of the ordinary."

"Thank the gods," Milo breathed.

"I'll want to do a full assessment of the pregnancy in a week or two to be certain," he continued, "but I doubt there's anything to worry about. The baby possesses its own magic, which likely protected it. In fact, it's possible that the baby's magic hid its presence from me while he was at the clinic."

"It's a warlock?" I asked, unable to help myself. I wanted to know everything about the tiny life-form inside Reid.

"And a shifter." Dr. Black smiled. "It's possible to be both, although it's rare. This baby will be quite powerful. Now, let me put the salve on."

He left the room and returned a moment later with a small case. He opened it, withdrew a glass jar filled with translucent white salve, and dipped his finger in. He dabbed the salve onto Reid's left wrist and then his right. When Reid whimpered, a growl tore through me.

"Be careful with that," I hissed.

"My apologies." He continued applying the salve, his touch even softer than before. When he finished, he wrapped a bandage around each wrist and taped them in place, then he pulled a small glass vial from the case, twisted the top off it, and held it to Reid's lips.

As soon as he emptied the liquid into Reid's mouth, Reid bolted upright, his eyes wide. He flinched away from Dr. Black and shuffled until his back hit the wall beside Milo. He was huddled in the corner farthest from everyone else. He drew his knees to his chest and wrapped his arms around them.

"I didn't mean to," he whispered, ducking his head as if expecting a blow. "I didn't mean to. I'm sorry."

Gods, did he really think we'd punish him?

The breath left me in a whoosh as I remembered that we *had* hurt him. Inadvertently, but still.

"It's okay," Milo murmured, staying close but not touching him. "You're okay."

Reid made himself even smaller and a wave of nausea rolled through me. I hated seeing him like this. It was so much better when he was prickly. At least then I didn't have to witness my mate brought so low.

"It was an accident," he said.

I dropped to my knees on the floor, hoping the subservient position would help him feel safe. "We know. You were scared."

I didn't understand why, but I'd do everything in my power to stop him from ever feeling such terror again.

His eyes were wild, the whites showing. "Did I hurt anyone?"

"No. We're all unharmed."

His hands went to his stomach. "What about my baby?"

"They're okay," Dr. Black assured him.

A shaky breath rattled between his lips and some of the tension eased from his body.

"No one was hurt," he said as if he was reassuring himself. "Thank the gods. I swear, I didn't mean to."

Behind me, Momma's breath caught on a sob.

"No one blames you." I clenched my fists, desperate to tug him into my arms even though I knew that laying a finger on him would only make this worse.

Dad backed out of the room, his footsteps retreating alongside Momma's.

"Would you like me to leave?" Milo asked, glancing at the door uncertainly.

"No!" Reid grasped his shirt. "Please don't go."

My heart throbbed, threatening to tear itself in two. I was glad that Milo being here helped reassure him but hated that he'd been taught to fear alphas so strongly.

"All right." Milo settled beside him, adjusting his position to get more comfortable with his pregnant belly. "I'll stay right here."

"Thank you." Reid rocked back and forth then looked down at his wrists. "What happened?"

"The cuffs burned you. I'm so sorry."

He nodded. "Please don't call my parents."

Shit. I didn't know what to say here. I wanted to assure him that no one would do anything he didn't want, but if he was letting shame or guilt keep him from his family then I didn't want to encourage that.

"Personally, I think your family would be grateful to hear you're alive. We don't need to ask them to come for you, but wouldn't it be nice to let them know that they don't have to worry? I'm sure they've been concerned for you."

Reid's teeth sank into his lower lip. "Please don't. They aren't... I mean, my family..." He trailed off helplessly. "Please just don't go looking for my family."

My gut twisted as his words sank in. "If you say no, then we'll respect that."

"Thank you," he whispered, barely audible. "Do I have to put the cuffs back on?"

"No!" The exclamation burst from me instinctively. I meant it though. I didn't know how we'd make sure he didn't pose a threat to anyone else, but I refused to allow my mate to be hurt like that again.

"I agree." Dr. Black sat back on his heels. He'd been so quiet I'd almost forgotten he was there. "As I've already told Zander, your baby seems to be functioning normally, but it would be ideal if we could avoid putting any extra stress on your body."

"I won't attack anyone." Reid lifted his head slightly and grimaced. "Not intentionally, anyway."

"We know you won't," Milo assured him, narrowing his eyes at Dr. Black and me as if daring us to disagree.

"I actually have an idea where that's concerned," Dr. Black said. "I've been doing some research because I knew the cuffs weren't a long-term solution. Have you ever heard of an honesty oath?"

Reid frowned. "No. What's that?"

Dr. Black cleared his throat. "It's a reasonably basic spell." He turned to me. "How much do you know about warlock magic?"

"Not a lot," I admitted. That would have to change now that I had Reid in my life.

"Would you like a basic rundown?"

"Yes, please."

He nodded. "Okay, then. So, every warlock possesses a certain amount of inherent magic inside them. Some have a lot. Others have so little it's barely perceptible. The types of magic they can do vary depending on how much magic they have access to."

"Okay, I'm with you so far."

Reid also seemed to be listening closely, which interested me. Surely he knew all of this.

"All warlocks, even those with hardly any magic, can draw and use magic circles—although the weaker warlocks will often invite stronger ones to bolster their efforts. Magic circles are complex, and minor differences in the symbols used can create massive differences in the outcome or intention of the circle."

"So, people have to be careful with them?" Milo asked. "In case they get them wrong?"

"Exactly. Warlocks can study for years or even decades to master them. Many of the more dedicated practitioners are those with less inherent magic because the use of complex magic circles can even the playing field against less knowledgeable but more powerful warlocks, at least to a certain extent."

At this, Reid made a sound of distress, but when I

glanced at him, he was looking down, his lips pressed firmly together.

Dr. Black also cast a concerned glance at Reid but went on. "Most warlocks can also use basic spells such as the honesty oath. These are generally verbal and sometimes include physical components. Then there are larger spells, such as large-scale warding, battle magic, or long-range seeking spells. Only those with more inherent magic can do them."

"I've seen seeking magic used before." Although not often. The Paranormal Bureau of Investigation, or PBI, employed many warlocks who specialized in tracking spells.

Dr. Black inclined his head in acknowledgement. "The most powerful warlocks—those with the largest reservoir of internal magic—can use magic intuitively. They can direct energy and the magical forces of the universe without the need for circles or spells. Isn't that right, Reid?"

"Sure," Reid agreed, but the way he'd blanked his features made me wary. I got the impression that this conversation made him uncomfortable, and I couldn't help but wonder where he fell on this warlock power hierarchy.

"Anyway, back to the oath." Dr. Black smiled. "As I said, it falls under the umbrella of basic spells. Essentially, a warlock uses their power to bind themself to an oath. Whatever the oath, the power ensures that it's fulfilled. So, say, if Reid promises under oath not to harm any resident of Grizzly Ridge, he's bound to keep that promise because of the backlash from the spell."

"What kind of backlash?" I didn't like the idea of putting him at further risk.

"It depends on the oath, but often the warlock will state up front what the consequences will be and they have to go into it with an honest mind. If they have bad intentions, the magic senses that and won't bind the contract."

I hesitated. "Let's talk this over with Dad and Momma."

It was a good idea, but it had complications. We'd have to ensure the consequences of breaking the oath were severe enough to stop Reid from doing so while also not risking his life.

TWELVE

R*EID*

"I'll come with you," I said, more because I didn't want any other people in my space while I was so discombobulated rather than because I actually wanted to tag along. Besides, if this conversation involved the safety of me and my unborn child, I should be involved.

The doctor headed into the hall and Zander glanced over his shoulder at me before following. I hauled myself upright.

"How are you feeling?" Milo asked quietly.

He seemed like a gentle soul. Perhaps if he was happy here then one day I could be too. Although he couldn't possibly be as damaged as I was.

"I've been worse," I said, and it was true. Although usually, I didn't have another life to worry about protecting. Only myself.

We padded along behind the others. Aaron and Melinda were in the kitchen. Melinda was in the process of kneading a ball of dough and she continued to beat on it as we entered.

Aaron, who scared the fucking crap out of me, looked at

my wrists and grimaced. I immediately put them behind my back, but then thought twice and clasped them in front of myself.

Perhaps if he felt guilty he'd be more likely to agree with Dr. Black's plan about the honesty oath.

"Doc has suggested an alternative to the magic-suppressing cuffs," Zander said, leaning against the wall and crossing his long legs at the ankles. His arm muscles bulged where they rested against his chest, and I had the strangest desire to bury my face between his pecs and let him wrap himself around me and take care of everything.

I wouldn't, though.

He wasn't someone I should seek comfort from. It was bad enough that I'd already allowed him to soothe me once. I needed to stand on my own.

"It's a spell." Dr. Black explained how the oath worked to Aaron and Melinda.

"We should do it," Melinda said as she set the dough aside and covered it with a dish towel. "If it ensures every-one's safety, including Reid's, then I don't see a downside. He's been hurt enough."

"More than enough," Milo agreed.

I ducked my head, tears pricking my eyes, and my throat constricted. I was touched by their concern, but I couldn't escape the ever-present shame of my situation.

I should never have been so easy to control.

If I hadn't been used to letting others rule my life, perhaps I would have fought harder when Trent kidnapped me. Perhaps I could have stopped him and fewer omegas would have been stolen from their homes and mistreated alongside me.

"Is there a way we can do this to mitigate the risks?" Aaron asked, obviously more reluctant to trust me.

Dr. Black cleared his throat. "It's my opinion that with

the appropriate consequences for breaking the oath, it will be safe. I've thought on the matter and I believe that the oath should be triggered if he attempts to harm anyone who is part of the Grizzly Ridge Clan. The consequences would be the temporary stripping of his magic."

The bottom dropped out of my gut and my heart slammed against my ribcage. What the hell? He wanted me to willingly agree to something that could strip me of my magic? Had he lost his mind?

"Doing this would protect whomever he was about to attack but would also avoid any harm to Reid or his unborn child," Dr. Black finished, looking quite proud of himself.

I backed up a step. Suddenly, this oath didn't sound so good.

Catching sight of my expression, Dr. Black added, "It would only be temporary, and if you don't try to hurt anyone then you won't have any reason to worry. Wouldn't you prefer to have access to your magic than wear those cuffs again?"

My airway constricted and I drew in a deep breath through my nose, blinking to dissipate the spots that had appeared in my vision.

"Reid?" Milo appeared in front of me, his bright eyes burning into mine.

"I need a minute," I snapped, more harshly than I meant to.

His features flickered at my tone but he backed away, giving me enough room to breathe and think.

Dr. Black was right. I didn't intend to harm anyone. I'd done more than enough of that on Trent's orders. Not to mention the fact I doubted I could handle it if they tried to put the cuffs back on me. I might scream or bawl or try to fight them off, and that would be humiliating because I'd never win in my current state.

"It's not a bad plan," Aaron said, giving it his tacit approval as Clan Alpha. "What do you think, Reid?"

"I... I..."

By the wall, Zander shifted, his muscles coiling and releasing, as if he was desperate to come to me but was holding back.

I appreciated that and, honestly, was once again caught off guard by his thoughtfulness. Having a massive shifter in my personal space right now would be too much and he seemed to realize that. Having Milo this close was all I could bear.

"I'll do it," I said, slumping.

"Then let's get to it." Dr. Black opened his satchel. "I've brought the necessary elements with me."

He retrieved a candle, a small brass bowl, a piece of notepaper, a pencil, and a needle. I took the pencil and paper from him and jotted down the oath I swore to keep, then showed it to Dr. Black for approval.

"How does this work?" Zander asked as I folded the paper and placed it inside the brass bowl on the kitchen countertop.

"It has mostly to do with the spell caster's intent," Dr. Black said. "I can't use magic myself but I understand it well enough to know whether the spell works as planned. Essentially, the caster writes the oath and consequences on a sheet of paper, adds a drop of their blood, and burns it, then says *iusiurandum*. If the right intention is there, the magic will slot into place."

All of a sudden, Zander stood between me and the doctor, his big frame vibrating. "He has to bleed?"

My eyes widened and my breath caught in my chest. Was it just me, or did he sound almost... upset? Like he was protective of me and didn't want me hurt.

My heart swelled and my throat clogged with emotion.

Did he actually care? Was he telling the truth about wanting me safe and happy?

Dr. Black held out his hands and took a step backward. "Only a pinprick. He'll barely even feel it."

Zander growled. "A pinprick is too much. I don't want him hurt *at all*."

I shivered and tried to ignore the way blood rushed to my cock. Had I ever noticed how broad his shoulders were before, or how his muscular form shielded me so well?

"This will hurt him less than the cuffs have," Dr. Black said, clearly trying to be reasonable.

"Not. Good. Enough." Zander squared those massive shoulders against the doctor as if he planned to tackle him if he took a step nearer to me.

Needing a distraction before I allowed myself to want things I couldn't have, I grabbed the needle, stuck it in the tip of my finger, and squeezed a drop onto the paper.

The instant the blood welled from the cut, an anguished roar tore from Zander. I flinched and immediately, he settled. He turned to me and seemed to shrink before my eyes, making himself smaller and less intimidating.

"Sorry," he said, his nostrils flaring as his gaze locked on my fingertip. "I'm so sorry."

"It's fine," I said automatically. Was it? Honestly, at this point everything was so topsy-turvy that I had no idea. "I'm sorry for upsetting you."

While Zander was paying attention to me, Dr. Black lit the candle with a lighter that Melinda handed him, then used the candle to set fire to the paper. Flames whooshed upward, then shot down as the paper rapidly burned up. I channeled my intent into the spell, murmured the word he'd said—hoping I'd gotten it right—and felt the spell descend on me like an invisible robe.

"Is it done?" Aaron asked, poised to grab Zander if he freaked out again.

"It's done," Dr. Black confirmed. "All looks well. I don't think we'll have any trouble."

"Thank the gods," Melinda said. "Reid, are you okay?"

"Fine." I backed up, somehow feeling both freer and more stuck than ever. Yes, the spell made it possible for me to use my magic, but it was also something I could never get rid of on my own. Only Aaron, as the Clan Alpha, had the ability to remove the responsibility of the oath from me.

"Wait."

I glanced at Zander, whose exclamation had halted my progress out of the kitchen.

"Can we talk for a bit?" he asked.

I narrowed my eyes and angled myself toward the door. I was overwhelmed, and my instinct was to escape back to the bedroom and get away from all of these people, but to my chagrin, I was intrigued by Zander. When he'd tried to defend me just now, he'd seemed so genuine. Part of me wanted to believe in his sincerity.

"We can stay here," Zander said, his deep brown eyes never leaving my face. "I know you're not comfortable with people in your personal space. Milo can stay too, if you want."

I hesitated, then asked, "Can I put a ward up around myself? It wouldn't be complicated. I only know the basics."

A deep groove formed between his eyebrows but he nodded. "Whatever you need."

"Then we're all right on our own."

"Are you sure?" Milo asked, still hovering nearby. "I don't mind."

"No, it's fine."

He studied me for a long moment, then nodded. "Okay."

Dr. Black tidied up his equipment and slung his satchel over his shoulder. He led the way out of the room and Aaron and Melinda followed, with Milo trailing behind. I was relieved when Milo left the door open.

I leaned against the kitchen counter, not willing to sit because doing so could slow my getaway if escaping became necessary. I didn't think it would, but trust was difficult for me, and Zander hadn't fully earned it yet, although his protectiveness today had been a step in that direction.

"How did you end up with Trent?" Zander asked, walking around the kitchen counter so that it was between us and sitting on one of the stools.

I relaxed a little. He was obviously trying to put me at ease by positioning himself in a less threatening way.

Sighing, I contemplated whether to ignore him or confess. The truth was, I was embarrassed, but if he wanted to discover how it had all happened, it wouldn't be difficult for him to find someone willing to spill their guts. I may as well let him hear it from me.

"I went out on a date with him," I admitted, keeping my gaze on Zander even though it was uncomfortable. I didn't want him to be able to surprise me if he moved quickly. "I grew up in a small town and I was isolated from others my age. When I met him, he was charming and I fooled myself into thinking we might be mates. I was just rebellious enough to sneak away for a date and he used the opportunity to drug and abduct me."

I hated myself for being so foolish.

"I'm sorry." Zander's voice was strained and his hands weren't visible above the kitchen counter, but I suspected they were squeezed into fists. Whether it was his intention or not, I appreciated him not putting on a scary display of alpha angst.

I shrugged. "I learned an important lesson."

Don't trust anyone. Even yourself.

A muscle in Zander's jaw twitched. He stood up and went to the kettle, flicking the switch to start the water heating. He grabbed two mugs from the cupboard and added a tea bag to one.

"Do you prefer tea or coffee?" he asked, poised with his hand above the box of tea, ready to grab another.

I cocked my head, wondering why the sudden change of tack. "Uh, coffee."

With a forced smile, he nodded and packed the tea away. "Is instant all right? I don't drink coffee so I don't know how to use the coffee maker."

"Instant is fine." I'd been lucky to even get that while I was living with Trent's pack.

He scooped a spoonful of coffee into the second mug. "Sugar? Cream?"

This was so strange. An alpha was actually preparing coffee for me.

"Creamer, if you have some. No sugar."

This time, his smile was genuine. "I don't consume much sugar either. My family likes to call me a health nut, but I think it's important to take care of my body. It's not as if I'll get another."

The kettle boiled and he poured water into the mugs, then added creamer to mine. I didn't have the heart to tell him that I did like sweet food, just not sweet coffee.

"Would you like a cookie?" he asked, stirring my coffee and sliding it over the counter to me. "I think I saw some in the cabinet. There's oatmeal raisin as well as chocolate chip, if you prefer something with more nutritional value."

"Chocolate chip?" I perked up before I remembered that

I wasn't supposed to be so obvious in my preferences because they'd been used against me in the past.

Zander smirked and plated two cookies–one of which he handed to me. "So, you do like some sugar, then?"

Hesitantly, I nodded.

"Do you have a favorite comfort food?"

I debated for a long moment whether to reply, but in the end, all he could do was withhold my comfort food from me. I hadn't had it for ages anyway.

"Fried chicken."

Mom used to make it for me back when she and Dad first started allowing me to be used like a battery by other warlocks. I think guilt had driven her to it. But she'd stopped feeling guilty a long time ago. I'd hardly even seen them in the last few years.

The cookie was good. While we ate, we chatted a little about nothing important and, gradually, the muscles in my back eased and I stopped looking for traps or potential pitfalls in every word spoken.

A while later, Melinda popped her head in and announced that it was time for lunch and we needed to either clear out of the kitchen or help.

Zander excused himself, perhaps sensing that I'd taken as much of his presence as I could for one day, and I fled to the doorway. I was hovering there, uncertain what to do, when Aaron appeared beside me.

I squeaked, my heart hammering and my muscles going taut once again.

"Sorry." He eyed me cautiously. "I didn't mean to frighten you."

"It's fine."

"I just wanted to ask…" His steady gaze held me captive and I couldn't help but wonder if it was some kind of Clan Alpha magic that made it difficult to resist giving him what he wanted. "What do you plan to do now that you're free from the Red Moon Pack?"

"I don't know," I whispered, and that frightened me.

I had nowhere to go. No one to turn to. No resources of my own.

And I was pregnant.

Honestly, I was in deep shit.

THIRTEEN

*Z*ANDER

My head throbbed and I rubbed at my temples as I got out of my parents' spare bed, my jaw aching with the strain of clenching it for hours on end. I'd woken in the small hours of the morning to the sound of whimpers and cries coming from the room next door.

The sour stench of an omega's distress would have driven my alpha side crazy even if he hadn't been my mate. I was certain that Dad must have been awake and suffering as well, eager to protect Reid from whatever plagued his dreams, but at least he had Momma to assure him that staying put was the right decision.

I'd second-guessed myself a dozen times over. It was difficult to believe that leaving Reid on his own was the best course of action when I could hear every sob and snif-fle. The poor guy hadn't even slept through it all. He'd woken every now and then, his heart racing as he tried to calm himself.

Everything in me wanted to go to him, but it was the knowledge that my presence wouldn't bring him the comfort he needed that kept me pinned in place.

After how much time we'd spent together yesterday, I didn't want to push my luck by forcing Reid to spend too long around me. I ducked out of the house before he stirred, grabbed a quick breakfast on the road, and drove to the police station.

When I entered, the lights were low. I went to the break room to make myself a cup of chamomile tea in the hopes it would ease my headache and found Garrick already in there, rinsing a coffee cup in the sink.

"What are you doing here so early?" I asked, sauntering over to the kettle and switching it on.

He sighed. "Trying to track the other omegas—the ones that the Red Moon Pack kidnapped and trafficked. I need to find them. It's like this itch under my skin. I can't handle knowing they're out there and in danger."

Assuming they're still alive.

I swallowed the thought. Some things were better left unsaid.

"Any luck?" I asked instead.

"Not yet. Everything is rumor and guesswork. It's driving me fucking crazy."

I grimaced. "I know how you feel. Listening to Reid's nightmares is almost unbearable. I wish I could bring Trent back to life just so I could kill him slowly. He deserved to suffer more than he did."

Trent's life had ended quickly. At the time, that had been the best thing for everyone in order to end the fight, but it would have brought me a sick sense of satisfaction if I'd had an hour alone with him so he could learn how it felt to pick on someone his own size. Someone capable of fighting back.

"No one could blame you for feeling that way." Garrick set his coffee cup down and cocked his head. "It sounds like you've got a bit of frustration to work out."

"Yeah." I put my hand on my hip, waiting to see where he was going with this.

"Well," he continued, crossing his arms. "I do too. Want to spar?"

A wicked grin stole across my face. "Fuck yes."

Sparring with Garrick was exactly what I needed. We were a similar size—although I was slightly bigger—and of similar strength. We could both give as good as we got and not have to worry about permanently maiming someone.

We made our way to the built-in gym. It was a long, rectangular space. One end was taken up by free weights and exercise machines while the other had a padded floor and was used for sparring and self-defense or combat-readiness refresher courses.

I stripped off my shirt and removed my shoes, setting them neatly aside. Sometimes, Garrick and I preferred to spar in our shifted forms, but we couldn't do that in here without shredding the floor. We'd have to keep to our human forms. He pulled off his overshirt but kept on his tank top. His shoes came off and the socks followed.

We circled each other on the mat. Garrick's amber-brown eyes assessed me for weak points as I did the same to him.

He struck first. Unsurprising. His internal alpha drove him harder than mine did. He was more inclined to aggression.

I deflected his fist from my forearm, pivoted, and tried to hook behind his leg with my heel. He bent his knees, leaned into me, and went to toss me over his shoulder, but I released him before he could throw me.

His grin had a maniacal edge and I was sure mine was the same as we leapt at each other with renewed vigor. We exchanged blows, but I scarcely noticed any damage until he cracked me across the face and the coppery taste of blood flooded my mouth.

I spat blood onto the floor, grimacing because I'd have to clean that later. We had a policy that people cleaned up their own messes, whether or not they were the boss. Being the sheriff wouldn't get me out of it.

I tackled Garrick and managed to pin him but he flipped us over and yanked me into an arm bar. I tried to find a way out of it, but when it became clear that the only way I'd escape was by dislocating something, I conceded.

Garrick flopped onto the ground beside me and we both lay there, breathing heavily. My face smarted and my knuckles ached but everything would be healed before noon.

"Did that help?" Garrick asked.

"Yeah." I held out my fist and he tapped his against it. "Thanks, man."

"No problem."

I sighed. "Reid needs comfort, but I don't know how to give it to him."

I didn't know why I was opening up to my one unmated brother about this. Perhaps because this could just have easily happened to him instead of me.

Garrick levered himself up. "Well, what does he like?"

I racked my mind. The little warlock had been close-mouthed and hadn't given much away. That said, I recalled that he'd said fried chicken was his comfort food. I couldn't be sure whether he'd been truthful, but I saw no reason for him to lie about it.

I clambered to my feet and offered Garrick a hand to pull him up. "Thanks. I've got an idea."

He nodded and didn't ask what I was planning even though he was obviously curious.

The rest of the day passed without any progress being

made in terms of discovering where other omegas kidnapped by the Red Moon Pack may have ended up. I tried not to take it to heart.

Instead, I headed home and searched the internet for a fried chicken recipe. When I found one, I did my best to follow it step by step, but I was smart enough to do a test run first. The final product definitely didn't look or taste like anything that anyone would want to eat.

Disappointed, I called Momma to ask for help. I talked her through what I'd done and she figured out where I'd gone wrong and stayed on the line with me until I managed to create several edible pieces.

I covered the fried chicken to keep it warm and carried it over to my parents' place. I knew they hadn't eaten yet since Momma had been on the phone with me, so I let myself in and went in search of Reid. I found his bedroom door closed.

"Reid?" I called, knocking softly so as not to startle him.

There was a shuffling and he opened the door, a crease on his cheek that indicated he'd been lying down for a while—perhaps even napping.

"What is it?" he asked, a furrow between his eyebrows.

I held up the plate. "I made you fried chicken."

His mouth fell open and he stared at me for a long moment before closing it. "You... made that for me?"

My tongue was suddenly clumsy. I hadn't screwed this up, had I? Perhaps he'd said he liked fried chicken but actually hated it. Nervously, I offered him the plate.

He narrowed his eyes at it. "An... *alpha*... cooked for me?"

Ah, so that's what his problem was.

With how poorly he'd been treated in the past, he couldn't fathom an alpha choosing to act in service of him. My heart twinged. If he gave me the chance, I'd dote on him for the rest of his life, so he'd never doubt how much he—and other omegas—should be cherished by their alphas.

"I'm not sure that it's any good," I said awkwardly. "I can cook, but I haven't used this recipe before."

He took the plate from me and unwrapped the tinfoil covering. He glanced at me, as if expecting me to yank the plate back from him and shout that it had been a joke. When I didn't, he hesitantly picked up a piece of chicken and nibbled on it.

His eyes widened. "It's nice."

My bear chuffed internally.

We pleased our mate.

I studied Reid's face, a little dubious. I couldn't imagine the chicken was particularly tasty. I saw no traces of deceit there though and he took a larger bite, keeping his eyes on me.

"Thank you," he murmured. "This is... really nice of you. I love it. I've been craving chicken all week."

Warmth filled me and my chest swelled. I fought the urge to preen, incredibly happy to have done something to nurture his unborn child and bust through his usual reserve.

"You're welcome," I said, tilting closer to breathe in his lovely scent with that hint of honeysuckle from the baby.

He glanced at the plate and then back at me before drawing in a deep breath. "Would you like to join me?"

I wanted to leap at the chance, but I reined it in because coming on too strong would only scare him. "If you don't mind."

He backed up and sat on the edge of the bed, patting the spot beside him. When I perched there, he offered me the chicken, and I took a small piece and ate it. I didn't want to eat his treat, but if I just sat there without doing anything, he might get uncomfortable.

"What food do you like?" Reid asked as he dug into another piece of chicken.

"Honey is my guilty pleasure, obviously. I love honey-roasted nuts. But usually, I prefer lean meat and vegetables. I'm a simple kind of guy."

He cocked his head and studied me intently. "There's something to be said for simple."

He didn't speak again as he finished the chicken. When he was done, he smiled at me hesitantly.

"Thank you, Zander. I haven't had fried chicken for years, and I really missed it." He blinked rapidly, his eyes shining with tears. "Stupid hormones."

"I'll make it whenever you like," I declared.

His answering smile hit me like a punch in the gut. I'd do anything if it meant he'd smile like that again.

I picked up the plate. We'd made progress tonight, but I didn't want to stay too long and wear out my welcome.

"I'll see you later," I said, backing out of the room. "Take care of yourself."

On the way out of the house, I ran into Dad. He grabbed my shoulder and whisked me into his office.

"What's up?" I asked, leaning against the wall as he closed the door behind himself.

He turned to me, his expression uncharacteristically hesitant. "Look, Zander. I know your mate made that oath and that he hasn't tried to hurt anyone, but I'm worried that he might. I don't want to make him feel any more like a prisoner than he already does, but I don't fully trust him either. Will you keep an eye on him for me?"

I stared at Dad, bemused. "Of course I will."

As if I'd ever take my attention off Reid now that I'd found him.

His shoulders slumped. "Good. I know I can trust you."

I nodded, but something niggled at the back of my

mind. He'd said he was certain he could trust me, but could Reid? My mate ought to be able to, but I'd essentially just promised to spy on him.

Damn, I had no idea what the right thing to do was in these circumstances.

As if sensing the direction my thoughts had taken, Dad's bear flashed in his eyes. "It'll be all right, son. I'm trying to get in touch with an old contact who specializes in magic and is familiar with this sort of situation. We'll figure it out."

I nodded, hoping he was right. At the moment, I worried that if I put a foot wrong, it could cost me my mate.

FOURTEEN

R*EID*

I gripped the edges of the toilet bowl and retched into it, unloading my breakfast inside. My abdomen ached, the muscles worn out from throwing up, and the bitter taste in my mouth made me retch again, even though I had nothing else left in my stomach and it squeezed like a wrung-out sponge.

"I need... fresh air..." I panted, tearing off a length of toilet paper and using it to dab my sweaty forehead and then around my mouth.

"Are you all right?" Zander asked.

He was hovering outside the bathroom and had been since I'd sprinted away from the dining table and dropped to my knees in front of the porcelain throne—as had become common for me over the past two days. It was like now that my mind knew I was pregnant, my body was throwing all of the unavoidable signs at me.

"Fine," I muttered, swallowing the temptation to ask whether I *looked* like I was all right. I was pretty sure that would be a no.

I staggered upright and snatched the glass of water

from his outstretched hand. I took a gulp, swirled it around in my mouth and spat into the toilet, then flushed the disgusting mess away.

"I have fried chicken," he said, motioning toward the kitchen. "Will that help?"

I retched again. For some reason, chicken was the last thing I wanted now, even though I'd craved it for several days.

"Okay, no chicken," he amended. "Crackers?"

"Pickles," I decided. "But I need to settle my stomach first. Being outside will help."

"It's howling out there," Zander said as I handed the glass back to him. "I think it would be best if you stayed in the house."

I straightened and bit back the reply that leapt to my lips. While no one here had harmed me, and I was beginning to think they never would, I was constantly worried that I might say the wrong thing and someone would lash. Then I'd finally have evidence that I was right not to trust anyone.

A dark part of me kept pushing at their boundaries, almost *wanting* them to snap so I'd have that evidence. It made no sense because I was warm and well-fed and being treated kindly for the first time in... well, longer than I could recall. I should just relax and enjoy it, but I was scared that if I did, the rug would be pulled out from under me.

"It won't be for long," I said calmly. "I don't want to risk my baby. I just need to feel the wind on my face."

I half-expected him to try to forbid me from doing it, but instead he nodded, although he clearly wasn't happy with the decision.

"Wait here," he said gruffly and disappeared into one of the bedrooms. When he emerged, he was carrying a bundle of clothing. "Here. Put these on."

I took them, baffled. There was a beanie, so I tugged it over my hair. I wrapped the scarf around my neck and slipped my arms into the sleeves of the jacket. It was massive on me, falling nearly to my knees, but I zipped it up and slid my hands into the gloves.

"Thank you." I breathed in. The fabric smelled of pine trees and bergamot, and it made me think of lean muscle and sun-bronzed skin.

Zander grinned. "Thank you for humoring me. Let's go."

I frowned. "You're coming with me?"

"Yeah." He stuck his ungloved hands into his pockets. "But I can keep my mouth shut if you need quiet. I know that can be difficult to find in this household."

I cocked my head. "If you're coming along, shouldn't you be wearing a jacket too?"

He shrugged. "Shifters run hot. A sweater is fine with me. If I get too cold, I can always shift. Bears have plenty of fur."

That was true, although real bears also usually hibernated through the worst of winter. I didn't argue though. I supposed he knew what he was doing and he didn't seem like the kind of guy who would make a big deal out of trying to seem tough and masculine. He drank herbal tea, after all.

"Do you need another drink before we head out?" Zander asked. "Or should I grab you a pickle to go?"

"Not right now." Honestly, if I put anything in my tummy, it would probably come straight back up again.

Zander tromped down the hall and I followed him. As we passed the living area, he called out to let Melinda know that we were heading outside. He held the front door open and I stepped through it and shivered as the wind blasted into my side. It was just as well he'd given me the jacket because it was one of those frigid winds that would have cut straight through my sweater and made me icy to the core.

Zander closed the door and moved alongside me. "Are you sure you want to stay out here?"

"Just for a little while. Don't worry, it won't be long."

I started along the path away from the house and turned left when I reached the road. I expected Zander to fall into step alongside me but instead he walked a few yards behind.

Perhaps he was giving me space. If so, I was grateful for it. Nevertheless, my thoughts lingered on the hulking bear shifter as I gazed around the cold, barren landscape of Grizzly Ridge. He'd been nothing but supportive and kind. I wanted to trust that he was exactly the sort of man he presented himself as.

Gods, I wanted it so badly.

But after seeing so much of the worst side of humanity, how was I supposed to believe it?

I looked around. Most of the houses had lights on in the windows, but the trees were bare, the gardens mostly empty, and there were no cars on the street. It was almost eerily quiet. I wasn't sure whether to think of it as a Hallmark-like small town or the setting of a horror movie right before everything went to hell.

I glanced over my shoulder, my gaze clashing with Zander's and strange heat lancing through me. His eyes were intent, and he didn't take them off me. He truly did seem to want me. But how did that work when I was pregnant with another alpha's baby?

Surely that was enough to put most alphas off. The ones I'd spent time around before never would have wanted to raise someone else's child. Yet he hadn't tried to influence my decision to keep the baby. Would that change?

A chill swept through me that had nothing to do with the frozen surroundings.

Behind me, Zander made a sound in the back of his throat, perhaps sensing my emotions. I drew in a deep breath, trying to calm myself. It wouldn't do me any good if he could smell everything that went through my head.

I paused at an intersection, taking a moment to check left and right as I collected myself. We'd gotten closer to the town center and a row of shops stretched ahead, some of them with cute facades and signs outside.

In the other direction, there was a bronze statue of a man in an old-fashioned hat. I wandered closer. The plaque was frosted over so I couldn't read what it said.

"He was the town's first mayor," Zander explained, having caught up to me at some point. "And the Clan's first Alpha."

"A bear shifter, I assume?" That would make sense, given the town's name.

He nodded.

I peeked at him out of the corner of my eye, revisiting my earlier thoughts. I honestly didn't believe that Zander would try to take my baby. He didn't seem like that kind of man. But if he or anyone else tried to do that, I wouldn't let them.

That's when it struck me, with absolute clarity.

I *wanted* my baby.

It had seemed so complicated, but it really wasn't.

This baby was mine. I'd raise them to be better than their kidnapping, assaulting father. I'd teach them about kindness and I'd never, ever use them the way I'd been used.

I blinked as moisture gathered in my eyelashes and wiped it away before it could freeze in place.

It seemed that deciding what to do about the baby

wasn't so difficult. Not when I couldn't handle the thought of being separated from them. Not when the baby deserved to know they were loved, and I could give them that. They'd never ever doubt their place in the world if I had anything to say about it.

I took off again and walked for a while longer, until a wave of nausea rolled through me and I bent over a nearby bush and emptied the pitiful contents of my stomach into it.

Zander approached and hesitantly stroked my back. "Can I carry you home?"

Straightening, I shook my head. My instincts screamed at me to just agree. To close my eyes and snuggle up to his broad chest. But I didn't let them get the best of me. Whatever my instincts wanted to believe, I couldn't afford to trust Zander completely or to be too vulnerable with him.

Maybe one day, but not yet.

CHAPTER

FIFTEEN

*Z*ANDER

"You look like you could use either a double shot espresso or a stiff drink."

I looked toward the doorway, where Garrick was leaning against the frame. "Coffee rots your gut."

I didn't know what else to say. I couldn't deny that the idea of either caffeine or alcohol appealed to me more than it usually would. It was the end of a long Monday and the station had almost completely emptied except for the night shift. I hadn't closed the curtains yet so the darkness outside was intruding on the otherwise well-lit office space.

Garrick sauntered into the room, frowning. "Seriously, you look rough. What's going on?"

I picked my hat up and flicked an invisible speck of dirt off it. "Same old."

He crossed his arms. "Come on, Z. Drop the act."

I sighed. Damn, he was too good at playing Alpha-with-a-capital-A. No wonder he was destined to take over leadership of the clan from Dad even though I was the oldest child.

89

"It's wearing on me to be away from Reid," I admitted, running my hands through my hair. "My bear wants to be with him constantly, but Reid is still cautious around me. Even if he did want to bond, he only just lost his mate, so the timing for anything to happen between us isn't right."

Garrick came farther into the office and sat opposite me. "Is it the emotional distance that's the problem or would just closing the physical distance help?"

I shrugged. "I don't know."

"Perhaps you should spend a little more time with him then. Just enough to ease your bear."

I rested against the back of the chair. "I've already been hanging around a lot. I don't want to overwhelm him."

"Maybe not." He cocked his head. "But you want him to know that you're there for him. You want him to know that he can come to you."

I stared at him, realizing he had a point. "I'll head over there now, just for a little while."

"Good." Garrick looked pleased. "If you want to go straight there, I can bring over a change of clothes for you since you won't want to stay in uniform."

"I'd hate to put you out." It didn't feel right to have the future Clan Alpha running around after me.

Garrick rolled his eyes. "You're not. You're my brother. It's what family does."

Something warmed inside me. "Thanks, G."

"No problem." He stood and clapped his hands together. "Get up. Off with you. That cute little omega is waiting."

I narrowed my eyes at him. "He's mine."

"All yours," Garrick agreed with a chuckle.

"As long as you know that."

I snatched up my hat, my bag, and grabbed my keys from on top of the desk. Garrick and I wandered out together and I bid farewell to the deputy on duty as we passed reception.

Outside, Garrick strode to his vehicle and I went to mine. I drove onto the main street and was about to turn toward the cul-de-sac where my family lived when a bauble in the jewelry store window caught my eye.

I slammed on the brakes and pulled into the empty parking spot outside the store. The jeweler was taking in the sign and he glanced over as I threw the door open and rushed out.

"What's wrong?" he asked, looking around nervously as though expecting robbers to materialize from behind the nearest street lamp.

"I need to buy that," I said, pointing at the thing that had caught my eye. From a distance, I hadn't been able to tell exactly what it was, but I'd had the powerful urge to give it to Reid. Up close, I could see that it was a black pendant necklace. Some kind of stone with a tapered crystal-cut end, bound in gold hung from the waxed cord.

The jeweler raised an eyebrow. "Jewelry emergency?"

"Something like that." I couldn't take my eyes away from the pendant, strangely certain that it belonged to Reid. It needed to be with Reid.

"All right. You're lucky you caught me. I was just about to leave."

I hesitated. "I can come back in the morning if now is inconvenient."

Not that I wanted to wait. My instincts were going haywire.

He shook his head. "It's no problem. Come in and let's get it packaged up for you."

I followed him inside and he put the pendant into a black velvet bag and handed it to me. I paid what seemed an exorbitant fee for what was essentially a black rock and didn't second-guess the decision for a moment, because I had no doubt at all that for some reason, Reid needed to have this.

Once I'd paid and the sudden, insistent brain fog had dissipated, I decided my subconscious might be onto something with this whole gift-buying thing.

I dropped by the minimart before it closed and picked up a few things I'd seen Milo use since he'd become pregnant. A special set of bath salts that promoted relaxation. Body oil designed to soothe Reid's skin as his belly grew. A soft, cozy blanket. A range of snacks because I wasn't sure what he liked best.

That done, I took my new purchases to my parents' place. I knocked on the door as I entered and called out to let them know I was coming in. I went through to the living room and laid out the items on the coffee table so Reid could see what they were, then searched until I found him in the kitchen.

"Hey," I greeted.

His eyes widened and he murmured a soft, "Hello."

"How are you feeling?"

He waved his hand from side to side. "Better than yesterday. I've only been sick once, so that counts for something, right?"

"Have you asked Dr. Black for nausea medication?"

"Melinda has." He looked down almost shyly. "And Milo has made a few suggestions for meals that might not make me throw up."

"I'm glad to hear it." Thank the gods my family had taken him under their wings. "I have something for you."

He tilted his head curiously. "What?"

"Nothing bad." I tried to subtly breathe him in, my bear overjoyed to be near him once again. I wanted to roll in his bed until I was coated with his signature ozone-and-concrete-during-summer-rain scent, but I refused to do anything that might scare him off. "Come and see."

Tentatively, he followed me to the living room.

I gestured at the offerings on the table. "These are for you."

He studied them for a long moment, his gaze flicking from one item to the next. He lingered on the pendant, which I'd pulled from the velvet bag and laid on top of it.

Slowly, his eyes met mine. "These are gifts? I don't have to offer anything in return?"

My heart clenched and my stomach dropped. "Nothing," I whispered hoarsely, hating that it ever crossed his mind that I might want some kind of quid pro quo. "You have no obligation to me if you accept any of this. I just wanted to do something nice for you." And, for some reason, my instincts had screamed that he needed that pendant.

He picked up the pendant and smoothed the pad of his thumb along one side of it. "This is obsidian. Do you know what it does?"

"No," I admitted. I knew that some crystals possessed properties that made them useful for certain spells but, having no magic myself, I'd never bothered to learn. "What does it do?"

Reid stared at the pendant, mesmerized, but he didn't reply. After several seconds ticked by, he reluctantly put it down again.

"The things are here if you want them," I told him, disappointed he hadn't been more enthusiastic about the gift.

One step at a time, I reminded myself.

Reid hadn't been able to trust anyone for a long time. He couldn't change that just because I wanted him to.

CHAPTER
SIXTEEN

EID

I snuck from the bedroom on feet made silent by a spell I'd learned during my tenure with Trent, when he'd hired that warlock to train me in a few spells that were useful to the pack.

Closing my eyes, I murmured the spell and concentrated on masking my scent as I made my way to the living room. I tiptoed to the coffee table and peered through the darkness, trying to identify each of the items that Zander had laid there earlier. A warlock's night vision wasn't anywhere near as good as a shifter's, but I didn't dare switch on the light in case someone noticed.

There, resting on the small velvet bag, was the obsidian necklace I'd been so tempted by. I hadn't been able to convince myself to grab it at the time. I wasn't brave enough. In my experience, showing someone that you wanted something just gave them a roadmap to your weak spots.

I didn't think Zander was looking for any vulnerabilities to exploit but old habits die hard.

I slipped the waxed cord around my neck and a weight

instantly lifted from my soul. I wrapped my hand around the crystal and basked in the wonderful sense of protection it offered.

Obsidian crystals shielded the person who bore them from psychic attack and repelled negative energy. Considering my situation, I couldn't think of many crystals I'd rather have. Perhaps this obsidian would help me stay hidden. At the very least, it would boost my personal wards and offer additional protection to my baby.

I smoothed my hands over my abdomen, noting the barest hint of a bump, and rearranged the items on the table to make it less obvious that something had been taken. I couldn't shake the feeling that Zander would notice. He was observant like that. But hopefully he wouldn't make a big deal of it.

I stroked the fluffy blanket. It was soft and when I raised it to my face, it smelled clean and new. After months of living in filth, it was so tempting to claim it. This would be something warm and cozy, just for me.

But no. I was already taking one thing. If I removed the blanket—by far the largest thing here—someone would definitely notice.

I froze, my hand still on the blanket.

Hold on. Perhaps I should take it for that very reason. If Zander noticed that the blanket was missing, he might not look further. The obsidian crystal might fly under the radar.

Snatching it up, I took the blanket back to bed with me. When I returned to sleep, I kept the necklace on and the blanket around my shoulders.

In the morning, I dressed in a high-necked T-shirt and hid the obsidian necklace beneath it. After checking my reflection to make sure it wasn't visible, I wandered out to the kitchen where Melinda was serving herself breakfast.

"Good morning, Reid," she said, glancing over with a smile.

"Hi, Melinda," I replied, helping myself to coffee and then filling a plate. I took it to the dining table, where Melinda had joined Aaron and Zander. I paused, caught off guard to find Zander here. I'd expected him to be at work already.

"Morning, Reid," he said, smiling warmly. "Did you sleep well?"

The corners of his eyes creased and my heart fluttered in response.

What was wrong with me? I shouldn't find the crinkles around his eyes or the flecks of gray at his temples sexy. He was an alpha. I couldn't afford to find anything attractive about him at all.

"I did," I replied, belatedly realizing that I'd hesitated for too long and made it awkward. "And you?"

"Like a log." He grinned and my traitorous heart gave another pitter-patter.

"How are you feeling today?" Melinda asked, leaning slightly toward me. "No lingering aftereffects from the reaction you had to the cuffs?"

I shook my head. "I seem to be fine."

The burns stung but whatever it was the doctor had put on took the edge off and sped up my healing. I'd peeked under the wraps earlier and saw that the new skin was already showing through where I'd usually expect the weeping sores to last for at least a couple of days.

"I'm glad to hear it."

"Have you given any thought to what comes next?" Aaron asked, echoing the question he'd raised a few days ago.

I sipped the coffee, relieved to have a delay tactic on hand. The roast was rich and bittersweet. Usually, I preferred creamer in my coffee, but I'd been too scattered to add it.

"Um, actually, sir," I said when I'd drawn out the coffee-drinking for as long as possible, "I thought perhaps I ought to move to the Omega House."

Everyone at the table stiffened. I looked down, the hairs on the back of my neck standing on end. I wasn't afraid of them, exactly, but I wasn't not afraid either.

"It's just that that's where it makes the most sense for me to be. I'm a pregnant omega without a place to live and I've been through something that makes it hard to, uh, re-assimilate. Isn't that the whole point of an Omega House?"

It made no sense for me to stay with Aaron and Melinda. At least, not on the face of it. They were the clan leaders. It wasn't their job to take in any stray who crossed their path. I was only here because they didn't trust me, but surely the oath would take care of that concern?

"I think it's best if you stay here for the moment," Aaron said, choosing his words carefully.

"Why?" I asked tentatively. "I'm not a threat, I promise."

Melinda started to reach for me but stopped.

"It's not that," Aaron said, laying his knife and fork down. "You've been through a lot and you'll have more support here."

I frowned. "Aren't those places set up to have support systems in place? And wouldn't the other omegas be able to help me with the pregnancy?"

I watched Aaron and Melinda exchange a look and realized that their reluctance definitely stemmed from their worry that I might hurt someone rather than out of any concern for me.

Reluctantly, I added, "If you need me to swear a specific oath not to harm anyone in the Omega House, I'll do it." I didn't want to bind myself more than necessary, but it wasn't as if I was planning to hurt any displaced omegas. After all, I was one of them. "I can even help with the protective warding. It's one of the few things I'm any good at."

Honestly, if Trent had ordered me to shield him the day the Grizzly Ridge clan attacked the pack house, we might not be in this situation right now, but thankfully, he hadn't.

"You'd be safer staying close to the Clan Alpha," Zander said, his attention laser-focused on me despite the cup of tea halfway to his mouth.

"Why?" It wasn't as if anyone would be coming for me—other than my parents, perhaps, and I had my doubts that a shifter would be able to run them off, no matter how strong they were.

"Because no one would risk a confrontation in my home," Aaron said, studying me as if I were a particularly fascinating insect. "Out there, we don't have the same guarantee."

I cocked my head. "Why would anyone confront me?"

Melinda's tongue darted out to moisten her lips. "Perhaps because of things you did while under Trent's control?"

My gut sank and I suddenly felt very small.

No matter how much I might like to tell myself that the things Trent had forced me to do weren't my fault, I couldn't completely avoid taking responsibility for them. Perhaps if I'd been smarter or stronger I could have escaped before he'd been able to turn me into one of his most valuable tools.

"That wasn't your fault," Zander growled, glaring at his mother.

She frowned. "Of course not. But some people might

not see it that way." She sighed. "Why don't you talk to Hamish, the manager over at the Omega House, and see what he has to say on the matter?"

"Thank you," I whispered, ducking my head so I couldn't see whether Aaron or Zander were displeased by her suggestion.

After breakfast, Melinda drove me to the Omega House and knocked on the front door. It was a turn-of-the-century style white villa with a gabled roof and a small front porch.

After a moment, the door opened inward to reveal the tallest, broadest omega I'd ever seen. He had close-cropped brown hair, a stubbled jaw, and muscular biceps that flexed as he crossed his arms.

"Alpha mate." He dipped his head respectfully to Melinda before turning to me. "And who is this?"

I liked that he asked. Considering this was a small town, I was sure I was the subject of a lot of speculation, but he didn't assume anything.

Melinda smiled at him. "Hello, Hamish. This is Reid. He's an omega warlock and he'd like to talk to you about the possibility of staying here."

"I'll help with the wards," I blurted out, eager to get on his good side. "I'm not good at much magic but I can do wards, as long as they aren't too specific."

Hamish arched an eyebrow but his expression gave nothing away. "You don't have to do anything to earn a place here, Reid. However, I do have to ask whether you pose a danger to any of the omegas in my care." His jaw tightened. "I don't tolerate danger to my omegas."

My heart flipped—not in a romantic way, but in a "*I want to be this guy when I grow up*" kind of way. I'd never met an omega who was so assertive. So sure of himself. Even the way he held himself showed that he wouldn't back down if threatened.

He was like a German shepherd, confident in his own abilities. Meanwhile, I was no better than a yappy Chihuahua, trying to convince everyone I could defend myself when they could all see how small and useless I was.

"I won't hurt them," I promised. "Not unless someone tries to hurt me."

There. That covered self-defense. Not that I expected to need it.

He nodded. "That seems reasonable. And you say you can help with the wards?"

"Yes." I knew where their weak spots were because I was the one who'd taken advantage of them to allow Trent's packmates to kidnap a pair of female omegas from here only a short time ago.

He tapped his chin and leaned against the doorframe. "Wouldn't you rather stay with the Clan Alpha and Alpha Mate?"

"We'd prefer that," Melinda said, drawing his attention back to her.

I gritted my teeth. "I want to feel like I have some control of my life," I murmured, hating that they were making me come out and say it. "I can't do that while I'm hanging in some weird limbo."

Hamish studied me for a long moment and I wondered what he was looking for.

"Come in," he said eventually. "Let me give you a tour."

SEVENTEEN

Z *ANDER*

I inhaled deeply as I neared my parents' place, expecting to smell the familiar ozone-and-summer-rain in the air but stopped short when I didn't find it.

Sure, Reid's scent was present, but it was diluted. At my best guess, he hadn't been home for several hours.

My heart beat a little faster and I hurried inside and strode down the hall, checking each door I passed, then headed upstairs and checked there too. The room Reid had been staying in was empty, the sheets stripped from the mattress.

Panic clawed at my chest and I raced into the kitchen.

"Where's Reid?" I asked Momma, who was peeling potatoes at the counter.

She glanced up as she rinsed a potato under the tap. "He moved to the Omega House earlier today."

"Just like that?" I was astounded. I'd assumed Momma would talk him out of leaving. Either that, or there would be a delay while they cleared a room for him and got his affairs in order. Not that he had much to get in order, I supposed.

"I'm sorry, Zander." She dried her hands and came over and scooped me into a hug. "We couldn't keep him locked up here if he wanted to go. That wouldn't be fair and it wouldn't endear you to him either."

"But..."

But what? I wanted him close?

That was selfish of me. If he wanted to leave, he had every right to do so. Just like I had every right to go there and visit him. After the day I'd had, I needed to see my omega, even if I wasn't able to pull him close the way I'd like to.

"I'll be back." I gave her one last squeeze and stalked away before she could try to talk me out of it.

I drove to the Omega House, parked outside, and jogged across the path and up to the front door, where I knocked briskly.

Hamish opened the door, his brow furrowed with irritation. "It's dinner time. What are you doing here?"

I ran my hand through my hair, thrown by the challenging glint in his eye. I'd forgotten how protective he could be of the omegas in his care.

"I need to see Reid," I said, shifting my weight from one foot to the other. "It won't be for long. I'm happy to wait until he's finished eating." I could sit in the car and reply to some emails while I waited.

"It's beyond calling hours." He tilted his chin up. "Since the abductions, we've instituted a new policy. If it's outside of daylight hours, there are no visitors allowed. It's for everyone's safety."

Desperation seized me. "I just want to see him and make sure he's okay. Won't you make an exception? I'm the sheriff so I'm hardly a threat and I'll be in and out within two minutes.”

Hamish narrowed his eyes. “Sheriff or not, you’re an alpha, and we’ve had enough of alphas pushing us around. It isn’t happening.”

The bottom dropped out of my stomach and sweat beaded at my hairline. I felt like a junkie who was about to go into withdrawals.

“I respect that. Could you...” I sighed, unsure how far to push my luck. “Could you just tell him I’m here and ask if he’ll come out to talk to me on the doorstep for a moment?”

Hamish stared at me for a long moment before huffing. “If it was up to me, I’d send you away. It’s nothing personal, but the omegas here need to know they’re safe from alphas. *All* alphas. That said, I know this must be hard on you and it’s Reid’s decision whether he wants to see you or not. I’ll pass the message along. Don’t make me regret it.”

“I won’t,” I promised. “Thank you, Hamish.”

With a grunt, he closed the door in my face. The lock snicked into place. The seconds ticked by as I stood there, waiting. A couple of minutes later, the door opened and my heart lifted as I realized the petite silhouette in the doorway was Reid’s, not Hamish’s.

He crossed his arms over his slender chest as he studied me. “What are you doing here?”

I smiled, the tightness in my chest already easing. “I just wanted to see you. How was your day?”

Reid cocked his head. “My day was fine. I’m sure your parents told you that I officially moved here.”

“They did.” I nodded, then felt like an idiot. “Are you settling in all right?”

One of his eyebrows hitched up ever so slightly, as if he didn’t quite know what to make of me. “My room is nice and I helped with dinner.”

He seemed proud of that. Perhaps we’d done him a

disservice by coddling him. We'd wanted to give him time to heal though.

"Is there anything you need?" I asked, wishing he'd let me help him. I'd noticed earlier that he'd taken the blanket I'd bought for him as well as the pendant, but he'd left everything else. It wasn't enough. He needed more.

He shrugged. "I have clean bedding, food, and shelter. I think the bases are covered."

I looked away so he wouldn't see me grimace. He deserved more than the bare minimum. *Everyone* ought to be able to live without worrying about having sufficient food or a warm, dry place to stay. The fact the bar was set so low made me sad for him. If he let me, I'd spoil him so damn much.

"What about clothes?" I asked, thinking quickly. "Surely you need new ones?"

He waggled his hand back and forth. "I can make do. There's a laundry machine here so I can wash my clothes as often as I need."

My heart ached. Reid shouldn't have to wash the same two outfits over and over. Especially when neither of them had been bought for him. They were just whatever had been available. He should have a closet full of clothes that brought him joy, be that jeans and T-shirts, skirts, or designer labels.

"What about maternity clothes?"

He paused. "I suppose I'll need some of those eventually."

I made a mental note to buy him some. "Did Momma give you any cookies to bring?"

"She left some for us to share."

He continued to watch me like he was waiting for the other shoe to drop. Perhaps he thought I'd come here to force him back to my place.

I backed away a step. "I won't hold you up for any longer. I don't want your meal to go cold."

The faintest hint of a smile flirted with the edge of his lips. "I've already eaten most of it, but thank you."

"Can I..." I ran my hand through my hair and drew in a deep breath. "Can I call on you again?"

Reid's teeth sank into his lower lip. He looked down at the ground and shuffled until he was back inside the house, safe beyond the wards.

"No," he said simply. "Not yet."

My chest cleaved in two. It was all I could do not to drop to my knees in front of him and beg.

Instead, my bear rippled beneath my skin and I bolted.

CHAPTER

EIGHTEEN

R*EID*

"Hey, Reid!" Hamish called from the Omega House kitchen.

"Yes?" I asked, sticking my head through the doorway to find out what he wanted. I was folding laundry in the adjoining living room while he and Jessie cleaned the breakfast dishes.

I'd managed to keep the meal down and, after eating a few pickles, was even feeling up to helping around the house. Since moving in, I'd learned that there was a roster of household chores to ensure that everyone did their part. I liked that. It made me feel like I was contributing.

I'd also learned that Hamish was serious about the boundaries. I hadn't seen any alphas inside the house—although Milo and Danny had visited to check on me, which was surprisingly nice.

I liked Milo. Danny was a bit more full-on, but there was something very calming about Milo's quiet presence.

Hamish dried his hands and hung the towel from a hook. "Will you go with Jessie to pick up the groceries?"

I glanced at Jessie. She was a pretty woman with dark

skin and braided hair that she often wore in a bun. At the moment, she was holding a piece of notepaper and a pen. A shopping list, perhaps.

"Sure," I agreed, smiling at her. "Now?"

She nodded. "We're running low on supplies."

"Okay, just let me grab a jacket."

I hurried back to my room and donned a jacket and woolen hat and pocketed a pair of gloves.

When I returned to the kitchen, Jessie had a pair of backpacks. She offered me one and I put it on. We told Hamish we were heading out and walked the mile or so to the shop. I burrowed deeper into the jacket and slipped the gloves on. I caught a whiff of laundry soap, but fortunately, it was faint enough not to turn my stomach.

I tried to make small talk during the walk, but it didn't go anywhere. While I'd apologized to Jessie and the others for the role I'd played in their abductions—and they'd accepted my apology—things were still stilted between us. Logically, they knew I was a victim just as they'd been, but convincing their hearts and minds of that wasn't easy. Jessie and the others would be wary of me for a while.

As we entered the shop through the automatic doors, a wall of warm air greeted us and I relaxed, the tension caused by the freezing wind dissipating. Jessie got out the shopping list and tore it in half, offering me the bottom piece. I took it from her, slung a basket over my arm, and went looking for the first item on the list: whole wheat pasta.

I'd half-filled my basket and was searching for the dairy-free milk options when I had the strangest sensation that something was off.

I stopped. The obsidian pendant was hot around my neck, reacting to something. But what?

Someone else's magic brushed up against my own. I

tripped over my own feet and dropped the basket, its contents spilling out onto the floor as I caught myself on my palms, the thud ricocheting up my arms.

The strange magic probed at me again, almost as if it was... tasting me? Maybe verifying who or what I was?

I didn't know, and I didn't like it.

The scent of ozone and mint filled my nostrils and I looked around frantically.

Was a warlock here?

Was someone using magic on me?

Then it struck me. There was something familiar about that combination of scents. I'd smelled it before. And anyone magical that I'd known previously wasn't someone I wanted to meet again. They had to be affiliated with either High Priest Hephaestes—the leader of my parents' coven—or Trent's pack.

No, no, no.

Whoever they were, they couldn't be allowed to know I was here. If they did, they'd come for me.

Magic exploded from my body in a wave of bright light.

I tried to draw in a breath but my throat had closed over. I clawed at it, begging it to open, but spots of light appeared in my vision.

The magic brushed over me again.

With no conscious thought, my energy flew outward.

Something crashed.

A woman screamed.

I covered my head. I couldn't let them take me.

You've got to fight. Get up and fight.

A blue glow started around me and I squeezed my eyes shut against the brightness, but a second later it was gone and I felt hollow inside.

"Reid!"

Someone grabbed me by the shoulder. I threw them off

and screamed. Another hand landed on me. When I tried to dislodge them, they wouldn't budge. I fought harder, knowing that if I let them take me, I was done for.

I wasn't strong enough to survive another round of captivity.

"Reid, it's me," Trent growled, which I knew was ridiculous because I'd seen him die.

I'd *seen* it. But it was impossible to convince my brain of that.

"Leave me alone!" I cried, throwing out sparks.

"No, don't," someone called, but I didn't think they were talking to me.

Something pinched the back of my neck and then my mind became foggy. My muscles loosened and I battled to stay upright but eventually keeled over, right into Trent's arms.

I jolted awake an instant later and shuffled away, crying out when my back hit something solid. I blinked rapidly, my vision sharpening, and realized immediately that I wasn't in the shop anymore. I was in a bed.

I looked around, trying to get my bearings. It was the bed in the medical center. The one I'd spent several nights in when they'd first captured me.

"You're okay."

I turned toward the voice. Zander was sitting on the opposite side of the bed, his forearms resting on his thighs, his hair ruffled as though he'd been running his hands through it.

"What happened?" I rasped.

He straightened and drew in a deep breath. "All I know is that you freaked out and started sending out shockwaves of magic in the middle of the shop."

"Oh, Gods." I felt for my magic, but it was gone. "No." Tears filled my eyes. "The oath stripped me of my magic."

Once again, I was powerless.

"It will come back," Zander assured me, reaching for me but then placing his hand firmly on his thigh instead. "As soon as you've calmed down, we'll make sure it's resolved. I know you didn't do it on purpose. It's obvious you panicked. What happened?"

"Wait, is my baby okay?" If I'd panicked and hurt them, I'd never forgive myself.

"Fine," he said quickly. "Dr. Black promises that the honesty oath would never cause ill effects on a baby, and according to him, your inherent magic will instinctively protect the baby as well."

At least that was something.

I pressed the heels of my hands to my eyes and tried to remember what had frightened me so much. "I sensed someone else's magic. There was something familiar about it. I thought it might be one of Trent's allies or..." Or Hephaestes and my coven. Not that I was about to say that out loud. "It was wrong. It shouldn't have been here."

Zander's dark eyes studied me intently. "You're sure you felt foreign magic?"

I nodded. "There was something off about it." An awful sense of foreboding. "Something bad is coming, Zander. Someone knows I'm here and they're coming for me."

I didn't want to be here when they found me.

He cocked his head. "You think it was some kind of seeking spell?"

"Maybe." I wasn't adept enough at reading magic to tell, but that was my best guess. "We need to find out who it was. Something terrible is about to happen, I can feel it."

"We'll look into it." His expression didn't change and I couldn't tell if he believed me or not.

"It needs to be now," I insisted. "Unless... do you think I'm making this up?"

Please say he believes me.

"Of course not." He wriggled his chair a little closer. "I told you we'll look into it and we will. We'll keep you safe, Reid. I promise."

I searched his eyes but didn't find the answers I wanted hiding within them. I couldn't tell if he meant it or if he was just placating me.

I wasn't wrong.

Something awful was on the horizon, getting closer with every second we didn't act.

CHAPTER
NINETEEN

ZANDER

I stood. "I'll go and start investigating now."

To my absolute astonishment, Reid lunged toward me and grabbed my arm before I could put any distance between us. His eyes widened and he let go of me almost immediately, as if he hadn't meant to touch me in the first place.

"Don't go yet," he said, his cheeks paling. "Please just stay for a little while. I feel... safer with... you here."

He choked out the word "safer" in a way that made me think he'd never associated it with an alpha before. My heart simultaneously ached and swelled. I hated that he'd had so few people to trust in his life so far, but I loved that for some reason he'd decided I was safe.

Even if he had told me I couldn't visit him again.

"Are you sure?" I'd take any excuse I could to spend time with Reid but I didn't want to overstep.

"Yes." He nibbled on his lip, looking not at all certain. "Where's Jessie?"

"She's back at the Omega House." I lowered myself onto the chair again. "She finished the shopping after we took you away. One of the deputies escorted her home to make sure she got there safely.”

“That’s good.”

Now that we were alone together, he didn’t seem to know what to do or say. His complexion was startlingly waxy and if the doctor hadn’t already cleared him, I’d be worried.

“Are you hungry?” I asked. After years in law enforcement, I knew that a snack could go a long way toward helping someone feel better after a panic attack, which was essentially what this was, just with an extra dose of magic.

He pursed his full lips. “A little, but I’m fine.”

“Let’s get you something.” I made a quick phone call to Danny and asked him to run a snack over from the bakery, then I pocketed my phone and gave my attention to Reid. “Do you have any idea whose magic it might have been?”

He looked down at his hands, his shoulders rounded. “It felt kinda familiar. Maybe it was someone tied to the Red Moon Pack. Trent had a few warlocks come through. The traffickers liked to use magic to keep everyone in line. I heard that sometimes they even put spells on their people to kill them or silence them if they were caught. Someone like that would be powerful enough for a seeking spell like this.”

He picked at his nails and the way he was determinedly not looking at me made me wonder if he was keeping something from me. Had he been involved with that kind of black magic?

Or was he suggesting that it might be an associate of Trent’s to draw attention away from who else might be looking for him? His family, perhaps?

That would explain the panic because he’d already shown that he became upset at the mention of his family. Maybe he was right and they were on their way to him at this very minute. And would that be so bad? Surely they'd be able to help him heal.

But they'd take him away from me.

Ours, my bear growled.

Yeah, I know, buddy.

I didn't get the opportunity to question Reid more though because Danny arrived with the food. He knocked on the door and eased inside, smiling cautiously.

"Hey, Reid," he said, greeting my mate first before dipping his head toward me. "I heard you like chicken. There's an egg and pickle sandwich in here. Perfect for those pregnancy cravings." He passed him a brown paper bag. "And I have a joyless low carb nut and seed slice for you, Z."

I took the other bag. "Thanks. What do we owe you?"

Danny flashed a grin. "On the house." He hesitated, his brow furrowing as he glanced back at Reid. "Are you all right? I heard you lost control."

"My magic is gone." Reid's voice broke on the last word. He sounded bereft. "You're safe. I can't hurt anyone."

Danny's face softened. "I wasn't worried about that, silly. I want to know if *you're* okay. That must be hard, having your magic gone, even if it's only temporary."

Reid nodded, and my heart gave a pang. I wished he didn't have to go through this.

Danny leaned against the doorframe and cocked his hip. "What say I bring the leftovers from the bakery to Omega House after work so you aren't by yourself? I'll ask Milo to come too."

Reid's eyes widened almost imperceptibly. "You don't have to do that."

"But I'd like to." Danny straightened. "Unless that's your polite way of saying you don't want to see us, which is also okay."

"I..." Reid swallowed. "I'd like that."

Danny flashed one last grin before ducking out. "Then I'll see you later. Take care, you two."

Reid stared after Danny as if he was an alien.

"I'll get you a glass of water," I said and set my bag down before following Danny out. I filled two mugs from the break room with water and returned with them, placing one on the stand beside Reid's bed and the other on a table on the side of the room.

Reid gulped the water down in just a few mouthfuls. I glanced at the other mug and, without a moment of hesitation, replaced the empty mug with my full one. He clearly needed it more than me.

His cheeks flushed and his gaze dropped. "Thank you."

Keeping an eye on me, he bit into the sandwich, chewed, and chased it down with more water. The sight of him enjoying something I'd provided, no matter how small, warmed my heart. I suddenly understood why Everett coddled Milo so much. The feeling was addictive.

Reid's eyebrows knitted together, and I realized I was staring at him. I opened my own bag, withdrew the bar, and ate half of it in one bite. For all of Danny's face-pulling about my tasteless choices, it was actually pretty good. Nutty and crunchy with just a hint of sweetness from the honey.

Gods, I loved honey.

We ate in silence until Reid had finished his filo. He wiped his fingers on a napkin and turned to me.

"Why are you bothering with me?" he asked.

The question struck me like a two-by-four, completely unexpected.

"What do you mean? You're my mate."

Of course I'd "bother" with him, as he put it. I'd literally do anything for my mate.

He shrugged. "I'm broken. Surely that's beyond obvious by now. I had a literal screaming meltdown in the supermarket."

I padded closer and sat near him but kept enough distance between us that he'd feel safe. "You're not broken. You've been through a lot."

He rolled his eyes. "I don't understand why you're being so nice to me. I have so many trust issues that I *tested* you."

I cocked my head, uncertain what he meant.

He sighed and absent-mindedly rubbed the gnarled scar where Trent had bitten him. "When I told you not to visit me at the Omega House, I didn't mean it. I just wanted to find out whether you'd listen to me. And... and you did."

Confusion laced his tone and it broke my heart. He shouldn't be so surprised to have his wishes respected. For the love of the Gods, that should be his bare minimum expectation.

"It's understandable that you'd have difficulty trusting people. You aren't broken," I repeated, injecting as much certainty into my voice as I could.

He raised his eyes and one side of his mouth hitched up. "You know, 'not broken' might be the most hopeful way I've heard myself described since... Well, since Trent."

I angled myself toward him. My fingers twitched, itching to reach for him, but I curled them into my palm, knowing he wouldn't welcome the touch. "So, you don't actually want me to stay away?"

"No." He slumped against the wall. "I like talking to you. I just... don't know whether I'll ever be the mate you want. I'm sorry."

"You already are, and there's no pressure to make any decisions quickly." I'd wait as long as it took if I eventually earned the privilege of calling him mine.

"How can I possibly be what you want?" he asked quietly.

"Because you're perfect for me." Slowly, I reached over and touched his arm. His breath stuttered and he relaxed into the touch. "You're brave and resilient. Clever and determined. Everything I could ever ask for."

He blinked rapidly and cleared his throat. "I don't feel brave."

"Well, you are. You've been through more than some people could withstand, and you're still holding your own."

He pursed his lips and stayed quiet. Eventually, he said, "I'm okay now. Can we go back to the Omega House?"

He'd avoided responding, but hopefully he'd at least taken my words on board.

"I'll just go and check with Dr. Black."

Once we were released, I drove Reid home. For once he didn't argue, and I appreciated that. Perhaps he was all too aware of the fact that he could be in danger because of whatever it was he'd sensed earlier.

When we arrived, I waved him inside and didn't push my luck by asking for an invitation to come in. Instead, I headed to my parents' place, parked outside, and went looking for Dad. I found him in his office, so I knocked softly and leaned against the doorframe while he finished whatever it was he was doing on the computer.

He glanced over. "Is all okay with Reid?"

I tilted my hand from side to side. "He's scared but physically unharmed. We might have trouble though. Do you know of any witches or warlocks who might be able to sense whether foreign magic has been used in the area?"

TWENTY

R*EID*

I knocked softly on Jessie's door, my heart beating faster than usual. I was afraid that she'd either ignore me or open it only so she could slam it shut in my face. After the drama I'd caused yesterday—and my role in her abduction—I wouldn't blame her.

When she didn't answer, I knocked again. The door swung inward and she flashed me a good-natured smile as she removed a pair of headphones from her ears.

"Sorry," she said, stepping aside so I could enter. "I couldn't hear you over the music. Would you like to come in?"

I wrung my hands and shuffled from foot to foot. "No, I just wanted to apologize for yesterday. I'm so sorry. I hope I didn't scare you, or... hurt you."

Hamish had assured me that Jessie was unharmed but it was difficult to believe that without seeing it for myself. I'd been throwing my magic around wildly—at least until the oath quashed it—and from what I'd heard, she'd been the first person brave enough to approach me to try to calm me down.

I just hadn't reacted to her. At all.

Apparently, I hadn't responded to anything until Zander arrived.

"I was scared," she began, her expression growing serious.

I nodded. "I understand if you don't want to talk to me anymore. If you need me to move—"

"I wasn't finished." Her lips thinned and she arched her eyebrow. "As I was saying, I was scared but only for your sake. It's clear that something intense was happening to you and I had no idea what. There was nothing I could do to help and I felt kind of useless."

I frowned at that. "You're not useless."

"And you're not a bad person," she shot back. "You didn't hurt me."

"Are you sure?"

Giving me a look, she stripped off her sweater and showed me her bare arms. "See? There isn't a mark on me."

I narrowed my eyes. There were still plenty of places that a burn could be hiding, but she didn't seem to be moving as though she was injured. Perhaps she was telling the truth.

"So." She put her hands on her hips. "What actually happened?"

I looked around, reluctant to say anything where someone else might overhear me in case I worried them unnecessarily. She gestured me into her room and I sat on the empty bed opposite her.

Another girl had slept here until a couple of weeks ago, but she'd relocated since it was too stressful for her to sleep in the room she'd once been abducted from.

I explained the strange sensation I'd had from the magic that seemed to be seeking me out. I even divulged how unsettling I'd found its familiarity. Fortunately, she seemed to accept my words at face value. No part of her expression suggested that she thought I might be paranoid.

"Do we need to be worried about someone coming here?" she asked, waving to encompass the whole of the house.

"Not unless they're strong enough to break through my wards."

"And how good are your wards?"

I considered this briefly. "Decent for a beginner, but the warlock Trent's pack hired only taught me the basics." He'd focused on personal shields so I could protect Trent if the necessity arose, but the principal was similar. I'd never let on to Trent that I was experimenting with larger wards. "There are others who are much better at them than me though."

She nibbled on her plump lower lip. "Is there a way we can make them stronger?"

"I can continue adding power to them whenever I have some to spare." Which, for me, was most of the time. "The trouble is that I can make them more potent, but if I've missed something when setting them up, it wouldn't be difficult for a skilled warlock to get around them."

It was like adding reinforcement to a building without knowing where its weak spots were. Against a blunt attack, it would do the trick, but anything more than that and the additional power would be more or less useless.

She grimaced. "That's not exactly what I wanted to hear but we should be safe, right? I mean, what reason would a skilled warlock have to try to break in?"

I nodded but didn't say anything because I didn't share her optimism. I was afraid that *I* was the reason someone might try to break in here.

No one in Grizzly Ridge knew it yet, but I was basically a

huge magical battery. I had more than enough power to tempt people who might want it for themselves.

"I'll go add to the wards now," I said, but then my gut dropped.

I couldn't add to the wards. My magic still hadn't returned after the oath had stolen it away.

Honestly, I wasn't even sure if the wards were working at the moment. Did they rely on me having my magic to keep operating, or would they be fine because I'd had access to magic when I'd created them?

My eyes stung and I blinked against the tears. I hated this sense of powerlessness. It made me feel like a sitting duck. What if someone came for me and my wards failed and I couldn't defend myself?

No wonder Dr. Black had chosen this as the consequence of failing to keep my oath. It was awful.

I walked the length of the house, holding the obsidian pendant in one hand as if that might somehow boost the wards despite my current situation. Even without training, I knew that a protection crystal could only do so much.

I sighed. Perhaps if I'd had an actual mentor, I'd understand the more intricate aspects of warding. Then I might know if we were safe right now or not. I had a lot of reasons to hate my parents, but my lack of magical education was one of the things I was most bitter about.

"I'll make sure you're taught everything you need to know," I murmured, running a hand over my little bump. "I don't know how, but I promise. You'll never end up like me."

I returned inside and helped prepare lunch. We ate together and I was focusing on keeping the meal down and finishing my drink when Hamish told me there was a delivery person at the gate.

I wasn't expecting anything and after yesterday, I was

reluctant to venture far from my safe space, so he accompanied me out and grilled the delivery person before accepting the small box.

The delivery person left, visibly grateful, and I opened the box. Nestled inside, on a bed of white tissue paper, was a small figurine of a bear carved from rose quartz.

My breath caught. I picked the figurine up between my thumb and forefinger. I knew without reading the note that this had come from Zander. Recalling our conversation about the obsidian—and how I'd asked him whether he knew what it did—I wondered whether he'd done his research this time.

Rose quartz was the crystal of love. It symbolized compassion, peace, healing, and unconditional acceptance. It was connected to the heart chakra.

It was beautiful, and I wanted it.

Last time, I'd stolen his gift in secret. This time, was I brave enough just to take it?

I wanted to believe there would be no strings attached.

I put the bear back inside the box and went looking for Jessie again. Jessie was like me. She'd been through some shit. She might understand my thought process.

I knocked on her bedroom door. When there was no answer, I wandered through the house and found her lying on the sofa in the living room, her feet propped on the arm of the couch, reading a book with a sexy bare-chested man on the cover.

I hesitated, reluctant to interrupt her, but she must have sensed me there because she looked up and smiled.

"Hey, are you okay?" she asked.

I wandered over and sank to the ground beside her, bringing my knees up to my chest. I grimaced as I realized that before long, I wouldn't be able to sit this way because my belly would be too big.

"Um, Zander had a gift delivered to me," I said, showing her the box but not what was inside.

"And that's a problem?"

I inhaled slowly. "I know that he isn't like the alphas from Trent's pack and I want to accept the gift but it's hard."

"Ah." Comprehension dawned on her face. "Yeah, I get that. Has he given you the impression he'll want anything from you?"

"No," I admitted. "He seems... good."

"Good" was such an inadequate description, but in my opinion, it was vastly underrated.

She slid a bookmark into the book and closed it. "I don't know Zander well, but he seems decent. Is there any way you can use your magic to tell what kind of person someone is?"

At that, I pinched the bridge of my nose. "I don't have my magic right now, and even if I did, I don't know how to use that kind of magic. If I did, I'd never have ended up with Trent in the first place."

Her dark eyes scanned me. "Then I guess you have to trust your gut. What does it say?"

I bit my lip, my hand tightening around the box. "That he won't ask for anything I'm not willing to give."

Gods, I hoped that was true.

CHAPTER

TWENTY-ONE

ZANDER

The doorbell jingled as I entered the bakery and I'd started to draw in a lungful of sweet-scented air when Danny raced out of the back room and nudged the woman at the counter aside. I came to an abrupt halt. This was uncharacteristic behavior.

"I can deal with this," Danny said, urging her toward the coffee machine. She raised an eyebrow but went without argument.

"I didn't expect you to be so excited to see me that you'd barge poor Skye out of the way," I said with a grin, even though I was slightly unsettled by his urgency.

Danny huffed. "I need to talk to you, that's all."

Immediately, I dropped the playfulness. "Is something wrong?"

Danny shouldn't be having any more troubles now that he was mated to Knox and his violent ex was locked away, but Gods only knew that chaos seemed to have descended on Grizzly Ridge recently. Perhaps something else had gone awry.

Danny's eyebrows knitted in thought. "Tell you what.

I'll take your order and Skye can put it together while I talk to you out the back." He turned to his coworker. "Is that okay?"

She nodded, although she looked slightly exasperated. She wouldn't stay annoyed with him for long though. No one ever did. Danny was simply too loveable.

I grabbed my phone out of my pocket and reeled off the list of coffees and snacks the other staff from the police department had given me. Gods knew when the sheriff had become their designated gofer.

When I was finished, Danny grimaced. "Are you sure I can't tempt you into something more interesting than a chamomile tea?"

I just looked at him.

He smirked. "I thought as much, but I had to ask. Come on back."

I followed him through to the kitchen, making sure to stay clear of the counters so I didn't bump or contaminate any food.

Danny leaned against the counter near the sink and crossed his arms over his slender chest. "So, I heard from Milo that Reid is refusing to leave the Omega House."

Guilt curled in my stomach. While I'd been patrolling near the Omega House at night, making sure there was no one unfamiliar in the area, I'd only visited once, reluctant to push his limits. I'd hoped that he'd come to me when he was ready for us to see each other more.

It would seem I'd been remiss. I should have noticed that my mate had effectively put himself under house arrest.

I rubbed my chest, hating the thought that Reid might be too scared to venture out. "That's... not great. That said, the Omega House is relatively secure with the new measures in place, so is there any reason to worry if he wants to stay somewhere he feels safe?"

Danny's expression said he thought I was an idiot. "He was held prisoner for months, Zander. *Months*. Then he was finally freed and came here, where we basically treated him like a prisoner again until we were sure he wouldn't hurt anyone. He should feel free to explore. It isn't right for him to continue to behave like a prisoner when he isn't one. He deserves better."

My insides twisted. "You're right. Reid deserves everything."

Danny nodded. "Then you'll make it right? You'll make him feel safe enough to leave the house?"

"I'll try."

Reid had been through a lot though. I wasn't sure my efforts, no matter how heartfelt, would be enough to soothe his fears.

"Thank you for letting me know," I added, making a mental note to pay closer attention to Reid's comings and goings. It was good that Danny had alerted me to what was going on but he shouldn't have to. I should be aware of the situation myself.

"Your order is ready," Skye called through the doorway.

I tilted my chin at Danny, acknowledging the conversation, then headed out. The order was waiting for me, the drinks carefully arranged so that I'd be able to carry the holder with one hand and the food bag with the other.

"Thanks, Skye."

She grinned. "You're welcome, Sheriff. Say hello to Angela for me."

"I will."

"So cute," Danny mouthed from behind her.

I hid my smile. Angela was a badass mountain lion shifter and a member of the search and rescue team. She and Skye had been dancing around each other for a while now. They weren't fated mates but they were, in my opinion, well suited to each other.

I took the goodies back to the station, handed them out, and passed along Skye's message to Angela. That done, I retreated to my office and paced the length of the room as I dialed Dad's number.

"Good morning, Zander," he said upon answering.

"Hey, Dad. Did you get in touch with your contact who specializes in magic? Can he help us?"

"He might be able to," Dad said, switching from friendly to businesslike as he noticed my tone. "He used to be employed as an investigator by the PBI."

"Is he retired?" A retired federal agent definitely sounded like someone trustworthy. He'd presumably have had to go through all the rigmarole of background checks already.

"Yes, he retired a few years ago after an injury left him unfit for field work. He's an independent contractor now."

"That's a shame." Not uncommon, though. Working for the PBI was dangerous. They investigated some of the most powerful paranormal criminals and underground organizations in the country.

"It's good for us," Dad said. "I'll give you his contact details."

"Thanks." I dropped onto my chair, grabbed a notebook, and jotted down the name and phone number he read out to me. "Is he expecting a call?"

"Yeah, I haven't explained the full situation, but he knows someone will be getting in touch."

"I'll let you know how it goes."

"You do that."

I ended the call and immediately plugged the new phone number into my mobile.

"Birch speaking," a male voice rasped.

"Nathaniel Birch?" I clarified, pen in hand.

"This is he."

"I'm Sheriff Zander Blackwood from Grizzly Ridge. I believe you're acquainted with my father, Clan Alpha Aaron Blackwood."

There was a rustle as Nathaniel Birch moved on the other end of the line.

"Yes, I know your father," he said, his tone impossible to read. "He's a good man. He said to expect a call but not much else. How can I help you, Sheriff?"

I explained the situation, making sure to emphasize both that I wanted him to confirm whether there was some kind of unfamiliar magical residue in the area and that we had a warlock who might require training.

Birch sighed. "I hate to delay, but I'm currently on a job. I can be there in about a week. Is that acceptable?"

I grimaced. Waiting for a week wasn't ideal if Reid was refusing to leave the Omega House, but it also wasn't too long, all things considered. "That will be fine. Thank you, Warlock Birch."

"Just call me Nathaniel. I'll sort out everything on my end and let you know when I'm on the way."

We hung up and I wandered out of the office and into the bullpen, the open-plan area where most of the officers were based.

"Has anyone seen unfamiliar paranormals around town?" I asked loudly enough that they all stopped what they were doing and gave me their attention.

"No, sir," Hawk said.

"Do we have any leads on the omegas?"

They all exchanged unhappy glances but no one spoke. I pressed my lips together and suppressed a surge of frustration. It wasn't their fault that we weren't getting anywhere.

"Keep trying, everyone. Sooner or later, something will come up."

It had to.

I strode back to the office and made yet another phone call. "Hamish, can you ask Reid if he'd like me to visit later today?"

TWENTY-TWO

R*EID*

"Won't you come and help me in the garden?" Jessie asked for the second time today.

"I don't feel like going outside," I replied without raising my head from the book I was reading. "It's cold."

She huffed. "You could wear a jacket, hat, and gloves. We have a communal supply if you don't have enough of your own."

"I don't have the energy. The baby has been keeping me awake." That was a blatant lie. While I did feel a bit flat, it wasn't because I was pregnant.

Still, it didn't matter what the reason, I wasn't interested in venturing outside. I was comfortable right here on the sofa with a book and a soft place to lay my head.

Here, it was safe.

The last time I'd left the house, I'd freaked out in the supermarket and lost the use of my magic for days. Being without that security blanket had scraped me raw, and I didn't think I could handle going through it again. Especially not when there were two of us I needed to protect. I couldn't afford to take any risks.

Jessie padded closer and knelt beside me. "The house will be in view and the garden is within the wards you set. That makes it pretty safe, right?"

"Ish," I mumbled, reluctant to acknowledge that she might have a point.

The garden was beyond the more intensive wards surrounding the house. Honestly, as comforting as I found my wards—which were definitely still in place because I'd powered them up as soon as my magic returned—each day I grew more worried that they wouldn't be enough.

All it would take to dismantle them would be a moderately powerful warlock with more training than me.

That was most of my former coven.

It was better to stay inside. Part of me knew I was being illogical, but my emotions weren't being logical right now. I felt safer inside—like my relative freedom and my magic were more protected—so inside I stayed.

Jessie sighed. "You know where to find me if you change your mind."

I kept my gaze firmly on my book until she walked away. I tried to continue reading but images of Jessie exposed and vulnerable kept popping into my mind. Reluctantly, I closed the book and walked through the house to the kitchen, through which I had a better view of both the garden and the street beyond.

Hamish glanced at me as I sat in the corner and I pretended not to notice the disappointment etched into his expression. "Didn't want to go out?"

"Not today."

Hamish was quiet for a long moment before asking, "Would you like to peel some carrots for dinner?"

"Sure."

I stretched and wiggled from side to side—my hips were a little achy—then went to the sink and rinsed the carrots. I made sure to check on Jessie through the window every couple of minutes. After I finished peeling the carrots, I started cutting them into slices. I was nearly done when I looked out the window just in time to see a black SUV cruise slowly past.

I stiffened. Something about that vehicle didn't feel right. When it disappeared from view, I told myself I was being paranoid and started washing broccoli to go with the carrots. But when the SUV drove past again, this time from the other direction, I froze and peered closer.

I recognized the driver. And Jessie was out there, all alone.

With a shout, I dropped a potato and raced through the house, flying toward the back door. I lunged through it, preparing my magic. As soon as I was outside, I flung blue sparks at the SUV.

They missed.

Tires squealed and the vehicle peeled away. I threw more sparks after it, hoping to burst one of the tires or prevent them from escaping, but they turned a corner before the sparks hit them.

"What the hell?" Jessie demanded, running over to me.

"That guy knew Trent," I said, bent at the waist, hauling in mouthfuls of air. "He shouldn't be here. He shouldn't be here." My fingers sank into my flesh hard enough to bruise. "Why is he here?"

"Reid?"

Hauling oxygen into my lungs, I looked toward Hamish, who'd appeared in the doorway, a phone in his hand.

"You need to call the police," I gasped. "That man is a criminal. They need to catch him."

A couple of the other residents appeared behind Hamish, who was entering a number into his phone. One of them sheltered behind Hamish's larger body and the other peered around him, obviously curious about what was happening.

Hamish began talking to someone.

"Is that Zander?" I demanded.

He shook his head. "It's dispatch."

"You need to take a breath." Jessie touched my shoulder lightly. "You're hyperventilating."

"I have to call Zander." It was all well and good putting in a generic call to the police but this needed the big guns. Someone who would actually care and not write me off as being paranoid.

"You can talk to him in a minute." She moved closer, her face filling my vision. Her dark eyes were worried, her mouth twitching as if it wanted to turn down but she was trying desperately to keep it curved up. "Let's make sure your brain has enough air for you to think clearly first."

Irritated, I tried to brush her off, but her grip tightened. Bright spots of light appeared in my vision.

"Breathe in for the count of four," she ordered.

Sensing that she wouldn't let me escape otherwise, I tried to draw in a deep breath, struggling because my chest was burning for oxygen.

"Hold it for seven seconds," she continued.

I only managed five before exhaling sharply and gasping for breath.

"I can't."

"Yes." Her jaw firmed. "You can. In for four."

I tried again and, at the top of the breath, slowly counted to seven.

"Now breathe out for eight seconds."

That was even harder than holding it, but I did my best.

We repeated the exercise several times over, until my vision cleared and I was feeling a bit more together.

"Thank you."

She nodded. "Go make your call."

I hurried into the house, snatched my phone from the kitchen counter where I'd left it, and found Zander's number. The call went straight through.

"Is that you, Reid?" Zander's rough voice wrapped around me like a hug.

"Yeah, it's me. One of Trent's friends just drove past the Omega House. I saw him through the window of his car. He was looking for me—or maybe someone else. He went past twice, so it wasn't a coincidence."

"Are you okay?" Zander asked, his tone sharper.

I took a moment to assess myself. Surprisingly, the breathing exercise had taken the edge off my panic. "Yeah."

"Good. Thank you for calling me. I was already on my way to see you, but I'll bring a uniform along. Are you certain it was someone Trent knew?"

"One hundred percent." I'd only met him a few times but I'd committed every face to memory in case I ever escaped.

He hesitated. "Are you sure? This isn't because you're worried about that magic you felt the other day?"

My heart sank. Gods, he thought I was paranoid too.

Poor, broken Reid, too badly damaged by the Red Moon Pack to trust what he saw with his own two eyes.

"You don't believe me, do you?"

TWENTY-THREE

ZANDER

My gut clenched at the desolation in his tone.

"I do, little one, but I know how panic can distort things."

"He was here," Reid insisted. "And I know I recognize him. I *know* it."

"Then I believe you."

"Do you really?" Hope and doubt twined together in his voice.

"Yes."

"Please come quickly."

"I will."

The call disconnected.

I gritted my teeth. "Fuck."

"Sir?" Hawk's voice burst through the radio. "We have a call about a situation at the Omega House."

I pulled to the side of the road and turned the car around. "Tell Bea to meet me out front. We'll assess and let you know if we need backup. Meanwhile, I want two units patrolling the township for any vehicles or people that don't fit."

He nodded. "Will do, sir."

Bea was an alpha shifter, but at least she was female and a bird species, which might render her less intimidating to the vulnerable omegas who lived in the home. She was relatively petite but could still pack a punch when needed.

I arrived outside the station just as Bea emerged from the building. She opened the side door and slid into the passenger seat.

"How much did Hawk tell you?" I asked as I pulled back onto the road.

"Hamish was preparing dinner with Reid when Reid became alarmed and ran outside. Hamish followed and found him magically attacking a car that had driven past. Reid claims that the car was being driven by an acquaintance of his late mate."

I growled. "That man wasn't his mate; he was his captor."

She ducked her head deferentially. "My apologies, Sheriff. I misspoke."

Thankfully, the drive didn't take long. Hamish was standing in the front garden, rubbing Reid's back. Reid, for his part, didn't look as panicked as I'd expected. Instead, his chin was up and he glared at me balefully.

"He was there," he said, yanking away from Hamish. "I saw him and I know I didn't imagine it."

A slight tremor rippled through him and I had to dig my partially shifted claws into my palm to stop myself from hauling him into my arms.

I closed my eyes and inhaled deeply, opening myself to all of the scents in the area. I picked up many familiar scents and a few less so, but none of them were completely foreign, which meant I'd either smelled them around Grizzly Ridge before or elsewhere.

"I can't detect anyone unfamiliar," I said gently.

His eyes narrowed. "He didn't get out of the car so maybe none of his scent transferred to the surroundings, or perhaps he has someone masking his scent. You know that can be done."

I did. After all, Reid had masked the scent of some of the Red Moon Pack wolves while they'd terrorized Grizzly Ridge.

"Besides," he continued, "if it was someone from within the clan then I would have lost my magic when I attacked them."

That was also an excellent point.

A raindrop landed on my forehead and I looked up. Dark clouds were gathered overhead and I was sure it would start pouring down at any second now.

"Let's get you inside," I said, trying to figure out how best to proceed.

"I'm not lying," he snapped.

"I don't think you are." I glanced at Bea and motioned for her to take Hamish inside and get his statement. "But that does raise some questions. Trent is gone, so what would his associates want with you?"

At that, he fell silent. A groove formed between his eyebrows. Most likely, he'd been so consumed by fear that he hadn't paused to consider that question.

He pressed his lips together and something dark passed across his face. Whatever it was, it gave me pause. It was clear that something had occurred to him but he didn't want to share his thoughts. Perhaps he feared I'd dismiss him.

"I need as much information as I can get," I murmured, silently pleading with him to open up to me. There were so many things he wasn't telling me and it made it difficult to protect him. I wanted nothing more than to keep him safe, but how could I do that if I didn't understand the threat?

Reid nibbled his lower lip and for a moment, I thought he might fold, but then he straightened his shoulders and said, "He was here. I can even describe him. I don't know his name but he's about five foot ten and built stocky. His hair is brown and he has a beard. I think his eyes are brown too and there's a sickle-shaped scar beneath his right eye."

"That's very useful." I smiled at him as another drop of water landed on the bridge of my nose. "We'll look into it. I'll run your description through the database and see if we get any hits."

Dark-haired, bearded men of that height were a dime a dozen in the area, but perhaps the scar would make it easier to find something useful.

"Can you…" Reid trailed off before squaring his shoulders and starting again. "Will you walk around the property perimeter with me before we go in? I want to feed some more power into the wards."

"Of course." Whatever he wanted I'd give it to him if it was within my ability to do so.

We wandered the edge of the property and I split my focus between him and our surroundings, wary of anyone who might be watching a little too closely.

For once, Reid seemed confident in himself. If anyone ever trained him properly, I was sure he'd become a force to be reckoned with.

Once he was satisfied with his efforts, I escorted him to the door. My heart panged in protest as he disappeared inside, but I kept my feet planted firmly on the doorstep. Hamish had been clear that I wasn't allowed in.

I only had to wait a minute or so for Hamish and Bea to emerge from deeper in the house. Bea was tucking her notepad into the front pocket of her uniform shirt and Hamish's face was set in harsh lines.

Hamish stopped a couple of yards from me and crossed his arms. "I hope you're taking this seriously."

"I promise we are. Your safety is our priority."

Hamish smirked. "Especially with your mate here."

I tipped my head, unable to deny that. "Speaking of." I looked around and lowered my voice. "I'm concerned about Reid's state of mind. Between that magical attack at the supermarket, him not leaving the house, and now this... Have you talked to him about seeing a therapist? It might help."

There was a gasp behind me.

My stomach lurched and I looked over Hamish's shoulder. Reid stood in the hall, his expression one of betrayal.

Fuck.

"I'm not crazy!" he shouted, then stormed away.

I started into the house, moving on autopilot, but Hamish blocked my path.

"Get out of my way," I growled. "My mate needs me."

He planted his hand on my chest. "He doesn't have his magic fully under control at the moment. Upsetting him will only make that worse."

I cursed, knowing he was right. Chasing Reid right now would only add to his distress and if he lashed out and lost access to his magic again as a result, there wouldn't be any consoling him.

"You've got a point." I closed my eyes as fur rippled across my skin and I struggled to suppress my bear's protective instincts.

We can't crowd him. He needs to feel safe, I reminded him.

Ours. Protect. Defend, he retorted.

I grimaced. Clearly, I was going to have to force him

down. I clenched my fists and channeled my energy into retaining my human form.

"I'll set up a watch," I said, clinging to the frayed remnants of my humanity.

Hamish nodded. "We'd appreciate that."

He closed the door and I strode down the path, dropped to my knees at the roadside and succumbed to the animalistic need to roar my frustration. Releasing that tiny bit of energy allowed me to find my phone and send a message to my family's group chat, letting them know we needed to be on guard, then I headed back to the station to make sure someone would be patrolling the town constantly.

No one would be getting near my mate again. I wasn't leaving his safety to chance, even if it meant doing things my human side found... questionable.

TWENTY-FOUR

R*EID*

I couldn't sleep, but it wasn't as if that was unusual. Ever since I'd seen that guy drive past the Omega House, I'd been on edge. Being used to it didn't make it any easier though. It was the middle of the night and I'd tossed and turned so much I thought I'd scream if I didn't get a moment of peace.

Frustrated, I got out of bed and went to check the wards. I padded around the interior of the house, probing the wards for weaknesses and adding more power to make them stronger.

That done, I leaned my back against the front door and sank to the floor. The encounter with Trent's associate wasn't the only thing unsettling me. I kept recalling Zander's expression as he'd asked Hamish about whether I was seeing a therapist.

He thought I was mentally unstable, and it hurt. Apparently, while I'd been growing to trust him more day by day, he still saw me as broken and unreliable. It made me question my judgment in letting him tiptoe into my heart. He'd worked hard to earn every inch of trust I granted him, but I still worried I'd made a mistake in allowing him to get closer to me if that was how he viewed me.

With a sigh, I rose to my feet and glanced out the window. My heart thunked painfully as I spotted a vehicle parked outside.

Holy crap. How had I not noticed that earlier?

My palms turned sweaty. Was it Trent's acquaintance? Had he returned?

Scarcely daring to breathe, I tiptoed closer and peered out. My weak eyesight allowed me to make out the silhouette of a vehicle parked on the roadside but not what type it was or whether there was someone inside.

I suspected there was.

Rain fell softly, trickling down the window and deadening any other sounds outside. Warily, I inched the window open and stuck my head through, hoping to get a better look.

It was a police car.

Zander?

My stomach fizzed and my pulse sped up. It did look like his vehicle. If it was, that meant my supposed mate was parked outside the house, in the rain, in the middle of the night.

But why?

I closed the window, uncertain of what to do. Should I wake Hamish and make him aware that an alpha was staking us out?

Yes, Hamish would know what to do.

I went to his door and knocked softly. When there was no response, I eased it open, crossed to the bed, feeling my way carefully so as not to trip over anything, and touched his shoulder.

He jolted, his eyes flying open. "What is it?"

His eyes were clear almost immediately, no hint of sleep

in them. I couldn't help wondering what had made him so hypervigilant. Was it just the knowledge that residents might need him or had something else happened in his past? I knew so little about him.

"Um, Zander is parked outside," I said quietly.

He relaxed back onto his pillow. "He was there last night too. Don't worry about it. Just go back to sleep."

I frowned. Zander was making a habit of staking out the Omega House overnight? Strange.

Hamish closed his eyes and his breathing became regular within the space of thirty seconds. I left his room, closing the door behind myself, and went instead to the front door, drawn as if by an invisible wire stretched from me to Zander.

I undid each of the locks and stepped outside. Rain landed on my bare skin and the hairs on my arms stood on end as I walked toward the vehicle.

What the hell was I doing?

I had no idea, but I couldn't stop myself from going to the driver's door and knocking on the window. Inside, there was a flurry of motion and then the door opened.

"Get in." Zander's voice was thick with sleep. "It's wet and I don't want you to catch a cold."

With the barest hesitation, I rounded the front of the car and climbed in the other side. It was slightly warm, as if the heater had been on at some point but he'd turned it off.

"What are you doing here?" I asked, cataloging his features in the dark. Deep brown eyes, hooded with shadows. Square jaw. The faint scent of pine emanating from him.

Even though I was alone with an alpha for the first time in weeks, I felt oddly safe.

Zander shifted, angling his big body toward me. "You're

my mate and there's a chance you're in danger. I'm here to make sure that nothing happens to you."

I gaped at him. Did he mean to say that he was sleeping in his car rather than the nice house across town because he wanted to *protect* me?

"But you think I'm crazy and I'm making it all up."

In fact, I'd been stewing over that for days, turning over what I'd seen and experienced. Strung together in the way he'd phrased it when speaking to Hamish, perhaps everything that had happened did seem unlikely, and I'd even begun to doubt myself a couple of times before I reminded myself that I knew what I'd seen, and what I'd felt.

I was sane, whether he wanted to believe it or not.

He sighed and stretched as much as he could in the cramped space. "No, like I said before, I don't."

I glared. "You questioned my mental state."

Groaning, he rubbed his temples. "I put it badly. I don't think you're lying. I just wouldn't be surprised if you have PTSD or other trauma-related issues after everything you've been through. It's reasonably common for victims to—"

"I'm not a victim," I snapped, feeling stung.

Was that how he saw me?

As damaged? Broken?

I shouldn't be surprised. I'd thought it of myself often enough.

"No," he said tiredly. "You're someone I want to protect and care for. I didn't mean to upset you."

I fell silent. Whether he'd intended to upset me or not, he had. But the fact he was here, parked outside in the dead of night when he had no way to know that I'd find him suggested that he was taking my fears seriously.

Maybe he did believe me.

And again, he wanted to keep me *safe*. He was giving up his cozy, comfortable bed for me.

No one had ever done anything like that. I didn't quite know how to respond. I'd initially assumed that Zander was an alpha who wanted something from me, but right now, there was nothing stopping him from claiming me except for his own sense of right and wrong. Still, he chose to respect my space and not push for anything.

Perhaps I wasn't so wrong to trust him, after all.

"Reid?" he asked, making me aware I'd been staring at him in silence for far too long.

I snapped my mouth shut. "It can't be easy sleeping out here."

He shrugged. "I can get by without much."

"Still." I swallowed, my words catching in my throat. I looked aside, reluctant to let him see exactly how much this meant to me. "Thank you. For being patient with me and for listening when I know that what I said might sound unbelievable."

Despite the darkness, I could see his expression soften.

"I'll always protect you," he said, quiet but clear. "Whatever it takes."

My heart gave a ka-thunk, and I offered him a shy smile. He smiled back. He smelled like a fall night and I leaned closer, holding onto his arm to steady myself. He stiffened but then exhaled slowly and relaxed.

I kissed his cheek.

His skin was warm against my lips and slightly stubbled. He radiated heat and feelings of safety. I wanted to burrow into him and beg him to keep protecting me, but instead, I made myself draw back.

"Thank you for trusting me, little warlock," he murmured, his eyes sparkling with an emotion I couldn't identify.

"Thank you for trying to take care of me," I whispered back.

I shivered, the water on my skin cooling me, and he turned the engine on and cranked the heaters up, then passed me a fleece jacket. I pulled it on, breathing in the piney scent overlaid with that familiar trace of bergamot. Just how much tea did Zander drink to smell that way permanently?

"Here," he said gruffly. "We need to keep you and the baby warm."

"Thanks." I was tempted to say that the best way to do that was to hold me in his arms, but if he actually tried it, I'd probably freak out. I might not think he was anything like Trent, but I was frustratingly aware of my own limitations.

We sat together in a pleasant silence for what could have been minutes or hours.

Eventually, Zander said, "There's a warlock coming to Grizzly Ridge next week."

Despite the gentleness of his tone, I tensed up. In the past, warlocks had never meant anything good for me. "Why?"

"To help us search for magical residue and see if we can figure out what's going on." He hesitated, then added, "If someone is searching for you or trying to psychically attack you, he might be able to work out who and where they are."

I nodded, relaxing a little. It was a relief that someone would be here who actually knew what they were doing. However, I couldn't shake the feeling of inadequacy that settled over me. If I'd been trained and wasn't just an overpowered magical battery, perhaps I'd have already been able to get the answers we needed without needing someone else to help.

"Hopefully he finds something." "If you say someone has been here, then I'm sure he will."

I sighed. "I wish I'd had more training so I could help."

"It isn't too late."

I didn't know what to say to that since warlocks who were willing to become mentors were hardly waltzing into my life on a daily basis.

My eyelids drooped and I yawned. "I should get back to bed. Apparently, my back will get more sore, so I should be trying to sleep as much as I can while I'm still able."

"Sweet dreams." Zander turned, his expression strangely sweet. "Can I visit you again?"

I jolted as I reached for the door, caught by surprise. "I... uh..." My cheeks blazed and I looked down. "I'd like that."

TWENTY-FIVE

Z ANDER

My heart was full to bursting as I recalled Reid's tentative but sweet expression as he'd told me I could call on him. I hadn't done so yet. I'd just remained outside the Omega House, and sometimes I could see his silhouette through the window if he moved around during the night.

I would, though. I was just giving him time.

"Why are you grinning into your herbal tea like a goof?" Clay asked, pausing in my office doorway.

I huffed and flashed him a smile. "Thinking about my mate."

He smirked. "You're so disgustingly smitten. Just wait until he accepts you as his alpha. You'll be unbearable."

I rolled my eyes. "There's nothing wrong with being happy."

"I know." His grin faded and his expression grew serious. "I'm happy for you, boss. We all are."

I rubbed my cheek, hoping he wouldn't notice the way heat rushed to them. "Thanks."

Clay shrugged. "It's just the truth. Anyway, I'm here

because we got a call about someone losing their shit at the supermarket. Don't worry, it wasn't Reid this time. I'm heading over to check it out."

"Do you need to take backup?" I asked, since he'd have a better idea of the situation than me.

"Nah, I doubt it. I'll call if it escalates but I don't think it's anything serious."

"Okay, thanks for letting me know."

He nodded and hurried away. I turned my attention to the report I was supposed to be reviewing and did my best to focus on it. However, only a few minutes later, Bea dropped by to let me know that a pair of wolf shifters had gotten into a fight after a road rage incident and she was taking Clay to help corral them.

Another half hour after that, Hawk raced out to deal with a teenager who'd gotten a hold of a rifle and was taking potshots at the neighbor's deer.

I wandered through the nearly empty station, baffled by the sudden uptick in violent crime. In general, Grizzly Ridge was a law-abiding town. We had a few speeding tickets and parking violations, but other than incidents like the ones involving the Red Moon Pack, violence was rare.

I looked out the window. Snow was falling steadily. Usually, behavior was worse during heat waves. On days like today, I'd expect people to be cooped up inside with a hot drink and a blanket, not out causing trouble.

I wandered up to join Nell at reception to ask if she had any idea what was going on, but before the words got out of my mouth, the front door flew open and Reid rushed inside, panting heavily, with Hamish close on his heels.

Reid bent over, his hands on his abdomen and his complexion a little waxy. He gagged then stumbled, his eyes wide and panicky. I inhaled and noted the sour scent of his fear in the air.

My arms twitched, eager to wrap around him and reassure him, but I joined my hands behind my back instead so as not to overwhelm him. He'd kissed me so sweetly the other night, but I didn't want to assume I could take liberties.

"What's wrong?" I asked, striding over to him and ignoring the way Hamish puffed up as if intending to protect him from me.

"I felt an influx of magic," Reid panted, straightening and mopping his sweaty brow. "I don't know who caused it, but there's not usually much magic in Grizzly Ridge, other than what you guys use to shift. This was strong and pure, like something from another warlock."

"Could you sense where it came from?" I asked, reaching for my radio. If he had a direction or point of origin, I could call for reinforcements and go to check it out.

But Reid shook his head. "It's like this wave of magic flooded the town, but I couldn't get anything useful from it." He bit his lip, furrowing his brow. "I'm sorry I'm not more help."

"No, this is useful," I assured him. "We just had a spate of violent incidents. I wonder if the two could be related."

At this, Reid's frown cleared away. "They could. When people aren't able to wield magic but they're inundated with it, they become agitated. That could easily show up as violence."

"Did you get a sense of whether the magic was good or evil?" I asked, mentally rolling through the options for how to proceed. Honestly, without a person or place to investigate, there weren't many. "Is the magic still present?"

He grimaced. "It left as quickly as it arrived while we were driving over here."

A thought struck me. Perhaps Nathaniel Birch had

arrived in town early. Would the arrival of someone like him cause magic to behave in such a manner?

I grabbed my cell phone and called his number.

"Birch," he answered.

"Hi, Nathaniel. It's Sheriff Zander Blackwood from Grizzly Ridge. We just experienced some kind of magical surge. Are you in the area?"

"As I told you previously, I won't arrive until tomorrow."

Damn. There went that idea.

"Do you think you'll be able to trace the magic even after twenty-four hours have passed?" I asked, needing some kind of lead to sink my claws into.

"Perhaps. Your local warlock, is he able to trace magic?" he asked.

I glanced at Reid. "He can't tell where it came from, and I don't think he's had any training in that space."

Reid mouthed, "I haven't."

Nathaniel hummed in thought. "Put me on speakerphone. We'll see if I can talk him through the process."

I switched the call to speakerphone and angled it toward Reid.

"Hello?" Nathaniel said.

"Hi." Reid stared at the phone dubiously.

"Are you Reid?" Nathaniel asked.

"Yes. Who are you?"

"Nathaniel Birch. Retired from the PBI. Do you have the capacity to use magic without a circle or a spell?"

His tongue darted out to moisten his lips. "Um, yes."

"Good. Are you sitting down?"

"No."

"Please do so." Nathaniel waited until Reid sat on Nell's chair and called out that he was ready before continuing. "Close your eyes. Feel the magic within you. You know what I mean. It's that tingle and warmth as it flows through you."

Reid nodded, glancing at me before closing his eyes. My heart swelled at the trust implicit in that gesture.

"Your magic will be aware of other magic nearby. It will have a certain hum to it. See if you can recognize that feeling."

Reid was quiet for a long moment, his hands resting on his lap, his eyelashes casting shadows over his cheeks. "I... I think I've got something."

"Good, that's really good. Now envision it like a cord and use your magic like a pair of tweezers to latch onto it."

A groove formed between Reid's eyebrows. It deepened the longer he went without responding and eventually he huffed. "I can't get it."

"Keep trying," Nathaniel urged. "Sometimes it takes a while. In your mind, picture the cord as being solid. Use your fingers to mime the motion of grabbing onto it if that helps. Some people are more kinetic when using magic."

Reid breathed slowly and deeply a few times, then reached out and pinched his fingertips together. He cursed and scowled, apparently failing, then tried again.

"I can smell it," he muttered, clearly frustrated. "Kind of minty. It's right there but I can't get it."

Nathaniel urged him to keep trying but a short time later, he called an end to it, accepting that it wasn't going to happen today.

"It was worth a shot," Nathaniel said as Reid's eyes fluttered open and he rubbed his temple. "I'm not surprised it was too much. Most warlocks require a lot of training before attempting such a thing, so don't beat yourself up about it."

Reid mumbled a response and we wrapped up the

phone call, but I could tell from the glossiness of his eyes that he was upset by the lack of result.

"Hey," I murmured, approaching him slowly in case I frightened him. I laid my hand on his shoulder and wished I could just scoop him into my arms. "We'll figure this out. You aren't alone."

He looked up at me and a tear trailed down his cheek. His mouth trembled and my gut clenched in response.

"Fuck it."

I pulled him into a hug, and my soul sang when he melted into the embrace, the slight swell of his belly pressed against me.

He'd allowed me to hold him.

Ours, my bear insisted.

CHAPTER
TWENTY-SIX

Z*ANDER*

My phone rang and I answered on autopilot, then perked up as I recognized Nell's voice.

"Warlock Birch is here, sir," she said, curiosity lacing her tone. "Should I send him down?"

"I'll be there in a couple of minutes," I told her, checking the time. "Tell him to wait."

I preferred not to have people walking through the station unsupervised.

"No problem, Sheriff."

She hung up and I quickly typed out a message to Dad, letting him know that Nathaniel Birch had arrived. It was generally a good idea to make sure the Clan Alpha was advised of all significant arrivals in Grizzly Ridge, and a powerful warlock certainly counted as that.

That done, I pocketed my phone and made my way through the station to the foyer, where a lean man around five foot ten stood near the desk, resting his weight on a silver and black cane.

His hair was black and scruffy with gray at the temples, and his deep-set eyes were also gray. His skin was a rich shade of copper, and I put him somewhere in his mid- to late-forties.

"Sheriff Blackwood?" he asked, limping across the distance between us, favoring his right leg.

I nodded in greeting. "Thanks for coming, Warlock Birch."

"Nathaniel, please."

"Nice to meet you, Nathaniel. I'm Zander."

"Aaron's son." He grinned. "I'm curious to spend time within Aaron's clan. I always got the impression he would be a good leader."

"In my opinion, he is, but I'm probably biased since he's my father and all."

Nell snorted. "He's a great Clan Alpha and you know it."

Nathaniel adjusted the bag that was slung over one of his shoulders. "Good to hear."

I cleared my throat. "Come on back. We can sit in a meeting room and I'll tell you about the issues we've been having."

"Thanks. I'd appreciate taking the weight off my leg. My old injury doesn't react well to long journeys in the car so I'm a bit achy."

I led him down the corridor, going slowly so as not to rush him, and into one of the meeting rooms. I pulled out a chair for him before circling around the small table to sit opposite.

Nathaniel withdrew a tablet from his bag and switched it on to a note-taking app. "So, you've been having some troubles?"

I leaned forward, my hands clasped together. "We have. It started in October last year. We had a few minor issues around town, nothing significant enough to make us worry, but things weren't typical. Eventually, that escalated into the kidnapping of my brother's mate, and shortly after that, to the kidnapping of several local omegas, including my brother."

Nathaniel's eyebrows shot up. "Were they safely retrieved?"

"Fortunately. My brother's mate, Milo, had been beaten, which was"—I clenched my jaw—"rather upsetting. Milo is a very gentle soul."

Everett had torn out the throat of the wolf who'd abducted Milo and I didn't blame him one bit.

"Who did it?" he asked.

"In the first instance, a feral wolf. In the second, a rogue pack that took up residence a couple of towns over. The omegas had been drugged or spelled and were scared but otherwise unharmed. At least, the ones from here were. We also rescued several who had been with the pack for longer, including Reid. They suffered far more than our local omegas did."

Nathaniel's expression tensed. "I've seen the sort of situation you're referring to. All I can say is that I'm glad Reid is safe now. Will you tell me more about him?"

"He's my mate."

Nathaniel's eyes narrowed. "Tell me you haven't claimed him."

I held out my hands, palms up. "I haven't. He's not in the right place for that. He was kidnapped, forcibly mated, and used as a weapon."

"Good." He relaxed slightly. "I've known some alphas who wouldn't have cared about that. What do you know about his life before he was abducted?"

"Not much," I admitted. "He's referenced his parents so I know he has them, but he hasn't said anything else about them. We offered to call them for him and he refused. When we pushed, he freaked out."

He nodded thoughtfully. "Not all covens are on the straight and narrow. You said he was untrained?"

"Either that, or his training is minimal. He hasn't said much about it other than that he wishes he'd had more training. Our local doctor says his magic is reactive as a child's might be."

"Interesting. What skills has he displayed?"

"He can ward, although he's told me his warding isn't particularly advanced. His abductor"—I refused to call that man his mate—"hired another warlock to teach him how to mask scents and make footfalls silent."

Nathaniel rested his cane against his leg and leaned back. "If that's the case, it's likely something isn't right inside his coven. All young warlocks should receive basic training. It's necessary to keep ourselves and others safe."

I hated that thought. Reid had been through so much in the past year. It didn't seem fair that his life before that might have also been less than ideal as well.

"I can tell you don't like that," Nathaniel said, and I realized I was growling.

"Sorry." I ducked my head. "My bear is very protective of him."

"As it should be. Now, about the supposed magical surge the town experienced yesterday. I will start investigating that this evening."

"Thank you." It was a weight off my shoulders to know we had someone reliable performing that much-needed task. I wished I could, but as a shifter, it simply wasn't possible for me to work such sophisticated magic.

"First, I'd like to meet Reid."

I stiffened. "Why do you want to see him today?"

We'd discussed the possibility of him assisting with Reid's training, but I thought I'd have longer to assess what kind of a man Nathaniel was before introducing him to my mate.

Nathaniel's lips twitched. "I can tell you're reluctant but trust me, it's better to make the introductions now than for him to sense another warlock in town and have no idea who it is or what's going on."

I supposed that was a good point. "Okay, but I'd ask you not to crowd him, and to respect his wishes if he doesn't want to engage with you beyond an introduction. He's still adjusting to life in Grizzly Ridge and his trust is... thin."

"I'll absolutely do that," Nathaniel assured me. "I've no desire to make him uncomfortable. Does now suit?"

I sighed. I had paperwork to do, but nothing that couldn't wait. "Now is fine. I'll just be a moment." I went to my office to collect my jacket, hat, and gloves, and then returned to the meeting room and escorted Nathaniel back to the foyer. "Do you want to drive there separately?"

He made a thoughtful sound. "I think that makes the most sense. Then I can continue on afterward without inconveniencing you."

I gave him the address. "I'll meet you there."

TWENTY-SEVEN

*Z*ANDER

I headed to my car and drove to the Omega House, the wipers working overtime to clear rain from the windshield. There was already a Jeep parked outside with a dog crate on the back, fortunately enclosed to protect the dog within from the elements. All I could see of it was a black and white splotched nose poking through a small slot in the front.

I got out of my car and grabbed the umbrella that lived in the back to shelter myself from the rain. However, the umbrella was made redundant only seconds later when Nathaniel stepped out of the car and created a shield around us that kept the rain and wind out. It was only now that I was closer to the car that I realized there was also a small bubble of protected air around the dog crate.

"This is Jilly," he said, reaching through the slot in the crate to pet the dog's nose. "Warlocks don't have familiars, but we can use animal companions to ground us when we perform magic and she's mine. It's her job to alert me if I start to push too hard, kind of like a service animal."

"I didn't know that."

He nodded. "We don't share it widely because we don't want our pets to be targeted. I'm telling you because in the future an animal like this might be helpful for your Reid." He motioned to the door. "Let's not hover out here long enough for them to get nervous."

I strode over to the front door and knocked. When Hamish answered, he had Reid at his side. Reid gave me that shy smile I absolutely adored—the one that lacked his usual sharp edge—and I warmed inside, reminded of how he'd felt in my arms.

Unfortunately, Reid's eyes widened as soon as his gaze landed on Nathaniel and he backed up, bumping into the door. A squeak of terror burst from him and even though I was confident that Nathaniel meant him no harm, part of me wanted to pin the other warlock down just for causing Reid distress.

Hamish's expression darkened. "Who is this man?" he demanded, stepping between Reid and Nathaniel.

A growl tore from my throat and I immediately ducked my head. "Sorry. My bear doesn't like seeing you between us and our mate."

Hamish's eyes narrowed. "Well, I'll be here until you explain."

I gestured to Nathaniel. "This is Warlock Nathaniel Birch. He's a retired PBI agent and he's here to help us with some of the problems we've been having."

Hamish's jaw worked, but he nodded as if satisfied and stepped to the side enough for me to see Reid. My little warlock tiptoed forward, visibly trembling but trying to be brave. My chest squeezed. I would never let anything happen to him.

"Can you sense the magic?" he asked quietly, his gaze darting between Nathaniel and the ground, as if unsure where to look.

Nathaniel tilted his chin thoughtfully. "I sense something that may be remnants of a magical surge, but I'll need to investigate further once I settle into my accommodation and unpack my tools. I understand that you're a warlock too, Reid?"

Reid glanced at me, his eyebrows flying up as if he were surprised the stranger knew his name. "I am."

Nathaniel hobbled forward a step, perhaps emphasizing his injury to make himself seem less threatening. "Are you interested in learning more about spell craft?"

Reid's eyes widened even further. "Are you serious?"

"Of course." He tilted his head consideringly. "Will you come out of the wards for a moment?"

"I'll protect you," I promised when he hesitated. I didn't know why Nathaniel wanted him outside the wards, but there must be a reason for it.

"You'd better not be up to anything," Hamish warned.

Nathaniel's lips curled. "I'm not, Protector. You can be at ease."

Hamish scowled, and when Reid began to move forward, Hamish linked their arms and kept pace with him. I was glad he was another omega. If an alpha had done the same thing, my bear might have seen it as a challenge.

"Hmm," Nathaniel said as they drew nearer. "Yes, I see the situation now. If you are willing, I would like to stay in Grizzly Ridge for a while and begin your training in earnest. It will take several months, at least."

I jerked, caught off guard not by the offer but by how long he expected it to take. He'd said he wouldn't mind going over the basics, but I'd thought he'd be here for a week or two at most.

Reid looked at me, his eyebrows knitted together, as if he expected me to object.

"If you want to, you should do it," I urged him.

He turned to Nathaniel. "I'm pregnant. Will training put my baby at risk?"

Nathaniel smiled softly. "Not at all. In fact, knowing how to use your magic will mean you're less likely to lose control and cause them harm."

Reid nodded decisively. "Then I'll do it. How would it work?"

Nathaniel grinned. "I'll come back tomorrow with a plan. How's that?"

"Okay." Reid glanced at me again and then straightened his shoulders. "I'll see you then."

We turned and made our way slowly back to the vehicles. Nathaniel smelled strongly of anticipation and I knew he wanted to share something with me, but he waited until the door clicked shut before doing so.

"Reid has one of the largest internal wells of magic that I've ever seen," he murmured, low enough that I only picked it up because of my shifter hearing.

"He does?"

"Yes, and the wariness he displayed wasn't just because I'm an alpha or a stranger. He was worried because I'm a *warlock*. That tells me he's scared of his own kind. Taking the sheer volume of his magic into account, I'd say it's likely he's been used by other warlocks for his magic."

"Wouldn't his parents have stopped that?"

Nathaniel grimaced. "Not if they were involved. Look, I could be wrong, but not all parents are like yours. There's a chance his are abusive. Warlock covens can be very hierarchical, and if someone in a leadership role took exception to how strong he is, he might have suffered because of it."

My palms stung and I looked down and jolted at the sight of blood pooling in them from where my claws had curled into the flesh. I quickly retracted my claws and wiped my hands on my uniform.

"Zander." He hesitated. "With as much power as he has, Reid could prove very dangerous if he isn't trained properly. That needs to be a priority, not an afterthought."

Ah, now his suddenly extended stay made more sense. He was unwilling to leave a ticking time bomb in Grizzly Ridge.

"Are you sure you're able to stay here for that long?" I asked, grateful to him but not wanting to disrupt his life too much. "If it doesn't suit, we can find someone else. Perhaps you even have a suggestion."

"No. I want to train him." He paused, then added, "But I also think I can help him in other ways too."

"How?" I demanded.

He pursed his lips and seemed to be second-guessing himself. "I don't want you to get carried away about this."

"About what?" I asked, confused.

He leaned closer. "With my magic, I can feel both his broken mating bond and the scarring that accompanies it. If Reid wants it, I can heal the scarring so the mate bite that was forced on him disappears."

My heart banged against the inside of my rib cage. "You can do that?"

"Yes." He clicked his fingers and a spark appeared. "Easy as that. I didn't want to mention it in front of him yet because he's so fragile, but it's a possibility."

Warmth filled my chest. He could remove that awful scar from Reid and cleanse everything it signified.

Hopefully, Reid would want that. And hopefully, some day, he'd allow me to replace it with a consensual mating mark.

TWENTY-EIGHT

Reid

I slipped the obsidian pendant beneath my shirt so that Warlock Nathaniel Birch wouldn't be able to see it. Hopefully, I wouldn't need to protect myself against him during our training session today, but if it came down to it, I wanted to have all the advantages I could.

"Are you sure you want to go with him?" Hamish asked, his brow furrowed with concern as he leaned against the wall in the living room, sipping from a cup of coffee.

"I want to learn how to use my magic better." I rubbed at the red skin that still encircled my wrists. It didn't hurt as much as it had, but it still wasn't pleasant. I had no desire to accidentally harm myself—or someone else, especially my baby—again just because my magic was out of control.

"But do we trust this guy?" he persisted.

I patted the spot where my shirt covered the obsidian pendant. "Zander does."

"And that's enough for you?"

I considered that. I doubted there was anyone I fully trusted, but between the hours sitting together inside his car—alone and vulnerable but safe all the same—and the nights he'd spent parked outside to protect me, I believed he wouldn't endanger me.

"For now."

It wasn't as if I planned to let my guard down around Warlock Birch. I'd keep a close eye on him and I expected he'd be doing the same with me. I doubted that I could out-fight him if the necessity arose, but I could certainly outrun him, even pregnant. I'd seen how he'd had to use a cane to support himself.

There was a knock on the door and I rose from the sofa, grabbed my jacket, and pulled it on. I'd packed a woolen hat and gloves into one of the pockets in case I needed them, as well as a small packet of dill pickle chips and my anti-nausea medication.

It wasn't raining or snowing outside, but I'd poked my head out for long enough to realize that it was bitterly cold.

"If you're gone for longer than a few hours, I'm sending the police after you," Hamish said, watching me go. "Will you message me every hour so I know you're okay?"

I paused, struck by the urge to hug him. I wasn't sure how much he actually liked me, but he was trying to keep me safe nonetheless and I appreciated that. I hesitated too long and it became awkward so I just nodded and hurried to the door, pretending the whole pause hadn't happened.

When I opened the front door, Warlock Birch stood there, resting his weight on his cane. A shaggy black and white dog sat at his feet, one ear cocked and the other floppy. She was alert but calm, and I didn't get any threatening vibes from her.

"Is she your support animal?" I asked, referring to the pet some warlocks kept to help ground them while they were using magic. I glanced at his cane. "Or perhaps a service animal?"

"She's a support animal," he said, taking the question in stride. Some warlocks were secretive when it came to their pets because they made an easy target if someone wanted to weaken an enemy. "Her name is Jilly. You can pat her, if you like."

I bent just a little and extended my hand toward Jilly. She sniffed my fingers and then, when I met with her approval, I scratched behind her ear. She didn't seem jumpy, which indicated that Warlock Birch probably didn't mistreat her. If he was kind to dogs, perhaps I had nothing to fear from him either, but I'd reserve judgment.

"I've scoped out an area near the woods where we can practice without being disturbed," he said, gesturing over his shoulder toward the National Park.

I stiffened. "Can't we just practice on the road?"

I didn't want to go far with a man I didn't yet trust.

He grimaced. "We can if that makes you more comfortable, but it would limit your ability to concentrate because you'd be on the lookout for traffic. And if something were to go wrong, there would be more people around who might get hurt."

I raised my hand toward the pendant again but stopped and dropped it to my side when I noticed how closely he was paying attention to the movement. "How far away is the area you found?"

He shrugged. "Perhaps a mile or so."

I could run that, if need be, and with shifters' enhanced senses, if I screamed, someone would probably hear. "Okay, but you'll need to give me directions so I can walk there."

Like hell would I get in the car with a warlock I didn't know. Even if my ward hadn't prevented him from entering —which indicated that he didn't mean me any harm— there were ways around that for skilled warlocks. It didn't necessarily mean his intentions were good.

Warlock Birch nodded as if this was totally understandable and he reeled off directions then added, "I'll drive there and get prepared while I wait for you."

"Sounds good." I stepped out of the house, closing the distance between us, and studied him discreetly for any indication that he might try to abduct me or use a draining spell on me.

As if sensing my unease, he limped back to his Jeep with Jilly on his heels. There was an enclosed kennel of some type on the back and he opened it. She jumped in and he secured the latch and rounded the vehicle.

I moved out from the shelter of the house and the wind whipped at me, stirring my hair and chilling the back of my neck. I shivered and unzipped my pocket to retrieve the gloves and hat.

I followed Birch's directions, cursing the dull ache in my hips but grateful that I wasn't carrying too much extra weight yet.

When I arrived I found him sitting on a park bench near the edge of the trees in an area of grass with a few picnic tables and a children's playground. The playground was bare since the kids were all in school. Even if they hadn't been it was too cold for little ones to spend much time outside.

Warlock Birch used his cane to lever himself up. "Has anyone taught you to shield yourself from the elements?"

"Um, no."

"Then I'll do that soon. I've been told that you've demonstrated the ability to do basic wards, to use electricity to attack, and to mask sounds and smells." He gestured toward a piece of cardboard that hung in the air midway between us and the trees. "I'd like to see where your skills are currently at so I know where to start from. Make sense?"

"Yeah."

He smiled and it softened his harsh features. "Aim your sparks at the center of the cardboard. We're going for finesse, not power. How's your eyesight?"

"Not fantastic, but I get by."

"If you look closely, there's an X in the center of the target. Aim for that."

I let out a breath and eyed the target, spotting a mark in the center. I checked to make sure both he and Jilly were out of the way and then sent a stream of sparks toward the target. When it stopped, we both stared at the result and I cringed. There was a scorch mark on the edge of the target but none where the X was.

"It's a start," Birch said, otherwise not commenting on my poor control. "Now I'd like you to send everything you've got at the target. I want the whole thing to go up in smoke."

That was easier. Less finesse required. I pointed at the target and it was engulfed by sparks and quickly caught fire. As the ashes started to fall, Birch did something to make them disappear before they hit the ground.

He came to stand in front of me. "So, your power is good, which isn't a surprise considering how inherently magical you are. Your accuracy leaves something to be desired. Next, let's test your ability to mask sound and scent. I'm going to stay here and I want you to use the spell you usually would and walk from here to the trees and back."

I mumbled the words of the dead language that started the spell and did as he said. When I returned, he was nodding approvingly. "I didn't hear a single thing. Will you hold out your hand to Jilly?"

I did and she sniffed me once again.

"Jilly, seek," Birch ordered.

Jilly trotted away, sniffing the ground. She stalled a few yards in front of us and wandered idly for a moment, then seemed to pick the trail up again and followed it perhaps fifty yards before becoming confused.

"Hmm." Birch called her back. When she came he rewarded her with a treat from his pocket. "Your scent-masking could use improvement but considering how little training you've had, you've done well."

My chest wanted to swell with pride, but I forced myself not to react. I wasn't going to fall into a trap just because someone fed my ego.

He sat on the bench again and rubbed his knee, as if it was bothering him. I couldn't help but wonder what had injured him so badly that he hadn't been able to heal himself. I wasn't well-versed in healing magic, but I knew that many warlocks could self-heal.

He patted the bench, indicating for me to join him. "Tell me what you know about wards."

I padded closer but before I reached him, the obsidian pendant warmed against my skin and the itch of foreign magic swept over me. Nausea coiled in my gut and I dropped to my knees and emptied my guts.

"Do you feel that?" I asked, panting for breath.

CHAPTER

TWENTY-NINE

*Z*ANDER

"Do you know where Reid is?"

Adrenaline spiked through me, sending my pulse through the ceiling. I hadn't looked at Caller ID when I'd answered the phone but I recognized the voice as Bea's and if she was looking for Reid, that meant something was wrong.

"Is he missing?" I demanded, bolting upright and snatching my hat from the desk out of habit.

"I went to the Omega House to look for him but Hamish said he'd left with that warlock who arrived in town yesterday," she explained, which didn't really answer my question. "Hamish didn't know where they'd gone and I'm not sure where to look."

I frowned. "You haven't stretched your wings?"

If Bea was really concerned, she could have shifted and flown over the town to search for him easily enough. If she hadn't and was resorting to other methods of tracking him, I had to wonder why.

"No, Sheriff." She lowered her voice. "There's a man

here claiming to be Reid's guardian. I called you right away."

"Thank you, Bea." Now I understood. Though she hadn't said the words, something about this man must have pinged Bea's internal alarms. Considering Reid's previous reaction to the mention of his family—and what Nathaniel had said yesterday—there was no way I was letting him anywhere near Reid without vetting him first. "Where are you?"

"He flagged me down outside the bakery. He's inside getting a hot drink. I'm waiting on the sidewalk."

"I'll be there in a couple of minutes."

I pocketed my keys, briefly considering whether to run straight over rather than drive, but if I ended up needing to escort this man somewhere—either to Reid or out of town—it would be best to have my vehicle on hand.

I hurried out to the car and drove the short distance to the bakery. Bea was standing outside, her hands in her pockets as she spoke with a long-limbed, dark-haired man.

I parked behind Bea and strode over, examining the man as I drew nearer. He turned toward me and strolled over with the insouciant walk of someone who knew he was good-looking and who probably had a nice full bank account to back him up.

"I'm Hephaestes, the High Priest of the Havlock Coven, and Reid Havlock's legal guardian." He offered me his hand. His sleeves were rolled up and his forearms were tattooed with layers upon layers of symbols and runes. A gemstone bracelet encircled his wrist and despite his edgy appearance, his hands were soft, like he'd never done a day's manual labor.

I studied him, searching for a trace of Reid in his features, but my little warlock was petite and light while this man was rangy and dark.

They couldn't be more different.

"Good day." I dipped my head politely. "I'm Sheriff Blackwood."

I discreetly scented him. He smelled of ozone, as all warlocks did, with a trace of mint and, beneath that, a darker note that reminded me of damp earth and rotting vegetation. It wasn't unpleasant exactly, but it unsettled me, bringing to mind the warlock ceremonies of old, which had involved far too much blood and death to be acceptable today.

Hephaestes grinned. "It's a pleasure to meet you. I must say, I'm relieved to have finally tracked down our Reid."

I stiffened, my bear rebelling at anyone considering Reid to be *theirs*. He wasn't theirs, he was *ours*. "I hope you won't mind me saying, but it's strange to hear that Reid has a guardian. He's an adult."

He just shrugged. "All High Priests consider ourselves to be guardians of our coven. It's our job to care for our members. Do you know where I can find him?"

I cocked my head, assessing him. If he wanted to come across as the nurturing type, he was falling short. Not only was his air the one of a man accustomed to getting what he wanted, but there was a hard gleam in his eyes that I didn't like. His smile never reached them.

"Has something happened to make you think it's necessary to track him?" I asked, ignoring the question. "It's my understanding that he left his home coven some months ago."

In fact, I knew damn well that it had been over half a year. If this Hephaestes was so concerned about Reid's well-being, then why hadn't he tried to help him while he was being held captive?

His smile tightened at the corners but didn't disappear. "Of course I looked for him when he first left us, but I immediately discovered that he'd mated with a wolf shifter. Since I know how protective shifters are of their mates, I didn't see the need to reach out to him if he wanted a little space." His expression turned wry and slightly self-deprecating. Nothing about it rang true. "Which I have to assume he did since he left without a word."

I exchanged a glance with Bea. This guy's story was just convincing enough that someone who didn't know Reid well might buy it.

But I didn't.

Perhaps his version of events was true in that the coven searched for Reid. If Nathaniel's guess was correct and they'd abused him, they might have backed off upon seeing he was mated to Trent, because no magic could overcome the mating bond. But now that the bond was severed...

Well, he was fair game again.

But that was only a guess.

I turned back to the High Priest. "I'll have to check with Reid before taking you to meet him. He's a resident here in Grizzly Ridge and we take the safety of our residents very seriously."

Hephaestes's smile faded and his eyes narrowed, burning dark like a coal fire. "He is under my protection, not yours. I haven't seen him for months and I won't be delayed a moment longer. Take me to him."

I jerked my head to the side and Bea moved away from Hephaestes. "Escort him back to Dad's place," I murmured, quietly enough that a warlock's less-sensitive ears wouldn't be able to make out the words. "I'm going to reach out to Reid. Something feels off about this."

THIRTY

R*EID*

"You don't have to worry," Warlock Birch said, the gentle tone of his voice contrasting with the intense look in his eyes. "I have a permanent shield around me that deflects seeking spells. Yes, I felt it, but there's no cause for concern. My shield repelled the spell and it won't provide the sender with any information."

"Really?" My shoulders slumped and I drew in a deep breath, finally able to breathe now that the tension in my chest had lessened.

Even just knowing that someone else had experienced the same magical poking that I'd been sensing on and off for days—if not weeks—was a relief because it meant that I'd been right.

It was real and I wasn't losing my mind.

He nodded. "I promise, they won't find us using that spell. However, it's a short-range seeking spell which means that whoever sent it is in the area. Why don't you and I go under the cover of the trees in case they decide to search another way?"

"That sounds like a good idea." I clambered to my feet. I

might not fully trust him, but I doubted he had anything to do with the magic I'd felt. He had no reason to seek me out because he already knew where I was. "Will you teach me how to make a shield like yours?"

He started toward the woods, moving surprisingly quickly despite his limp. Jilly ran ahead of him, her nose to the ground. "I can but it's quite advanced. It might take a while before you reach that level."

"I'll train hard to get there." I was sick and tired of being a victim. If I knew how to wield my power effectively, I'd never be forced into that role again.

He glanced over his shoulder. "I know you will. You're a quick study."

As we entered the woods, the shadows lowered the temperature and I shivered.

"If you concentrate, you can ward us against the elements and warm us," Birch said. "Close your eyes and imagine the warmth of a fire. Not the fire itself because we don't want to start a forest fire, but envision the heat wrapping around you and warming you all the way through, then say *calor*."

I stopped walking and tried to concentrate on imagining warmth. "*Calor*."

When he cried out in alarm, my eyes flew open just in time to see him stomp a flame out of existence.

"I'm sorry!" I raced over, looking helplessly down at the ash on the ground. There was nothing I could do to help. The problem had been dealt with, but I felt like I had to do something.

"It's okay," he soothed, his hands out as though I was a skittish animal. "It was just a little fire. No harm done." His phone rang and he reached into his pocket to get it without taking his eyes off me. He answered with, "Birch."

He relaxed a little. The caller must have been someone

he knew. Jilly nudged my hand and I petted her absent-mindedly.

"We're in the woods near that playground on the edge of town," Birch said, and then nodded. He hung up. "Zander will be here soon."

My heart lifted and I was taken aback by the strangeness of the emotion.

I was looking forward to seeing him.

It was so strange. I was excited to see an alpha. Less than a month ago, I'd happily have gone my entire life without encountering one again.

"Why don't you try the warmth spell a second time?" he prompted.

I chewed on my lower lip. When Jilly bumped against me, I buried my hands in her fur. "What if I start another fire?"

"Then I'll put it out. It's the middle of winter, and despite appearances"—he gestured to his leg—"I'm a reasonably strong warlock. There's nothing to worry about."

I bit back the retort that we were surrounded by trees and that forest fires could happen at any time of year. I had to believe that if he said there was nothing to worry about then that meant he really could handle anything that might happen.

Closing my eyes, I breathed evenly and instead of imagining a fire, I pictured sitting in front of a heater, the warmth radiating outward. No flames, just heat. Slowly, the air around me became less frigid and I stopped shivering.

"*Calor.*"

"Nice work," Birch said.

I opened my eyes again. "I did it?"

He grinned. "You did. I think Zander is here so let's meet him halfway, shall we?"

I glanced at his leg, thinking that perhaps it would be kinder to him if we made Zander come all the way over here, but I didn't want to say the wrong thing. This was the closest I'd ever been to having a mentor. I kept my mouth shut and followed him out of the trees.

Zander's tall form appeared ahead of us, his hat atop his head like always, and although he wore a jacket it was nowhere near enough for the conditions. At least, it wouldn't be for me. Especially not without a woolen hat, gloves, and a scarf.

As his features became clear, I noticed that his forehead was furrowed and his lips were pressed firmly together.

"What's wrong?" I asked.

He opened his mouth but hesitated for so long that dread curled in my gut. Whatever it was, it must be bad. "There's a man in town claiming to be the High Priest of your coven. He's tall with dark hair and tattoos... hey, are you all right?"

I swayed from one foot to the other, my blood rushing in my ears. White lines danced in front of my eyes and my vision blurred.

I tried to concentrate on Zander but his voice was a deep drone in the back of my mind. I couldn't pick out individual words let alone figure out their meaning.

No. No. No.

They'd found me.

They knew I was here.

I tried to draw in a breath but my throat was too tight. I clutched at it, my fingernails digging into the skin, pinpricks of pain helping me to focus enough to meet Zander's eyes as he knelt in front of me.

Knelt?

When had I sat down?

"Breathe," he urged, putting my hand on his chest and

inhaling deeply, his rib cage expanding beneath my finger-tips. "In and out, sweetheart. Come on, you can do it."

I sucked in a lungful of air, just enough to make my head spin.

What was the exercise that Jessie had taught me?

In for four, hold for seven, out for eight.

With Zander murmuring encouragement, I inhaled as slowly as I could and counted through the beats. The lines in front of my eyes started to dissipate. I inhaled again, held it for seven seconds and let it go bit by bit. On the third breath, my ears cleared with a pop.

A hand was rubbing circles on my back. Considering Zander was in front of me, it must be Warlock Birch.

My face burned. How humiliating. I'd had a breakdown in front of a badass former PBI agent.

Zander must have read my expression because he frowned. "Hey now, none of that. There's no need to be embarrassed. Panic attacks happen. I'm just sorry I brought it on. I assume that means you don't want to see this man?"

I shook my head vigorously. "No, please no. Don't let him anywhere near me."

"I won't." Zander's face darkened, but it didn't scare me. Perhaps because I knew his anger wasn't directed at me. "I know you wouldn't have reacted to hearing about him like that for no reason. If he's a threat, I won't let him anywhere near you."

I stood on wobbly legs and when he straightened too, I threw myself into his arms. "Thank you."

The muscles of his broad chest were firm beneath my cheek and his heart pounded a steady rhythm. I clung to him, for once comforted by the fact I had a big, strong alpha who'd decided I was his mate. Even though we weren't bonded, I somehow knew that he wouldn't let Hephaestes take me away.

For the first time, something warm stirred inside me—a thread of trust that wrapped around my heart and tightened like a hug. I pulled him closer, reveling in his strength and in the knowledge that, for whatever reason, he *wanted* me.

A spark flickered to life—one I'd never expected to feel again. I rocked against him, needing to feel him, wanting to be as close as two souls could be.

Behind me, Birch cleared his throat. "Would you like me to shore up the wards on the Omega House so that no one unwelcome can get through them?"

I flinched and released Zander, my cheeks burning as I realized I'd been all but dry humping him. "Yes, please."

I focused on the matter at hand and tried to ignore the hormones going haywire in my body. Was this a side effect of pregnancy, or was it something to do with the mate connection I was beginning to believe we might actually share?

Birch circled me, his weathered eyes creased at the corners, his eyes shining with kindness. "Shall we do that now?"

I cleared my throat, embarrassed. "If that's okay."

Having his wards around the house would make it so much safer against the collective knowledge and skill of the Havlock coven than my own basic efforts.

The Havlock coven was dangerous. Honestly, I shouldn't stay here now that they'd found me. I should run and hide so that they didn't pose a threat to the people of Grizzly Ridge. But the thought of leaving made me heavy-hearted and I wasn't sure I'd be able to do it.

"Actually, let's wait," Zander cut in. "Bea called Hamish at the Omega House before calling me to alert me so your..."

"High Priest."

"Okay, so your High Priest knows you've been staying

there. I asked Bea to take him to Dad's house but if he resists, Bea won't be able to force him to go. We'd be better off keeping you elsewhere for now. Perhaps at the police station." He sighed and shook his head. "No, not that either. He knows that I was coming to speak with you so he'll expect that too and we can't take him to my place because it's too near Mom and Dad's."

"What about the Children's Home?" I suggested, but then immediately realized that was a bad idea. I didn't want to endanger the children. "Scratch that."

"No, it could work," Zander mused, scratching his jaw. "I doubt anyone would think to look there. Nathaniel, could you hide our presence there and shield the children if need be?"

"No problem," Nathaniel said. "I won't let anyone hurt a hair on a child's head."

Zander touched the brim of his hat. "Then let's go."

"But..."

Neither man acknowledged me as they turned and trudged toward the road. I hurried after them and Jilly danced around my feet, apparently at ease despite the tension in the air.

I was given the choice to drive with either man so I climbed in with Zander since I trusted him more. He led the way to the Children's Home and he and I waited in the car, parked on the roadside, while Warlock Birch performed a spell of some kind and Jilly stood beside him like a sentinel.

When he finished, we got out and went to the front door. Zander knocked and the door opened only a few seconds later.

George smiled out at us, but his chocolatey brown eyes were wary, especially when they landed on Warlock Birch. Considering that he was one of the omegas my old pack had tried to kidnap, I could understand his caution.

Birch gave a quick intake of breath and a yellow glow flickered around his hands. George's eyes widened and he took a step back.

"Hey, George." Zander stepped forward, trying to put him at ease. "Do you mind if we borrow a room for a little while?"

"S-Sure," he stuttered, his gaze darting from Zander to Birch and back again. His hands fisted at his sides, then loosened.

I looked down, hating how raw and exposed his obvious fear made me feel. *I* was part of the reason he wasn't comfortable even here in his workplace. I'd helped someone hurt him—and many others—and it would take a long time before I properly came to terms with that.

George led us down a corridor and into a small playroom. "I'll keep the children out. Is there anything you need?"

"Not right now," Zander told him.

I kind of wished I could spend time with the children. Perhaps I'd have to return later. I didn't have much experience with them and that was something I should probably change considering I'd be a father soon.

I stepped into the room and Zander followed. George turned on his heel and hurried away.

Warlock Birch closed the door and light flickered around his hands again. "I think that sweet human is my mate."

CHAPTER
THIRTY-ONE

R*EID*

I gaped at Warlock Birch, who was looking thoughtfully at the door. I hadn't seen a non-shifter recognize their mate before. At least, not in real time.

I knew that warlocks had fated mates, but finding them was less common than it was for shifters because a warlock's instincts were weaker. A simple scent exchange wouldn't be enough to identify them, but something about George must have triggered this reaction.

"Tread carefully," Zander said quietly. "George is a good man but he survived an attempted kidnapping only a few weeks ago. He may not be ready for a mate."

Warlock Birch nodded. "I'll be patient." He glanced between us. "Can I leave you alone while I speak to him?"

"Of course." Zander took off his hat and sank onto the sofa. "I think Reid and I need to have a conversation too."

I looked down at my gloved hands. I didn't want to talk about my birth coven or my parents, but if I wanted him to protect me then I'd have to.

"Reid?"

I looked up, surprised to find Warlock Birch still hovering there, his expression making it clear that he wasn't leaving me alone with Zander unless I agreed to it. Something warm unfurled in my chest. I'd barely met the man and yet he was trying to keep me safe and comfortable.

Perhaps I didn't need to be so wary of him.

"You can go," I told him.

He searched my gaze for a long moment and I was awed at his willpower. Most shifters lost their minds when they first met their mate, but he was being very controlled. Hopefully that meant he wouldn't frighten George.

I drew in a breath and summoned my courage. "Please don't push him."

Warlock Birch's features softened. "A mate is a precious gift. I would never push. I give you my word."

I ducked my head awkwardly. "Thank you."

He left the room and closed the door behind him. I hovered, unsure whether to sit beside Zander or on the floor.

"Would you like a drink?" Zander asked, moving over to create more room on the sofa. "Or a snack? I know you had a shock."

"No, thank you." I slinked closer, settling onto the cushion beside him but keeping at least a foot of space between us. "Later. I don't think I could eat now."

"Just tell me when."

"Okay." I kicked my shoes off, lifted my socked feet onto the chair, and wrapped my arms around my knees. "I guess I'd better get talking, huh?"

Zander rested his elbow on the arm of the sofa and angled himself toward me. "Only share as much as you're comfortable with."

I bit my lip. At this stage, there was no point keeping anything to myself. He'd find out sooner or later anyway.

I opened my mouth but couldn't find the words. I felt adrift, unanchored at sea. Needing something to ground me, I shuffled closer to him and reached out.

As if sensing what I needed, he took my hand. His was so much larger than mine and hotter too. I focused on the sensation of his callused skin against my softer palm and used the connection to stay in the moment.

I couldn't let the memories pull me under.

"My coven realized how powerful I was when I was very young." My voice was startlingly loud in the quiet room and I dropped it to a whisper. "In some covens, they would have trained me to be their next leader and used all of their resources to make me as educated and skilled as possible, but not in mine."

He gave my hand a squeeze. "What happened?"

I looked down at our joined hands because that was easier than meeting his eyes. "The High Priest was intimidated by me. He didn't see me as a protégé but as someone who might usurp his place. So instead of training me to use my power, he paid off my parents and the entire coven was allowed to use me as a magical battery."

"They *what?*" Zander growled, a soft menace in his voice that made the hairs on the back of my neck stand on end.

I curled my fingers around him more tightly. "They created a room with a magical circle that allowed others to siphon my power. The High Priest used me most often and he put limits on how much others were allowed to take but as long as they stayed within the limits, he was happy."

Closing my eyes, I warded off memories of that awful room. The chains drilled into the concrete to keep me in place when I fought. The spells that rendered me unable to protect myself. The utter hopelessness that would sink into my bones any time I was taken there.

I'd stopped fighting after a while. When I was complacent, I earned some small freedoms. At the time, I'd loved being able to leave the compound for short periods. Eventually, that was how I'd met Trent and ended up in a whole other form of hell.

"You said he paid your parents off, but where were they during all of this?" Zander's tone was rough, barely human, and when I peeked at him, his eyes were amber, his bear close to the surface.

"Around. They were loyal to the High Priest. My father was one of his enforcers and my mother... Well, they might have been lovers at one point. I was never certain but she was closer to him than she should have been."

"So they just allowed you to be used like that?" Zander practically vibrated with rage and part of me liked it. I couldn't help tensing because he was a strong alpha and those had never been good for me in the past, but he was angry on my behalf and that was kind of nice. "You don't have to worry about that anymore. My clan will protect you. *I'll* protect you."

A small flame of hope burst to life inside me.

I wanted to believe him.

I *yearned* for his words to be true.

"Thank you," I whispered, leaning closer to him and drawing comfort from his presence.

Maybe this time would be different.

Maybe this *man* was different.

If so, my baby and I might be able to have a life I'd always been too afraid to dream of.

Zander lifted my hand and brushed his lips over the back of it. Goose bumps rippled down my arm.

"I have to send that asshole away," he said. "I'm going

to call Everett. Do you need a few minutes to process things first?"

"No." The sooner Hephaestes was gone, the better. "I want to check on George."

I didn't think Warlock Birch would mistreat him but alphas had surprised me before and rarely in good ways.

We stood and I tried to pretend I didn't notice that my hand was still in Zander's as he opened the door and held it for me. The corridor was narrow but we fit side by side as long as we stayed close together.

Warlock Birch and George were in the kitchen. As soon as we entered, a knot in my gut loosened. All it took was a glance to see that Birch was already smitten and George seemed relaxed with him. The human omega had a sparkle in his eye and a sassy sway to his hips as he moved that certainly hadn't been there earlier.

George looked over and smiled. "Would you like a drink?"

"Can I get a glass of water?" I asked, offering him a hesitant smile in return.

He opened a cabinet, pulled a glass down, filled it and passed it to me. "Here you go. My mate tells me that you've been training with him."

Ah, so that answered the question as to whether or not Warlock Birch had told him they were mates. The connection was even more difficult for humans to recognize than it was for warlocks, although I'd been told there was an undeniable draw to the person in question.

"We haven't done much yet," I replied, not wanting to give anyone the idea that I was more skilled than I was.

The side of Birch's mouth hitched up. "We'll get there. It's all one day at a time."

I looked between the two men and found myself hoping that he meant it, both for George's sake and for mine.

Zander cleared his throat. "Reid, I'm going to ask Everett to come and wait with you while I get rid of that... *monster*."

THIRTY-TWO

*Z*ANDER

Reid's big blue eyes met mine and his teeth scraped over his bottom lip. "He's really powerful. Do you think you can actually make him leave town?"

"I can and I will. I promise." The words settled into my soul. They weren't locked into place with a spell like his oath not to harm anyone from Grizzly Ridge, but they were binding nonetheless.

A promise to my mate that I would do anything I could to keep him safe and happy. I didn't care what it took. Hephaestes might be a strong warlock but our clan was nothing to sneeze at—especially with Nathaniel here too.

"And you won't let him near me?" The terror in his voice shredded me inside.

I hated it, just like I hated the way he'd shrunk in on himself as he'd explained his life before Trent. He'd seemed so small. He shouldn't ever have to make himself appear as less than he was to protect himself.

If I had my way, Reid would get whatever training he needed to become the most powerful warlock in the state so he'd never have to live in fear again. Although if all he wanted was to live quietly and avoid garnering any extra attention, that was fine with me and I'd still stand proudly at his side.

I just wanted him, in whatever shape he came.

"Never, sweetheart." I kissed his cheek and then stepped outside to call Everett. "Are you at headquarters?"

"Yeah. Need something?"

"The leader of Reid's former coven turned up in town. He's…" I gritted my teeth as fur sprouted along my arms and I forced my bear to back down. "He's abusive and I don't want him anywhere near my mate. We're lying low at the Children's Home. Could you come and stay with Reid while I make sure the asshole leaves?"

"Sure." A rustle indicated that he was already moving. "Be there in a few minutes. We'll keep your omega safe."

I thanked him, then hung up and called Bea. It took several rings before she answered.

"Sorry, boss," she said breathlessly. "I had to leave the room. What's the story with Reid?"

"He's not interested in seeing Hephaestes." I spoke quietly, hoping the sound wouldn't travel to anyone else who might be listening in on the other end of the call. "Don't tell the High Priest that. I don't want him to leave before I get there. Are you both at Dad's place?"

"We are. I'll try to keep him here without being obvious but he's restless. I've smelled ozone pretty strongly a couple of times. I think he's trying to use a seeking spell and doesn't realize we'll notice."

"Fucking hell." I went to grab my hat and realized I'd left it inside. Damn, I'd have to return for it later. "Probably because warlocks don't smell magic the way we do. Do your best and if he makes a move, let me know straight away."

"On it, boss."

I ended that call and pocketed my phone as Everett

pulled up on the road outside the house. When he got out, I saw that Knox had come with him. Together, they made an imposing pair, and my bear settled a little. He didn't want to leave our mate but at least Reid would be well-protected.

"I hear you've got a problem," Knox called, crossing his arms and scowling as if he'd like nothing more than to bash some heads. "If it's fine with you, we thought we'd take Reid to the bakery so he can sit with Danny. Being around another omega might comfort him and if he stays here and the coven leader comes looking, the children might be in danger."

I grimaced. That was a good point. "Fine. But don't let him out of your sight."

Everett stopped in front of me and patted my shoulder, which was basically a confession of love where he was concerned. My stoic brother wasn't the most affectionate type, other than when it came to Milo. "We've got this."

"Thanks." I nodded briskly. I couldn't afford to be emotional at the moment. "Warlock Birch is inside with them. He's Dad's PBI contact and it seems like he's also George's mate."

Everett's eyes widened. "Really? Will George be comfortable if we leave them here together? Milo tells me he's been nervy lately."

I shrugged. "Ask him yourself but he seemed happy enough. I'd better go. I don't want Hephaestes trying to leave before I get there."

"Be careful," Knox called as I strode to my car. "Warlocks can be tricky bastards when they're angry."

I narrowed my eyes, fur rippling over my skin again. It didn't matter how "tricky" Hephaestes might be. I was fucking furious and an alpha bear protecting his mate wasn't something to be trifled with.

The drive to Dad's place didn't take long. I went straight inside and headed toward his office but Momma caught me in the hallway before I could open the door.

"I don't care what that man says, there's something not right about him," she hissed, jerking her head toward the office. "Do not let him anywhere near our precious Reid."

"I won't," I replied softly. "He's told me enough to know that he's better off here. Don't worry, Momma. I'll keep him safe."

She released me reluctantly and I went to the office, opened the door, and entered. Dad sat behind his desk, his posture relaxed but his eyes flickered to that of his bear's so I knew immediately that he didn't trust Hephaestes any more than Momma did.

The man in question was perched on a padded black chair with his legs crossed at the ankles, visibly relaxed even though the scent of ozone lingered in the air.

Bea stood at attention between him and the door, not obviously blocking his path but there in case she was needed.

"Sheriff." Hephaestes straightened and sauntered toward me.

Bea stiffened and moved closer, obviously concerned he might attack.

"I've been waiting an awfully long time." He smiled as if we were old friends. "I'd really like to be taken to Reid now."

I glanced at Dad and hoped he could read the subtle warning in my eyes to be prepared in case the situation went awry. "Unfortunately, Reid doesn't want to see you." I tried to sound apologetic but I really wasn't. I just wanted to avoid a scene in my parents' home. "I think it would be best for you to leave Grizzly Ridge."

A muscle in his jaw ticked and the smell of ozone, mint,

and decomposition filled my nostrils. It dissipated quickly so whatever he'd done must have either been unintentional or short-lived.

He drew in a sharp breath. "I've been trying to do this the nice way, but really. This is ridiculous. He's a member of my coven and you have no right to keep me from him."

"Perhaps not." I inclined my head. "But he has the right to choose to stay away from you."

"He's misguided." He rolled his eyes and turned to Dad. "Young people often are. But you're the Clan Alpha. You can override him. It's in Reid's best interest to come with me."

Dad's eyes followed him like a predator stalking prey. "I doubt that."

Hephaestes shook his head and tsked. "Other people are looking for him and if you don't hand him over, they'll bring all kinds of trouble to your doorstep. Do you really want that?"

"He's my *mate*," I growled, barely avoiding the urge to grab him by the shoulders and shake him. "And I am the Clan Alpha's eldest son. We will stand by him. He won't be sent away. Do you understand?"

At that, he frowned. "I sense no mating bond."

"It will be there soon enough." Dad blithely ignored the possibility that Reid might never come around to the idea of mating with me. We both wanted to believe that he would. "Zander is correct. We will protect his mate against any threat."

Even you, his dark gaze seemed to say.

Hephaestes's jaw clenched and he reached into his jacket pocket. My hand went to my gun and Bea had her Taser out and aimed at him in two seconds flat.

He huffed. "It's just a business card." He held it up to show us and then dropped it onto Dad's desk. "Call me when you realize that you're in over your head."

With that, he stalked out.

"Follow him," I muttered to Bea. "I want eyes on him until he's well outside the town's boundaries."

"Yes, sir." She followed Hephaestes out.

Not satisfied with that, I sent Nathaniel a message, requesting that he use his magic to confirm when Hephaestes departed in case he tried any illusion magic on Bea.

Dad motioned for me to join him. "What was all of that about?"

THIRTY-THREE

ZANDER

"Which part?" I asked, taking a seat.

Dad considered that for a moment. "Why is he so determined to get to Reid?"

I inhaled slowly and deeply to calm my riled bear. Even the thought of our vulnerable mate in that man's possession made me want to carve his innards out. "My guess is that it's because his coven used to use Reid as a magical battery."

Dad's breath hitched. "Excuse me?"

I nodded grimly. "He has a lot of magic. Nathaniel told me as much. Apparently, when he was born, Hephaestes was threatened by him so he allowed the coven members to drain his magic as they pleased—provided none of them took more than him, of course."

Dad's thick fingers drummed on the desk and his claws curled from the ends. As if sensing his mood, Momma walked in and went straight over to him. She sat on his lap and he wrapped his arms around her. As usual, her presence steadied him.

My heart ached. I wanted to have a relationship like

theirs so much. Hopefully, one day, Reid would be ready for that. The baby steps we were taking gave me hope.

"His parents didn't stop this mistreatment?" Dad growled.

"No," I confirmed. "They're both loyal to the High Priest and put his orders above Reid's well-being. According to Reid, he paid them off as well."

"That isn't right," Momma said, shaking her head. "The poor boy. No wonder he's as he is. Even before he was kidnapped, no one took proper care of him."

Her steely tone told me that she was determined to rectify the situation and be the kind of mother Reid had never had. I wished her luck. Perhaps, being an omega and a woman, she'd be able to get through to him more easily than I could.

My phone vibrated and I checked it. "Nathaniel says he's out of town."

We all relaxed a little. I doubted we'd seen the end of him, but at least for now, Reid was secure.

"Get back to your mate," Momma urged. "He'll need you."

I dipped my head in acknowledgement and took my leave. The drive to the bakery seemed to take forever because I was so eager to lay eyes on Reid again. I trusted my brothers to watch over him, but I wouldn't rest easy until I saw him myself.

The front of the bakery was as busy as usual. I nodded to Skye, who was behind the counter, and pointed to the door through to the kitchen. She sent me a thumbs-up while taking an order and I let myself through. Everett stood just inside and he moved to let me pass.

As soon as I saw Reid, my stomach plummeted. He was pressed into the corner of the room, his knees drawn up to his chest, his chin resting on them. Danny hovered over him, fidgeting and obviously unsure what to do. Knox was guarding the outer door and looked just as lost as Danny.

Reid was breathing in a strange, slow rhythm and staring blankly into space. He was shivering even though the ovens kept the kitchen warm, and he was twisting something around and around with one of his hands. When I dropped to my knees in front of him, I could just make out the shape of the black necklace I'd given him.

"No one will make you go back," Danny murmured, awkwardly rubbing Reid's back. He met my gaze and relief flooded his eyes. "Not you or your baby. I promise. Thank Gods you're here. He's been like this since just after he arrived. He said he felt the High Priest's magic touch him or something."

My chest tightened. "He's not in Grizzly Ridge anymore." When Reid didn't respond, I debated whether to touch him but I didn't want to frighten him more. "Reid?"

He just kept breathing.

I closed my eyes and focused on the invisible tether between us. Even though we hadn't bonded, the connection was still there and I plucked on it like a guitar string. His eyes lifted to mine immediately.

"What if he wants both of us?" he asked, his eyes wide and despairing. "I can't let anyone use my baby the same way they did to me. I can't."

"We won't," I promised, my chest aching. "Hephaestes is gone. One of my deputies followed him out of town and Nathaniel confirmed it. He isn't here anymore."

Reid unwound and threw himself at me. I caught him, my knees protesting as my weight rocked backward onto them. His arms circled around my neck and he clung to me, plastered to my body, shaking from head to toe.

"Shh." I buried my face in the side of his neck and

inhaled his scent. "Shh, sweetheart. I've got you—both of you. It's all okay."

I met Knox's eyes and he, Danny, and Everett slipped out of the kitchen, leaving us alone. Carefully, I shifted position until I was sitting on the floor and Reid was cuddled on my lap. I kissed the top of his head and murmured sweet words, encouraging him to relax.

His tremors eased gradually, and when they finally stopped altogether, he let me go and rested his cheek on my chest, drawing comfort from me without clinging so urgently.

Progress.

When he'd calmed more fully, Everett escorted us back to the Omega House. Nathaniel had already been by and added to the wards. Apparently, he'd warded the Children's Home too.

I waited outside with Danny while Hamish gathered the omegas in the living room and Everett checked through the rest of the house to make sure there were no signs of trouble.

He confirmed that the place was clear and I walked Reid to the door. Hamish met us and wrapped a protective arm around Reid's shoulder. My mate still wasn't his usual self and I was tempted to ask him to get back in the car and come home with me, but he'd chosen to live here and I had to respect his wishes.

"Call if you need me," I told him.

As I started to walk away, he reached for me, grasping my shirt. He tugged me closer and I went willingly, dipping my head as he stretched onto his toes and—as my heart slammed against my ribs—brushed the softest of kisses over my lips.

"Thank you," he said. "Be careful, okay? Hephaestes is dangerous."

"I will." I cupped his face and kissed his nose. "And I mean it. Call for anything, okay?"

He nodded. With difficulty, I left him and got back into the car.

Everett and I returned to the police station but later that evening, I found myself parked outside the Omega House once again, all senses on alert in order to protect my mate.

THIRTY-FOUR

R*EID*

"Are you okay?"

I glanced up, surprised to find Jessie hovering in the bedroom doorway.

"I... am. I think." I patted the bed beside me and she wandered over and perched on the edge of the mattress. I motioned to the brown paper bag on the nightstand. "Help yourself."

She picked it up and looked inside, one of her eyebrows rising. "From the bakery?"

"Yeah. Danny gave them to me." He'd thrust the bag into my hands on the way out the door. He really was a sweet guy. I'd been put off by his bouncy extroversion at first but it had become apparent that he genuinely cared as he'd fussed over me earlier.

I was a sucker for people who cared. I hadn't known enough of them in my life.

"Is anything off-limits?" she asked.

"Eat whatever you want."

While I appreciated the gesture, I didn't have much of an appetite for anything other than pickles and pickle chips. She reached in and pulled out a small slice of something that smelled strongly of honey and took a bite.

"So." She watched me as she chewed. "Your old High Priest turned up in town."

I flinched, not expecting such a direct comment. "Yeah."

She kept eating, that steady gaze never leaving my face. "I take it he's horrible."

I looked down at my hands. "That's an understatement."

"But he's gone? They sent him away?"

I nodded. Thank the gods they had or I had no idea what I'd have done.

"Will he stay gone?"

My stomach twisted painfully. "I doubt it."

I hoped he would. Prayed for it with every fiber of my being. But Hephaestes had spent more than twenty years siphoning power from me, and he wasn't about to give that up because a couple of shifters chased him out of town. Especially if he'd sensed my pregnancy and knew there was a possibility of scoring *two* magical batteries for the price of one.

He might not be reckless enough to attack them without a plan but he'd reassess and return later.

I should leave.

If I didn't want to endanger any of my new friends, it only made sense for me to run and not look back.

But I didn't want to. It was selfish of me, but the people here were kind, and I'd only just begun to let them in. I'd hate to lose them already.

Jessie finished her treat and wiped her fingers on a napkin. "Have you decided whether you trust Zander yet?"

Closing my eyes, I tuned out the sound of her rustling the paper bag and the doughy aroma of baked goods and turned my attention inward.

Did I trust him?

I was reluctant to say that I trusted anyone completely, but he'd protected me today, even after I'd made it clear that Hephaestes was dangerous. He hadn't considered giving me up even once, and despite my meltdown, I'd never really believed that he would.

I was more worried for his safety while he'd gone to send Hephaestes away than I was scared he'd change his mind and betray me. And when he'd come to find me at the bakery, I'd thrown myself into his arms without thinking twice.

So yes, I thought it was safe to say that I trusted Zander.

"I do," I whispered. "Is that bad?"

Her mouth curled into a slow smile. "No, honey. I'd say it's probably pretty good."

"But what if I bring danger to Grizzly Ridge? I don't want him hurt because of me."

He wasn't the only one I feared for either. There was sweet, gentle Milo with his unborn child and Melinda, who might be the closest thing to a proper maternal figure I'd known.

Kind, determined Jessie. Protective Hamish. Good-natured Danny.

What kind of person would it make me if I stayed and put them at risk?

"Zander is strong."

I jumped and almost knocked myself out with my kneecap. I'd been so absorbed by my thoughts that I hadn't heard anyone approach.

"Milo!" I exclaimed, spotting the figure in the doorway. Danny hovered just behind him. The two could often be found together. "You scared me!"

His expression became apologetic. "I'm sorry. I didn't mean to. But you should know that Zander and his brothers aren't pushovers. I've seen them fight." He shuddered. "It's not something I'd recommend, but they know what they're doing. If they say they can handle something, then they can."

"They saved us," Jessie pointed out, reminding me of the hellscape I'd witnessed that day in Moonlight Cove. The shifters had been savage. But facing magic was different from fighting with teeth and claws.

"Don't you dare even think about leaving. We'll come after you and drag you back. We won't let anything happen to you," Danny said fiercely, one hand propped on his hip. "If you trust Zander, then trust him to know the best course of action. Strategy is literally in his job description."

I grimaced, not having realized that of course he'd have heard the earlier part of our conversation with his enhanced shifter hearing. He had a point though. It wasn't fair of me to assume that Zander and his family didn't understand the threat posed by a coven of warlocks led by someone as power-hungry as Hephaestes.

Zander had likely seen more of the world than I had. Of course he'd know what warlocks were capable of—and even if he didn't, Nathaniel did.

Something warmed in my chest.

Zander *was* strong.

He was brave and clever and all he'd ever done was try to protect me and my unborn child, who he seemed to accept without reservation. He'd stood between me and danger, and he'd held me together when I needed support.

If anyone was trustworthy, it was him.

"Okay," I conceded. "I'll stay."

I only hoped I wouldn't regret it.

THIRTY-FIVE

R*EID*

"Follow the thread," Nathaniel—he'd insisted I call him that—urged as I did my best to trace the last wearer of the shirt he'd handed me this morning. "You've said the words. You've got the connection. Now picture it as a fine gold string in your mind's eye and follow it back to its origin."

I envisioned the thread as he'd instructed, but when I tried to follow it, I reached a broken-off and fraying end. I opened my eyes and blinked against the glare of the cloudy sky. We were out near the woods and although it wasn't particularly cold, I wasn't exactly enjoying the weather either.

I huffed. "I can't make it work."

Nathaniel took the shirt from me. "Perhaps because it's been too long since it was worn. Let's try something else." He passed me a button. His hands were gloved so as not to interfere with the spell. "This was handled only an hour ago. See where it leads."

I took the button from him, uttered the words of the spell, and closed my eyes. This time, the invisible string connecting the button to the last person who touched it was larger and stronger—more of a rope than a thread.

I mentally seized hold of it and pictured following it down the street, past the playground, around the corner, and all the way to the Children's Home.

"It's George's," I said with certainty, opening my eyes again.

I was proud of the progress I'd made since he'd begun teaching me. I just wished I could relax enough to enjoy it. I'd been tense every day since Hephaestes left, waiting for the other shoe to drop. That first night, I'd woken screaming because I could sense his magic searching for me, but thanks to Nathaniel's shielding spells, it hadn't locked on.

Nathaniel grinned. "Very good, Reid. I want you to keep practicing that spell. You can use it on nearly anything, and the more you practice, the fainter the signals you'll pick up on and the more accurate your spell will become."

"Okay, I will." I'd track every freaking thing I came across if it would give me better control over my magic.

"Speaking of mates..." He trailed off, as if uncertain whether to continue.

"What?" I wasn't sure if I wanted to know,

"If you ever want that mating scar removed and the remnants of the bond cleared away, I can do that for you."

The breath punched out of me in the best possible way. "You can?"

"Yeah." He gave me a soft smile. "Just think about it. There's no rush. I could do it anytime. The magic won't be dangerous to your baby. If you want me to do it right now, I can, or if you'd like to wait for a while, that's fine too."

My mind spun, flipping through the implications. I'd never have to see that awful scar again. I'd lose the permanent reminder of Trent.

"Yes," I exclaimed, more loudly than I'd meant to. "Please get rid of it."

He chuckled, and Jilly leaned against his leg, her head tilted up questioningly. "Now?"

"If you don't mind."

"Of course not. Can I see it?"

I grabbed the collar of my shirt and tugged it aside to expose the damaged skin. My stomach rolled and I rubbed my belly, silently assuring my little one that we'd be better without a connection to the shifter who donated his sperm.

He wasn't a father, and he never would be.

Nathaniel laid his hand gently on the scar and closed his eyes. After a moment, my skin warmed, and then he murmured a handful of words from the dead language. I gasped as, before my eyes, the skin knitted itself back together, absorbing the scar tissue as if it had never been there and leaving a smooth, unblemished shoulder behind.

Tears filled my eyes and I blinked rapidly, my throat tight.

"Thank you. You have no idea how much I needed that."

He moved his hand away and smiled softly. "You're most welcome."

Movement in the corner of my eye caught my attention and I turned toward it.

A pair of men were strolling along the side of the road a couple of hundred yards away. It was a strange place to be out for a walk. Reasonably far from the center of town, with nothing commercial around. Perhaps they were just out for some air.

I squinted at their faces. My stomach plummeted when I recognized one of the men. It was the same associate of Trent's who I'd seen in the car outside the Omega House.

My heart raced; I was grateful that Nathaniel was a

warlock rather than a shifter or he'd definitely have sensed my panic.

I opened my mouth to tell him who they were but then closed it without saying a word. Maybe they hadn't noticed us, but if we started discussing them, that would change immediately. They'd be able to hear us even from that distance.

"Nature calls," I said, then got up as casually as I could and walked into the trees. I kept going until I was out of Nathaniel's line of sight and muttered the spell that silenced footsteps, hoping it might also soften voices. I phoned Zander.

"Hey, Reid." His voice was warm and reminded me of hot chocolate on a cold night. "Is everything okay?"

"Two wolves who knew Trent just walked past the place where Nathaniel is teaching me magic," I whispered, knowing that there was a chance their sensitive ears would hear me. Hopefully they were too far away for that.

Zander's breath caught. "Are they approaching you?"

"They weren't when I was with Nathaniel but I went into the woods to call you so they might be now." I lowered my voice even further. "I didn't say anything to him. I was worried they might hear. Was it wrong of me to leave him alone?"

"He knows how to take care of himself," Zander assured me.

"Listen, Reid, I'm going to come straight over. Can you return to Nathaniel? He's powerful enough to protect you if they try anything."

I bit my lip, reluctant to venture back out there, but it wasn't as if I'd be able to outrun a shifter, so if they came after me, it would be best for me to have protection.

"Fine." I sighed, hoping I wouldn't regret it. "See you soon."

I hung up, turned, and trudged back out. The wolves had reached the end of the field and were just standing there, talking.

I didn't trust them.

"Is everything all right?" Nathaniel asked as I drew close enough for us to speak without shouting.

"My tummy is a bit unsettled," I lied, afraid that the wolves might be able to hear me and that if they knew I was on to them, they might step up their plan—whatever that was.

"Would you like me to take a look at it? Healing magic isn't my specialty but all PBI warlocks get basic healing training. Kind of the equivalent of a workplace first aid course."

I shook my head. "No, it's fine."

I glanced at the wolves again and jerked when I realized they'd started walking back toward us, having turned around for no apparent reason.

That didn't bode well.

Nathaniel frowned and looked over his shoulder. "Are they—"

I put my finger to my lips, motioning for him to be quiet, then transitioned the movement to cover my mouth as if I was yawning, hoping that neither of the wolves would have noticed. I looked at him meaningfully, silently willing him not to ask questions that the men might overhear.

Just as they were almost level with us, the sheriff's vehicle came into sight and parked at the curb. A deputy spilled from the passenger side and Zander leapt out from behind the steering wheel. Both of them made quickly for the men, who immediately started stripping their clothes.

One of the wolves shifted and bolted for the woods. The deputy tried to tase him but he was too far away. Frustrated, the deputy tore off his uniform, shifted into a large grizzly bear and lumbered after him.

Meanwhile, the other guy—the one I recognized—had tripped over his pants while trying to remove them, and before he was able to recover, Zander leapt on him and pinned him to the ground.

THIRTY-SIX

Z ANDER

I slammed the asshole onto his front, straddled him, and wrestled him into a pair of cuffs.

Hauling in a ragged breath, I fixated on the back of his neck. My bear wanted nothing more than for me to shift and sink my teeth into his flesh. This man had frightened our mate—perhaps even done worse than that.

He didn't deserve to live.

"Zander!"

I growled, not recognizing the voice.

"Zander, if you kill him, you won't be able to get any information from him."

I glared at the man limping toward me, using a silver and black cane to support himself. It took a moment for my brain to make the connection because my bear was trying to take control.

"Birch." I panted.

He nodded. "Your mate is here with me." He motioned to Reid, who stood beyond him and to his right. "He's safe. If we can question this person—who I assume is a threat of some kind—then we can keep him safe. How's that sound?"

I gritted my teeth at his patronizing tone but also knew that he was appealing to the only thing that could get through to me in my current state: my protectiveness of Reid.

My jaw cracked and my fangs started to descend. I turned to Reid and met his gaze. To my surprise, he held his head up and didn't cower. He was clearly scared—I could smell it—but I didn't think his fear was of me.

I growled. This wolf was frightening my mate.

And from the look in Reid's eyes, he'd be happy for me to kill him. Unfortunately, Nathaniel was right. Dead men couldn't answer questions.

With an effort, I retracted my fangs and got to my feet. The wolf tried to scramble away. I put my foot on his back and perhaps pressed him into the ground a bit more firmly than needed.

"I can knock him out magically," Nathaniel said, edging closer. "It won't do any long-term damage but might make him easier to transport. May I?"

I grunted, and taking that as an assent, he muttered something under his breath and the man went limp beneath me. I rolled him over to check that he was fully unconscious, then hefted him up and dumped him into the back seat of my car.

Clay emerged from the woods in his bear form, trotted to his discarded clothes, and shifted. "He outran me," he called as he began tugging on his uniform.

Damn.

At least we'd caught one of them.

"Can I escort you two to the police station?" I asked, turning to Reid and Nathaniel. "I'll need a statement from you both and your assistance might be helpful, if you're willing."

Reid glanced at the guy in the back of the car, his brow furrowed. "Will he stay unconscious for long enough to get there?"

Nathaniel touched his shoulder reassuringly. "He'll remain out cold until I reverse the spell."

Reid worried his lower lip. "Can I ride with you, please?"

My bear, still close to the surface, chuffed his approval. Reid trusted us over his new mentor. I knew that we'd keep him safe. My chest started to puff out and it was only the knowing look in Nathaniel's eyes that stopped me from preening.

"Clay, do you mind riding with Nathaniel?" I asked as Clay—now fully clothed—joined us.

"Sure thing." He bent to pat Jilly and gestured toward the Jeep. Nathaniel gave me a warning look and hobbled over to it.

Reid followed me to my car and got silently into the passenger seat. I got behind the wheel, checked that our captive was still unconscious, and started the engine.

"Are you all right?" I asked as I pulled onto the road and performed a U-turn.

"I'm okay."

He sounded shaken so I doubted that was the truth, but at least he'd trusted me enough to call me. I hated to think what might have happened if the wolves had tried to abduct him. Nathaniel should have been able to protect him, but nothing was certain when it came to magic.

When we arrived at the police station, I hauled the captive over my shoulder and lugged him past reception— ignoring Nell's startled gasp—and into an interview room, where I cuffed him to a chair that was bolted to the ground.

That done, I locked him in to keep him out of the way while I escorted Reid to Bea's desk so she could take his statement. I would have liked to do that myself but too many other things needed my attention.

"Will you be all right here?" I asked, reluctant to leave him.

"Yeah." He shrugged. "But I want to watch you interview that guy. I want to know what he has to say."

I grimaced. I'd rather he not watch the interrogation, but I couldn't deny him what he wanted. "Bea, once you've recorded his statement, will you take him to the observation room?"

Bea's eyes widened but she didn't question me. "Yes, sir."

"Thanks."

I radioed the patrol officers and asked them to meet Clay at the playground to begin a search of the woods for the escapee. A quick visit to Garrick ensured that the Search and Rescue team would soon join them, and then I called Dad to update him on the situation.

Finally, I went in search of Nathaniel, who was in the process of giving his statement to another deputy, and motioned for him to join me. "Would you mind waking him up?"

"Of course."

I showed the warlock to the interrogation room. With a muttered spell, the man at the table roused. Nathaniel slipped out and I followed just long enough to check that Bea and Reid were in the observation room.

"Are you sure you want to watch?" I asked Reid. "I can call Momma to come and pick you up. Maybe take you to their place or to the Omega House, whichever you'd prefer."

He lifted his chin, so brave in the face of the monsters from his past. "I want to be here."

"Fair enough then."

I returned to the interview room and sat opposite the prisoner. "What's your name?"

He didn't respond. At first I thought perhaps he was groggy, but on closer inspection, his eyes were clear and his heart rate was normal—slightly elevated because of stress but otherwise unremarkable.

"How did you know Pack Alpha Trent?" I tried, mentally cataloging his features. Dark hair, receding hairline, eyes a nondescript brown, scruffy facial hair.

No answer.

"Why are you in Grizzly Ridge?"

He just smirked.

My hands curled into fists beneath the table but I kept breathing slowly. I couldn't let him know that he was getting to me. "Who do you work for?"

It went on like that for an hour. He didn't say a word and even when I threatened to start chopping off fingers, he didn't budge. Perhaps that was because he knew I wouldn't cross that line, being a man of the law, or perhaps his employer was even scarier than a pissed-off grizzly shifter.

Eventually, I got up and stalked to the door.

"Giving up so easily?" he asked, speaking for the first time.

"Not a chance." I shut the door. As I'd suspected, Nathaniel had joined Reid in the observation room. "Can you use a truth spell on him?"

"Yeah. Just maybe turn the video camera off. I'm supposed to have approval from the higher-ups before performing magic on suspects."

He started to get up but his leg buckled. I went over, wrapped my arm around him to help support his weight and together we made our way back into the interview room.

Nathaniel withdrew a pen from his jacket pocket. "I need to write on him."

As we approached, the prisoner jerked against his cuffs and tried to push his chair back. It was fortunate we'd used magical cuffs because otherwise he'd have busted out of them already.

"You can't do that to me," he snapped, his eyes wide as he stared at the pen. "I know my rights."

"You were sniffing around my mate," I informed him, my tone low and lethal. "I don't care much about your rights."

Nathaniel drew a rune on the back of the man's hand and murmured a spell. "It's done. I'll sit beside you. It's most effective if I stay close."

I assisted him into the spare chair before addressing the prisoner again. "Who do you work for?"

He gritted his teeth and the veins of his neck pulsed angrily beneath the surface, but he couldn't stop himself from replying. "Ace Amato."

A thrill ran through me. We had a name. Fucking finally.

"What do you do for Ace Amato?"

He leaned back, putting as much space between himself and Nathaniel as he could, but it didn't seem to lessen the effect of the spell. "I... find... fuck! I find and secure omegas. Especially valuable ones."

My gut roiled at the implication. "Are you part of an omega trafficking ring?"

"Yes." His eyes watered and I had no doubt that, if not for the magical cuffs, they'd already have shifted. Probably his fangs and claws too. "Trent was one of our main suppliers."

"Trent is dead," I told him calmly.

"I know." His hands fisted and his heart rate picked up. "Ace knew about Reid. He's a valuable omega. Magical, with the face of an angel, and the potential to create powerful offspring. Ace has a client who would pay out the ass for him, so he ordered me to bring him in."

My gut twisted, threatening to throw up everything I'd eaten so far today. It sounded like he was talking about sex slavery, or potentially being used as breeding stock. How could someone talk about another person like they were a commodity?

"Does the man who was with you today also work for Amato?" I asked.

"Yes."

"I want his details."

"All I know is his name."

"Then give it to me." I noted down his answer so I could pass the name along to Bea to look into. "Is Amato in the area?"

"No. I don't even know if he's in the country. He—" He cut off abruptly, a jolt running through him like electricity.

"What was that?" I demanded.

Nathaniel frowned. "Perhaps some kind of silencing spell. Whatever it is, it's buried deep. I can't quite get at it."

"Fucking hell." If his tongue was magically tied, how were we supposed to get any information?

"Give me a moment." Nathaniel closed his eyes, his lean frame radiating tension. "I can see the general shape of it. The spell is very specific. You might be able to get some further information. It's been crafted to stop him from mentioning particular things, but not others."

I tapped the pen against my chin, considering this. It made things more difficult, but surely we'd still be able to get something to go on.

"It could escalate," Nathaniel added. "Often spells like this will start with a warning and the consequences will gradually become more severe."

"Can you remove it?"

"Perhaps, but it would take time."

Okay, so that was worth looking into but wasn't an immediate priority.

I met the wolf's gaze. "Tell me everything you know you can share without triggering the spell."

Thanks to the truth spell, he started talking.

By the time I left the interview room, I was ready to tear out Ace Amato's throat and that of anyone who answered to him. There were layers of evil in the world, but human traffickers and those who hurt people weaker than them were the worst of the worst.

My hands were shaking as I locked him in, gave Bea her orders, and turned to Reid.

I dragged him into my arms and gazed down at him. His eyes were large and wounded and angry all at the same time, as if that asshole wolf shifter had stirred up the emotions he'd been trying hard to bury. He reminded me of a kitten who'd been kicked one too many times and was afraid to hope for anything better.

"I will keep you safe." I held his gaze, hoping he would see how serious I was. "I swear it on my life."

CHAPTER

THIRTY-SEVEN

R *EID*

"Don't say that." I shook my head and tore my eyes from Zander's. "I don't want anyone risking their life for me or swearing on it."

I didn't want anyone to be hurt or in danger because of me, period.

"I mean it." He cupped my cheek and I stubbornly kept my face turned away. "I will do whatever it takes to make sure you don't suffer another minute of your life. Any alpha mate worth his salt would do the same."

"I'm not important enough to throw everything away for. I'm broken. Even if I was ready to bond with someone, surely they expect better for the Clan Alpha's son."

Zander stared at me, disbelief etched in every line of his face. "You're not broken. You're fucking perfect. I've wanted you since day one, but after everything you've been through at an alpha's hands, it's understandable that you'd have a hard time trusting another."

The slight bump of my belly brushed against his flat abdomen, reminding me of the last time I'd trusted an alpha I shouldn't have. I'd never believed I'd trust another alpha

217

but against all odds, I did, even if I was freaked out about being in the crosshairs of an omega trafficking operation.

Believe it or not, that wasn't the most pressing concern I'd taken away from the interview. Yes, it sucked, but I was relatively safe where I was. Meanwhile, according to the man they'd been questioning, at least twenty omegas were being held in a facility waiting to either be placed in a brothel or auctioned off to the highest bidder.

"Do you really think he knows where the other omegas are being held?" I asked Zander. "Because we need to find them and help them. We're going to, right? We won't just leave them."

Zander tilted his head. "I think that Nathaniel is a powerful warlock and his truth spell should have gotten all of the information the man is capable of giving. It's possible he knows more but can't say it without the spell being removed."

"So we're going to do that, right? Nathaniel can remove it?" I wasn't sure exactly how that kind of magic worked.

"Yes. I've asked him to look into it, but he thinks it may take a few days, and he wants to loop in one of his old PBI colleagues for help. Apparently, removing someone else's magic is complicated."

I rubbed my temples and bit my lip so hard I tasted blood. Zander's eyes flickered golden-amber and his nostrils flared—probably because of the metallic smell.

I moved a little closer, swallowing the lump at the back of my throat. "We need to find them."

"And we will." Hesitantly, he raised his hands and rested them on my shoulders. "We'll make sure he goes through all of the proper channels and that we extricate every piece of information that we can. Once that's done, a rescue party will be mounted—probably led by the PBI because this is beyond the scope of a small-town Sheriff's department."

My breath caught. All of that sounded like it would take time—more than a few days—and those omegas might not have much time to spare.

"They can't wait." The words burst from me and sparks flickered in my peripheral vision.

I closed my eyes and inhaled slowly, trying to calm myself. The reminder of what had happened last time I'd lost control was like a splash of cold water.

I couldn't risk doing anything to make myself that vulnerable again.

"Every minute we wait, someone could be getting beaten or raped." I raised my chin, my mouth trembling as I forced myself to go on. "You don't know how that feels, but I do, and if I can save a single person from experiencing what I did then I have to. I *have* to. I can't just leave them there."

A growl rumbled from Zander's chest and his eyes remained amber. He opened his mouth, then seemed to second-guess himself, drew in a shuddering breath, and reined himself in. "We can't help anyone if we're too upset. I'll call my contact at the PBI to report what we've discovered and get the wheels in motion, then I'll bring you a nice cup of tea. Will you go and find Bea in the bullpen and wait with her?"

I nodded when all I wanted to do was scream.

He didn't understand. No one could—not unless they'd lived through the same hell as me.

Zander gave me a long, lingering look before striding toward his office. I waited until he was out of sight, then cast a spell to cover my scent and the sound of my footfalls. I hurried down the corridor and out the front door.

There had to be something I could do to help those omegas. I didn't know what, but I'd figure it out.

Halfway down the block, I ran into an invisible wall.

I frowned, reached forward, and touched something I couldn't see. Confused, I tried to circle around it, but the barrier seemed to continue.

"Reid!"

I spun around. Zander was standing right behind me with Nathaniel farther back. He had his hand outstretched, and I realized too late that he must have created the blockade.

I backed up, my heart hammering wildly, and bumped into that invisible force. I wanted to turn and bolt but I suspected all I'd end up with was a bloody nose if I tried.

I raised my chin, the urgency in my gut heating and morphing into something other than fear for the unknown omegas.

I was so goddamn tired of having others dictate my life.

"I thought I was allowed to make my own decisions." I was proud of how steady my voice was. "I thought you weren't going to control me. I should be able to leave if I want to."

Zander looked torn. He started to reach for me, but I dodged to the side since I was unable to go backward. "You're in danger. I can't let anything happen to you. You mean too much to me."

"What about those other omegas?" I challenged. "Will you let something happen to them?"

Because I wasn't sure I could. If there was anything I could do to save someone from a fate similar to mine, I had to do it.

I'd prayed so many times for someone to save me, and they finally had—even if it hadn't gone exactly how I'd have liked.

By the time my rescue had arrived, it was too late.

But I could save someone else.

I *had* to.

Otherwise, what good was I?

"We'll save them," Zander said, but his voice lacked the conviction it had when he'd talked about protecting me. He cared about me more than them and that was nice—it maybe even made me feel things I was scared to acknowledge—but I needed him to be just as motivated to rescue the other omegas.

"Come back," he urged. "Everett just called. He and Garrick caught the other wolf and they're bringing him in."

That gave me pause. The other wolf might know more than his friend, or he might not be subject to the same spell. Maybe he could tell us where the omegas were.

"Fine," I said. "But I want to watch him be questioned too."

Zander nodded and extended his hand. I hesitated for a few seconds, then laid mine on it. When his hand closed around mine—so much larger and warmer—I shivered. Hopefully, he wouldn't notice. Knowing shifters and their senses, he probably had, but he didn't say anything about it as he led me back to the station.

A Range Rover pulled over to park outside just as we reached it. Garrick was driving so I assumed the wolf was in the back.

Knox, Danny's scary wolf shifter mate, hauled the other wolf out through the side door and dragged the struggling man inside.

Garrick circled around and gave me a small smile. "Are you hanging in there, Reid? Is there anything I can do to help?"

Zander growled and Garrick held his hands up. "Whoa, Z. I'm not trying to steal your mate."

"I know," Zander gritted out. "You can't help acting like a Clan Alpha, trying to look out for everyone, just like I can't help reacting because I'm protective of Reid."

They stared at each other for a long moment and the tension leaked away. Thank the gods. The last thing I needed right now was to be subjected to alpha posturing.

By the time we got back to the interview room, Knox had manhandled him inside and was dragging him down the corridor. The man was spitting profanities. Knox ignored him and just hauled him into another interview room and shoved him into a chair.

At that point, they left my line of sight. Zander motioned to the door of the observation room and I went in. I sat and watched as one of the deputies cuffed the guy to the chair, then both he and Knox left the room.

Zander entered and held the door open for Nathaniel. Perhaps they were going straight for the truth spell this time. I hoped so. We didn't have any time to waste.

Nathaniel repeated what he'd done to the other guy earlier and then he and Zander sat facing him, side by side.

"Do you know where the omegas you captured are being held?" Zander asked, getting straight to the most important point.

The man—who was beefier than his companion—slowly turned red in the face. "Y-Yes."

Butterflies filled my gut. Finally, something that might be useful. I leaned forward, eager to hear what came next.

"Tell me where," Zander ordered.

The man opened his mouth, closed it, and then convulsed. His eyes rolled back in his head and he slumped in his seat, completely motionless.

THIRTY-EIGHT

R*EID*

Zander leapt up and rounded the table, grabbing a hold of the man's shoulder and tilting him back. His head flopped to the side and his eyes were open and staring.

My gut dropped and my hand flew to my mouth.

Oh my Gods, was he dead?

Nathaniel hobbled around the desk as Zander pressed his fingers to the man's pulse point in his neck. He held them there, counting as the seconds dragged painfully on.

I should be doing something.

Fuck. Why was I just standing here?

That man might be our only lead to finding the other omegas. We couldn't lose him.

I raced out of the observation room and yelled, "We need medical help! Someone call an ambulance!"

Bea glanced over, then reached for her phone and dialed. She motioned to let me know that she was getting help.

Garrick barreled down the corridor from the Search and

Rescue headquarters with an enormous first aid kit in his hand. "What is it?"

I pointed to the door. "They're in there. The man they were interviewing passed out. I think…" I swallowed. "I think he's dying."

Garrick rushed through the door and dropped to his knees. At some point, Zander and Nathaniel had moved the man to the floor and Nathaniel was hovering over him, murmuring spells, while Zander thrust rhythmically against his chest.

I was frozen to the spot, unsure of what to do. I didn't know enough first aid to be useful and my grasp of healing magic was nonexistent. If Nathaniel couldn't heal him then I had no chance. I could attempt to funnel my magic into Nathaniel to make his stronger, but I didn't know how to do that without a magic circle—if it was even possible at all.

"Is he responding to CPR?" Garrick asked.

"No," Zander replied.

Garrick opened the first aid kit and pulled out a defibrillator. Nathaniel stopped his spell for a moment and uttered another. The man's shirt vanished from his chest and reappeared on the floor near my feet.

Garrick stuck the defibrillator pads to his chest and they all backed away. A few seconds later, an electrical pulse jolted the man's body.

He didn't respond.

A second pulse passed through him, and his head lolled to the side, his mouth hanging open.

I wanted to close my eyes and forget his slack-jawed expression but for some reason, I couldn't make myself look away.

Garrick grimaced. "That's it for the defibrillator. Keep up CPR."

Footsteps thundered down the corridor and I leapt

aside as Dr. Black rushed in with Nurse Allison in tow. They used some sort of equipment I didn't recognize to take readings, but it was only a couple of minutes before Dr. Black shook his head.

"He's gone," he said reluctantly. "As far as I can tell, it wasn't poison but a spell, and as soon as it activated there was no way to save him." He looked up at Nathaniel. "Would you agree?"

Nathaniel's mouth was a thin line. "Unfortunately, yes. We saw evidence of spell craft with the other suspect, but it didn't escalate this far. Someone didn't want this man sharing locational information and they put a safeguard in place to ensure he never would."

I dropped to my knees, stunned. If we weren't able to find the truth from him, then how were we supposed to rescue those omegas?

If this was the same spell that was on the other wolf, I had to assume that he'd also die if pushed for information about the location of the captive omegas. Perhaps it was just as well that Zander had asked him for whatever information he could share rather than pressing for details.

Zander suddenly seemed to realize I was standing there and he stood and ushered me out. "I'm sorry you had to see that."

I bit my lip, still struggling to believe everything had gone wrong so quickly. There had to be another way to save those omegas. Something that didn't depend on risking another life—even that of a criminal lowlife.

I wouldn't give up.

And I wouldn't wait for days—or perhaps even weeks—for all the godsdamn bureaucratic bullshit to be put in place first.

"I'm going back to the Omega House," I said, keeping my eyes lowered.

"No, it's not safe."

I scowled. "Nathaniel added to the wards. It's probably the safest place in town."

I needed him to let me go so I could get started on my own plan. If he and the department were so determined to follow the letter of the law, then I needed to get away so I could figure out how to save those omegas quickly.

"Reid, look at me."

I kept my eyes down.

He sighed. "Will you try to run off on your own?"

"I can set the wards to alert me if he leaves the property," Nathaniel said, emerging from the interview room.

"How accurate is the alert?" Zander asked. "Can it be tampered with?"

I felt two pairs of eyes boring into the top of my head, but I wrung my hands and picked at the skin around my fingernails. It irritated me that they would try to trap me somewhere; however, I couldn't bring myself to hate it when I knew it came from a place of caring.

"Not without me sensing it," Nathaniel replied.

"Fine." Zander huffed. "I'll drive him there and you do what you've got to. I don't want there to be any chance of Reid ending up in danger."

I fought the tiny smile that wanted to burst forward because of the small win and kept my head down as Zander guided me out of the police station, calling to the receptionist that he'd be back in a few minutes.

I got into the back of the car because it would be easier for Nathaniel to sit in the passenger seat, and Zander drove us to Omega House. I remained where I was while Nathaniel amended the wards. I watched, trying to discern what he was doing, but it was beyond my comprehension.

Finally, Zander told me I could get out and escorted me to the front door. He touched my shoulder and I flinched, caught off guard because I'd still been doing my best not to look at anyone or anything.

"Sorry," he mumbled, immediately retracting his hand. "Please stay safe. I couldn't stand it if someone like those assholes got their disgusting paws on you."

Something cracked in my chest and I couldn't resist raising my chin and offering him a small smile. I took hold of my pendant and ran my fingertips over the smooth surface of the stone. "I'll be careful, I promise."

And I would.

At least, as much as I could. It was a novelty to have someone who cared about me. I didn't want to damage the fragile trust between us, but I also couldn't leave those omegas where they were for a second longer than necessary.

He squeezed my shoulder gently. "Thank you. Keep yourself and the little one inside where it's safe."

He turned and left.

I let myself into the house and locked the door, then I slipped away to my bedroom and sent a message to Danny.

Please come to the Omega House, ASAP. It's an emergency. Bring Milo.

THIRTY-NINE

REID

I lied to Hamish that Milo and Danny were coming over to discuss the ups and downs of pregnancy. I hated being untruthful with someone who had always treated me honestly, but if he knew what we were really meeting about, he'd have been on the phone to Zander within a minute.

Instead, I had to endure his proud smile as I escorted the two omegas to my bedroom. It made me feel two feet tall.

"Are you okay?" Milo asked, one hand curled protectively around his belly as he slumped on the opposite bed. "Everett said someone tried to kidnap you."

"I'm fine." Or at least, as fine as I could be. "No one actually tried to take me. We spotted them before they could make a move."

"Thank the gods."

Danny sat beside Milo and cocked his head curiously. "Why do I get the feeling we aren't just here for moral support?"

I squirmed, wondering where to begin. It had seemed

so straightforward in my head. If the alphas wouldn't help, then surely the omegas would. Especially these two, who both knew how it felt to be held against their will.

I closed the door and sat on the other bed. "One of the men admitted that they're part of an omega trafficking ring."

Milo gasped, his eyes wide, and Danny turned a faint shade of gray.

"Apparently, they find omegas and take them back to the people in charge. Trent and his pack were supplying them." The thought made me sick.

"Do the police know where the others are?" Danny asked, leaning forward before grimacing slightly and adjusting his position. Being tall, he wore his pregnancy better than Milo and it was easy to forget he was carrying another life in there. Suddenly, I felt guilty for calling these pregnant omegas to help me. They wouldn't only be risking themselves but their babies too.

"They don't, but I'm sure they'll figure it out," I muttered, looking down at the faded denim of my jeans. "Maybe you guys should call one of your mates to come and get you. It might be dangerous for you to be away from home."

Danny huffed. "You aren't getting rid of us that easily. You called us for a reason, right?"

I fidgeted, instinctively running my fingertips along the scars on my wrists.

"We want to help," Milo said, his voice gentle, his tone sincere. "Is there something we can do?"

My stomach rolled nauseatingly, reminding me that they weren't the only ones pregnant. "I don't want you to get hurt."

"We won't do anything dangerous," Milo assured me. "There must be some way we can help though."

I sighed. "At least one of the men knew where the omegas were but he was killed by a spell before he told us. The others want to wait and go through all the proper channels before questioning the other man further in case the same thing happens."

Danny's eyebrow twitched. "That could take days, if not more."

"I know." I gripped the blanket and clenched my hands in it, hoping that it would ground me enough that my magic wouldn't go haywire again. "Nathaniel has been teaching me a tracking spell. He's much better than me, but if I had something the dead guy touched—especially something he kept close to him for a long time—then I might be able to trace the locations where he's spent most of his time."

Milo nodded his understanding. "And if one of those locations is where the omegas are being kept, then we'd find them."

"Exactly. I just..." I stared at the fabric of my jeans until my vision blurred and hot tears stung my eyes. I blinked rapidly, not wanting them to see my weakness. "I can't leave them there. Shouldn't they be more important than some federal paperwork and the safety of one of the monsters who kidnapped them?"

The mattress shifted beside me and then an arm wrapped around my waist. I stiffened instinctively but relaxed when I dared to glance sideways and realized Milo was... hugging me. Kind of. His head was next to mine and his small frame trembled.

"You're right," he murmured. "They should be our priority."

Danny sat on my other side and took my hand, sandwiching me between them. One of the tears I'd been holding back streaked down my cheek, dripped off my chin, and soaked a small, dark circle on my jeans.

"What do you need from us?" he asked, squeezing my hand.

I drew in a shuddering breath. "I know this is asking a lot, but would it be possible for one of you to get something that belonged to the dead guy so I can use it as a focus for the spell? Perhaps his wallet or his phone since he would have taken those with him everywhere."

"Why don't you get it?" Danny asked, confused but not accusatory.

I squeezed my eyes shut and inhaled slowly and deeply, trying to stop the way my chest quivered and the back of my throat ached. "Nathaniel did something to the wards so they'll alert him if I try to leave. If I go anywhere, they'll know, and they'll come looking for me."

Danny's hand tightened around mine. "Excuse me?" he demanded, his expression outraged. "You're not a prisoner! How dare they treat you like one!"

My heart pounded in a way that wasn't entirely unpleasant. I wasn't used to having omegas defend me. Most of the ones I'd spent more than a few days around either resented me because of my role in their imprisonment or pitied me because of how badly I was used.

"They want to protect him," Milo said quietly. In moments like these, it was obvious that he was the more levelheaded of the two. "But you're right, it isn't fair."

"We'll get you what you need," Danny said, meeting my gaze. "Or rather, *I'll* get it. Milo will stay here with you."

Milo snorted. "I'll come with you, thank you very much."

"It might not be safe," Danny said pointedly.

Milo raised his chin. "Which is why it should be both of us." He removed his arm from around my waist and scooted back far enough for us to look at each other comfortably. "I'll drive Danny there and I'll distract the others while he gets what you need. When we come back, we'll sit with you while we do the spell. You have to promise not to try to go after them on your own though. It isn't safe and none of us can afford to put our babies at risk."

I nodded. "I understand, and I wouldn't ask you to. If I manage to get the information, hopefully that will be enough to convince someone to investigate."

It had to be, right?

I couldn't do all of this for nothing.

FORTY

R*EID*

When Danny and Milo returned, I met them at the door and motioned for them to be quiet until we were in my bedroom. Danny's expression was tense and Milo was jittery, as if he'd had a couple of energy drinks and hadn't burned off the buzz yet.

"Did you manage to get something?" I asked as soon as I closed the door behind us.

Danny reached into his pocket and pulled out a thin leather wallet. "I'm pretty sure this belonged to the dead guy. Obviously, I couldn't ask anyone to make sure, but given where I found it, I think it's the right one."

I took it. "Thank you." Hopefully he was right or else I'd involved them for nothing. "Honestly, thank you so much for your help. You guys should go now. If you hurry home, they might never know you were part of this."

Danny crossed his arms over his chest. "Like we said earlier, we're staying with you."

"But I don't want you to get in trouble," I protested.

Milo smiled softly. "And we want to save those omegas

and to... to make sure nothing happens to you. You're our friend."

I pressed my lips together, not entirely sure that last part was true, but deep down, a part of me wanted to believe him, so I didn't question it. "The spell shouldn't be dangerous. I've done it a few times now and I've never had any problems."

"Great, then there's no reason to leave," Danny said. "Are we doing the spell in here?"

I shook my head. "Outside would be best. There's less potential interference. You can wait inside though, if you'd prefer."

He just grinned. "Not a chance. It's a good thing I kept my jacket on."

I tucked the wallet up my sleeve to hide it from sight. "Come on then."

I wandered through the house, feigning nonchalance, and slipped through the door that led to the garden. I spotted Jessie in a room we passed, but she was too engrossed in her book to notice us. Fortunately, we didn't encounter Hamish.

Once we were outside, I slid the wallet into my palm, closed my eyes, and searched for the thread that would trace its movements through the world. Since the wallet had been handled often, its thread was strong. I traced it back to the police station in my mind's eye and then continued farther, to the park, and then out of town.

I was vaguely aware of cold seeping through the fabric of my jeans. I must have sat down.

I followed it to the town of Moonlight Cove, where Trent's pack had last resided. The trail lingered there for a while before venturing first to a truck depot at the nearby city of Grayton and then to a series of sprawling buildings in a rural area perhaps twenty miles outside of Grayton.

I tried to search for details that would allow me to identify the location. When I spotted a truck, I focused on its license plate and committed the number to memory.

My energy was rapidly waning, the vision in my mind's eye blurring at the edges. It was strange. That had never happened before.

I dug my fingernails into my palms to ground myself and pulled back until I reached the roadside. I checked the number on the mailbox as everything flickered and went dark.

When I opened my eyes, the light seared my retinas like I'd looked straight at the sun and I squeezed them shut, my head pounding.

"Reid!"

An arm slid under me and propped me up. Nausea rolled through me and I retched but fortunately didn't throw up.

"Are you okay, sweetheart?"

I squinted, relieved to find it was slightly darker than before. Something soft was behind me—a cushion, perhaps —and whatever I was sitting on was soft too.

Definitely not the cold, damp grass outside.

"M'okay," I mumbled, trying to focus on the owner of the deep, concerned voice. I could somehow tell it was Zander even though I hadn't seen him and could hardly bring myself to concentrate on anything.

"You damned well are not," he snapped, but someone shushed him and he didn't say more.

Gentle hands rested on my thighs and warmth suffused me, spreading from my legs to my core and out to my fingertips, ridding me of the chill I hadn't even noticed until it was gone.

"He actually is all right." This time, the voice was Nathaniel's. "Exhausted, yes, but unharmed."

"Thank fuck." Zander again. "Danny. Milo. What the hell were you two thinking?"

"We had to help those omegas," Danny replied tremulously. Whatever had happened, it had clearly shaken him. "We thought it would be fine."

"There's no way anyone could know how much energy a spell like that might require." Nathaniel was the calmest of the bunch. "It depends on a lot of different factors. In this case, it would seem that Reid underestimated. Given these consequences, I'm sure he won't do it again."

"Did you find them?" Milo asked. "They must be so scared. Maybe even hurt."

"I... might have." I couldn't be certain.

"You have to be more careful!" Zander exclaimed. "All of you. We can't lose you. You're too precious. When I saw Reid on the ground like that, I... *Fuck*."

My heart squeezed. He almost sounded scared. As if he was as shaken as Danny and Milo.

Perhaps he really was.

I forced my eyes open and blinked as my vision adjusted. Zander was hovering in front of me, on his knees, the lines of his face deeper than ever and his eyes seething with emotion.

"I'm sorry," I whispered. "I didn't mean to worry you. I just... I had to try."

He took my small hand between his larger ones. "I understand, but you need to remember that people care about you too. Not to mention your little one. What if the spell had used up too much energy and tried to siphon some from the baby as well? Or what if you'd fallen and hurt your abdomen? So many things could have gone horribly wrong."

My breath hitched and an icy sensation trickled down my spine.

He was right.

"I didn't think. I'd done the spell with Nathaniel, and it seemed fine then, so I thought it would be the same."

But it wasn't. My thoughtlessness could have cost me my baby.

I buried my face in my hands. I didn't deserve to be a father.

"Hey, now." Zander edged closer, the heat radiating from his big body bringing me comfort. "Don't spiral. You got lucky this once. Let's just not push our luck again, okay?"

I nodded numbly. "Will you call Dr. Black please? I'd like him to check that my baby is safe."

"He's already on his way," he assured me.

"Did you find anything?" This question came from Nathaniel. When Zander glared at him, he scowled right back. "What? You're right that it was a foolish thing to do, but if he discovered something useful then we should know about it."

"I, uh, found a couple of places." Ignoring the heat of Zander's gaze burning into me, I explained the locations I'd seen to Nathaniel, pausing while he made notes on his phone.

"Thank you." He smiled warmly. "We'll do recon for those sites and decide whether they're worth pursuing." He paused, glanced at Zander, and then continued, "You may have misjudged the energy expenditure, but I'm impressed by what you were able to achieve."

"Let's just not do it again soon," Zander added, a growl in his voice. "I've got enough gray hairs as it is."

I studied him. Sure, he had flecks of gray at his temples and a few silvers sprinkled throughout, but I thought they suited him. Made him look distinguished. I kind of wanted to take off his shirt and find out if there were any silvers in his chest hair, too. Or if he had chest hair at all.

"I like them," I murmured shyly.

Zander's eyes widened and his nostrils flared, but then he schooled his features. "I like *you*, so how about you don't frighten me again?"

I wanted to protest. I didn't like being treated like either a child or a prisoner, but I could see he was genuinely scared on my behalf and that was a balm to my ego, so instead, I kissed his cheek.

He inhaled sharply, his eyes flashing amber, and then something seemed to settle inside him and he gave me a look so tender I thought I might cry.

FORTY-ONE

ZANDER

"Dr. Black is here," Hamish called from the doorway. He stood with his arms crossed, his face etched in a scowl. "I don't like all of these alphas in my house. How long until you've got everything you need?"

"Not much longer," I told him, straightening from a crouch. Perhaps I should have arranged to transport Reid elsewhere, but according to Nathaniel this was the safest building in town, and that's exactly where I wanted my mate to remain.

I waved to Nathaniel. "Why don't you head out to make room for Dr. Black?"

Nathaniel nodded and brushed out past Hamish. "We'll be out of your way soon, Protector."

Hamish's eyes narrowed. "Glad to hear it."

Behind him, Dr. Black tsked. "Not all alphas are bad, Hamish. Some of us only want to help."

To my utter astonishment, Hamish's cheeks turned pink and he ducked his head, mumbling something incomprehensible as he hurried away down the hall.

Huh.

Did big, tough Hamish have a thing for the handsome older doctor?

Dr. Black entered and I moved out of the way so he could approach Reid. I watched him closely, my bear on alert for any potential threat to our mate.

The lack of mating bond chafed and I wished I could sink my teeth into his shoulder and claim him as fate had intended, but I'd never forgive myself if I hurt him or rushed him. I just had to clench my jaw and summon a level of patience I'd never known I'd need.

Dr. Black examined him thoroughly but kept his touch clinical—probably the only thing that stopped my bear from plucking him away from our little warlock.

"As far as I can tell, the baby is fine," he said, standing and giving Reid the kind of look a stern parent might. "But that's purely down to luck. You're overtired and dehydrated. I want you to focus on resting and getting plenty of fluids over the next twenty-four hours. Preferably water but I'll leave some flavored electrolyte powder you can add if you'd like."

Reid nodded, then winced. "Thank you."

Dr. Black's lip curled. "You can thank me by taking it easy, okay?"

"Yes, sir."

Dr. Black packed his case and left. I glanced at Milo and Danny, who were both lingering with guilty expressions and their heads down, like scolded children.

"Can I trust you to take care of him?" I asked them, not entirely certain they could be relied upon to ensure he didn't use his magic again.

"Yes, Z," Danny said, scuffing the carpet with one foot. "We'll look after your mate."

I narrowed my eyes at him and then at Milo, the weaker link.

Milo's eyes widened and he nodded furiously. "We won't leave his side."

"Good." I was sure Everett and Knox would appreciate their omega mates also being secure in the safest building in town.

Reid reached for me, his fingers brushing my sleeve. "Will you let me know what you find?"

I bit the inside of my cheek to prevent my instinctive reply. I wanted him far away from any trouble, but if I tried to hide anything from him, there was every chance he'd find some devious way to learn the truth without me. "I will."

His gaze searched mine and then he settled, apparently satisfied. "Thank you."

I looped my fingers through his and gave his hand a slight squeeze, then released him and headed out.

I drove Nathaniel back to the police station. The deputies were hard at work in the bull pen, Bea on her computer while Hawk was discussing something heatedly with Neil, the cop who usually worked the night shift.

"Any luck on those sites?" I asked, speaking loudly enough to be heard by everyone. I'd asked Clay to send them the details Reid had shared so they'd be able to get a head start.

"The rural site looks promising," Bea said, motioning to her computer screen.

I strode over and looked at the satellite imagery that showed a cluster of buildings in the middle of nowhere, with a long gravel drive and a country road that passed by.

"I'm almost certain this is the location that Reid described. The address matches, there's a similar number of buildings, and it's about the right distance from Grayton. See these"—she pointed at several long rectangular structures—"they're shipping containers. If I was going to hold omegas captive, that's where I'd put them."

My back teeth ground together and my stomach plummeted as I imagined Reid being kept in one of those ugly metal boxes. Were there other omegas inside at this very minute? If so, what kind of condition would they be in?

"Send the address to my phone," I told her. "I'll let the feds know."

Nathaniel touched my arm. "They won't have gotten a warrant yet and they might not be pleased that a tracing spell has been done without approval, or that evidence was stolen to do it."

I grimaced. "I still have to tell them."

Surely the PBI had bigger fish to fry than a desperate, traumatized omega warlock who only wanted to help.

Nathaniel hesitated, but then nodded. "Ask for SSA Rainier."

"Thanks." Already getting my phone from my pocket, I headed to my office and called the main contact line for the PBI.

When it connected, I asked for SSA Rainier as Nathaniel had suggested and explained that a tracking spell had been carried out and a location of interest identified. SSA Rainier grumbled about not following protocol but he gave me less trouble than I expected—perhaps because I'd name-dropped Nathaniel.

"Will you investigate?" I asked him after he'd finished quizzing me.

He sighed. "We'll follow up, but we have a strong —*authorized*—lead on another trafficking ring that we're preparing to infiltrate. That's our current priority. Once the operation has wrapped up, we'll shift focus and by then, we might have got the sign-off to use the information your source provided."

"But Amato will realize his guys are missing soon," I protested, knowing as I did that it wouldn't change anything. "What if they move up the auction or relocate the omegas?"

There was a moment of silence.

"We don't have solid evidence that omegas are being held there," Rainier said eventually. "I know it's hard to sit on your hands and wait, but the other case is urgent and can't be delayed. I'm sorry."

I accepted this, unsurprised but still frustrated, and said a brief goodbye before ending the call. As soon as the call disconnected, I rang Dad and asked him to come down, then I headed to the Search and Rescue base of operations and gathered Garrick and Everett in a meeting room. Knox accompanied them, apparently sensing something was up.

Once Dad arrived, I explained the situation.

"I understand where the feds are coming from, but it doesn't sit well with me," I tacked on when I finished. "Right now, I doubt the traffickers will realize they've been compromised, which means we have a window of opportunity. As soon as that changes, we might lose any advantage we have over them."

Dad rubbed his jaw, his palm rasping over the stubble as his eyes flashed gold. "This is likely only one site of many. If we were to attack it, there's no saying what might happen to omegas being detained at other sites."

"We can't abandon them!" Everett growled, claws bursting from the tips of his fingers.

"They might not even be there," Garrick said, proving once again why he was the next in line to become Clan Alpha. He was less hotheaded than Everett and more willing to play games than me. "As the PBI said, we don't know for sure. We need more information before we decide on our next steps. How can we get that?"

I tapped my chin, thinking quickly. "I'll ask Hawk to fly overhead."

Everett paced from one side of the room to the other, fur sprouting and retracting along his bare forearms. "Will it take long?"

I considered the distance. "Perhaps an hour."

Dad nodded. "Do it."

I radioed Hawk with instructions and waited to get the affirmative before moving on. "Say he does find omegas there. What then?"

Everett started to speak but Knox held up a hand to cut him off.

"We go in with stealth," Knox said. "We make sure we capture a couple of the higher-ups so we can extract information about the organization, then we free the omegas."

Everett rumbled. "The omegas should be our priority."

Knox hurried to agree. To be fair, if anyone disagreed, Everett looked like he might take a swipe at them.

"Perhaps Nathaniel can mask our presence so no one realizes anything is wrong and reports back to Amato, at least for a couple of hours," Garrick said thoughtfully. "If he does a truth spell on anyone we take prisoner, we might be able to get answers quickly—although we run the risk of them being subject to the same silencing spell as the others." He turned to Dad. "What do you think?"

Dad's brow was furrowed with concentration and he looked older than his years, reminding me that while he was a strong and capable Clan Alpha, he wasn't accustomed to leading our usually peaceful clan through situations like this.

After a while, he inclined his head. "I don't like to risk losing the element of surprise. If the plan goes wrong and news gets back to Amato, he could go to ground. But we also need to rescue those omegas and the PBI is busy with something else. Let's make a plan to go ahead with the infiltration but wait until we hear from Hawk before confirming our course of action."

"Right." I straightened. "I'll get Bea to print a map of the terrain and brainstorm methods of entry to the compound."

Half an hour later, I received a call from an unknown number.

"Boss, it's Hawk," a quiet male voice said as soon as I answered. "I have bad news. There are omegas being held here, but a truck just arrived onsite and it looks like they're going to be moving them soon. Perhaps someone tipped them off that we're onto them."

"Fuck." If there was a leak in the feds, we'd never catch them if we waited. "Lie low, Hawk. I'll be in touch. Can I call you on this number?"

"Yeah. Be quick."

I hung up and cleared my throat to draw everyone's attention. "The omegas are there, but they're moving them. We need to go."

And damn, that meant I had to call Reid as I'd promised to update him. Hopefully he wouldn't do something ridiculous like try to insist he come too.

FORTY-TWO

*Z*ANDER

I leaned against the wall and closed my eyes against the bright overhead lights as the call connected. I dreaded the upcoming conversation but there was no avoiding it.

"Zander?" Reid's voice was small and tired, although clearer than it had been earlier. Perhaps he was beginning to recover from his overuse of magic.

"I have an update." My gut tangled in knots. Every instinct I had was blaring at me to bundle Reid in a blanket, lock him in a cozy bedroom, and not let him out until this whole situation was dealt with.

"What is it?" he asked, his tone growing sharper.

I rubbed my eye with the heel of my palm. "One of the locations you found is a holding site for trafficked omegas."

There was a quick intake of breath, then, "Will you be going in to rescue them?"

"Yes," I confirmed. "Tonight. We don't have clearance from the PBI because the proper approvals haven't gone through yet and they have other priorities, but Hawk reports that they're preparing to move the omegas so we need to act soon. Hopefully I'll have good news for you later tonight or perhaps tomorrow morning."

"I want to know when it's done."

"I'll get in touch as soon as I can. I promise." That was much easier than I'd expected. Perhaps the consequences of overextending himself had hit harder than I thought.

"Thank you." He hesitated, then added, "Come back to me safely, okay? I... I don't want anything to happen to you."

My heart warmed at the care in his tone. "I will, sweetheart. Stay with Milo and Danny. I'll have Momma come over so you can keep her company too. She worries when Dad's away."

"I'll need a bigger room soon."

I laughed and said goodbye. I was heading out of my office to coordinate with the others when Nell came rushing down the corridor.

"Sheriff," she called, waving frantically. "Melinda just called. She was driving down the main street when she saw two warlocks. One of them smelled of that High Priest you kicked out of town. It wasn't him, but they'd been in contact recently."

My breathing stuttered. Damn, that was bad. "Does she have eyes on them?"

"Not any more. She's circling back around, but she said they were on the move."

Raised voices approached from the other direction.

"Warlocks are in town." Nathaniel moved toward me far more quickly than I'd seen before. "I sensed their magic. At least three."

Shit, that meant that the two Momma had seen weren't the only ones here. Perhaps Hephaestes was too.

I cursed internally. How was I supposed to leave on a

rescue mission when my own omega's worst nightmare was practically knocking on his door?

"Do you think they're here for Reid?" I asked Nathaniel.

He nodded, his expression grim. "I can't think of any other reason they'd be here. My guess is they've been keeping an eye on things and saw that we're all distracted by the two wolves and the trouble they brought to town. They probably think it's the perfect time to try to snatch him while we're not paying attention. I'd say that's why they only sent a few. They want to be in and out before anyone notices them."

"But they underestimated Momma's nose, and didn't account for you," I concluded. Thank Gods. "Reid will be safe in Omega House though, won't he? You've warded it."

Nathaniel grimaced. "I've warded it well, but I'm only one warlock. If a group of them works together, they could probably break through. It might take a couple of hours, but if we leave town, they'll have that and more."

"Fuck." I couldn't leave when Reid was in danger, but if we didn't go, then who knew how many other omegas would be sold into a fate worse than death? I motioned down the corridor. "Come on."

We strode down to the bullpen, where the others were waiting. I explained the situation as briefly as possible.

"Should we split forces?" I asked Dad, because that was the best option I could think of. Some of the clan's warriors could stay to protect Reid while the rest went after the traffickers.

But Dad shook his head.

"We don't know how much firepower the traffickers have," he said, his mouth twisted and his expression dark. "If we halve our force, it could be a suicide mission. I can't justify sending people to their deaths, can you?"

I deflated. "No." The last thing I wanted was to

endanger my friends and family. "Can we chase the warlocks out of town again?"

Nathaniel grimaced. "If you did, they'd only come back as soon as we left again."

I dug my fingers into my hair and tugged at the roots. Fuck, there had to be an answer that wouldn't result in anyone being killed or sold into sex slavery.

"What if we take Reid with us?" Bea suggested.

I stiffened and rounded on her. "Did I hear that right? You want to take my pregnant mate into danger?"

Her eyes widened but she stood her ground. "Forgive me for saying so, sir, but if we aren't willing to leave the trafficked omegas for the PBI to deal with, then it seems like the only solution."

"I will not—"

"Hold on." Dad raised his hand. "Hear her out. Go on, Bea."

Bea darted a glance at Dad, ducked her head, and continued. "If he stays and we go, then the warlocks will probably be able to overcome the wards eventually. They might not if Nathaniel stays, but I'm of the understanding that we need his magic to help us infiltrate the compound, so we can't leave him behind."

Reluctantly, I nodded. We were relying on his stealth spells to sneak in undetected.

"If half our team stays, then both halves are weakened and everyone is at risk." She swallowed, her slender throat bobbing. "But Nathaniel can ward things other than houses, right? If we take Reid with us, Nathaniel can ward the vehicle, and he'll be just as protected by the ward as he currently is at the Omega House, but he'd also have us nearby for backup. Someone could stay with him as another layer of protection, and it would also remove the threat to the other omegas at Omega House."

I frowned. "What do you mean?"

She shrugged. "Reid isn't the only omega there. Others live there, and Milo and Danny are with him too. If the wards come down, all of them are at risk, not just Reid. The warlocks might be angry at us for keeping Reid from them, and they might take that out on our omegas."

My stomach tangled in knots. Much as I hated to admit it, she did have a point.

"She's right," Dad said, and the knots pulled tighter. "Nathaniel, will you be able to ward the vehicle as she's suggested?"

"I can." Nathaniel looked torn. "It isn't foolproof. I like the idea of extra backup from a predatory shifter. Another point you might not have considered is that if he comes with us, he's within my shielding spell, and he'll be more difficult for them to track. Right now, they probably know exactly where he is."

Dread curled down my spine. I closed my eyes and concentrated on breathing. I really, really didn't like the sound of this.

"Then we'll bring him with us," Dad said.

And then it was final.

FORTY-THREE

Z ANDER

An hour later, we were all packed into vehicles and traveling in a convoy to the site. I'd had the fucking fright of my life when Reid called in a panic because the warlocks were working on breaking the wards at the Omega House.

I'd kept him on the line while Nathaniel warded the vehicles, and then we rushed over. Everett drove straight at the row of warlocks—three, as Nathaniel had guessed—and when they scrambled, unable to attack the warded vehicle, I parked right at the gate so Reid could dart from the warded property to the warded car.

We'd screeched away, but as I looked in the rearview mirror, I'd noticed the warlocks running for a nearby car. They probably thought to follow us, knowing we couldn't stay in the vehicle forever.

Momma soothed my scared mate while Nathaniel leaned out the window and worked some sort of magic— hopefully to earn us a better head start. If we could put some distance between us and the warlocks, they might not be able to hunt us down.

I had no doubt that we could take on three warlocks if the need arose, but the trafficked omegas needed us to get there quickly and in good shape. Battling warlocks would jeopardize that.

"I can't see them," Nathaniel said, closing the window and belting himself in. "I think we've got a solid lead."

"Thank the gods," Dad muttered from the passenger seat. He had his phone out and was messaging with someone from the other vehicle. "Knox can't see them either."

"Good."

Hawk reported in. He'd set up spikes on the road outside the property in case they tried to leave before we arrived. Hopefully we'd get there before that became an issue.

Reid was quiet. So much so that it worried me, but unfortunately, we'd have to deal with the fallout of facing his old coven again later. I was grateful to Momma for keeping a close eye on him. She'd insisted on coming and serving as his protector while everyone else went onto the compound. She had teeth and claws and knew how to use them.

There was nothing Momma wouldn't do to protect Reid now that she considered him one of her own.

We made good time to Grayton, cruising around the edge of the city, and turned toward the address Hawk had confirmed. He called again on his "borrowed" phone and confirmed that the omegas were still on site. The traffickers seemed to be waiting for something.

Nathaniel reported sensing a seeking spell at one point, but there was no more sign of the warlocks. We were lucky. There were only so many enemies we could deal with at a time.

When we arrived at the compound, it was after

midnight. I turned off the car's headlights a couple of miles from the property and parked a few hundred yards down the road, behind a stand of trees.

I turned toward the back seat just as Reid opened his mouth to say something. I motioned for him to be quiet. Nathaniel had spelled the vehicles to be less obvious than usual, but until we were all subjected to silencing spells, I didn't want anyone to make more noise than necessary.

Nathaniel's lips moved and he did something I didn't quite catch. My ears popped.

"I've silenced noises you make so they won't be heard by anyone more than five feet away," he said, speaking at his normal volume. "They also won't be able to smell you until you get close. Wait here. I need to do the same for the others, then we'll have to move as quickly as possible because maintaining the spell at this level of potency—as well as the wards on the vehicle—will quickly use up my magic reserves."

"Is it too much?" I didn't want him to risk his health—or his life. Especially not with him being newly mated to George. He was part of our clan now and that made him our responsibility to care for.

He shook his head. "As long as we've done what we need to within thirty minutes of casting the spell, it should be fine. At that point, the efficacy of the spell will begin to wane."

He opened the door and ducked outside. I glanced in the mirror and squinted as he made for the vehicle behind us, which carried Everett, Garrick, Knox, Clay, and Bea. Farther back, Angela, Yuri, Francis, Li, and Dr. Black were squeezed into the last car in the convoy.

Yuri and Francis weren't trained to fight like the rest of us, but they were strong shifters and could hold their own. Li, Yuri's mate, was skilled with healing poultices and energy transfer magic so he and Dr. Black were also to remain in the car but be available if there were any casualties.

I returned my attention to Reid, who was sitting upright and very much awake now, his bright eyes sharp with focus. "Promise you'll stay here?"

He nodded, wide-eyed. "I don't want to endanger my baby. I'm staying right here."

"I'll be with him," Momma reminded me.

"Thank you."

I had to trust them to be sensible. If I allowed myself to worry about Reid, it would distract me from the mission, and I couldn't afford to be distracted. Dad had decided to have him here, and I'd gone along with it. Too late for second thoughts now.

Nathaniel tapped on the window and I opened the door and got out. The others were already assembling their gear so I checked that my bulletproof vest was in place and that my gun was in its holster. I didn't bother carrying a knife because my claws could shred flesh just as easily.

"Ready to move in?" Dad asked quietly.

I looked around at the brave souls who'd volunteered for this unauthorized and dangerous task. "Looks like it. Let's go."

Knox and I each led a team as we snuck up the road and onto the property. With Knox's military training and prior career as a mercenary, he was also well-placed to make decisions under pressure.

We moved in from the sides like a scorpion's pincers. There was a guard walking the length of the driveway and I took him down with a blow to the head. A bullet would have been more effective, but we were trying to keep as many traffickers alive as possible so we could gather intel from them afterward. Clay cuffed and gagged him.

Another guard stood beside the cab of a massive cargo truck. Knox swept in like a fucking ninja and choked him until he fell unconscious, then stepped aside for Bea to secure him.

There were noises coming from inside the truck. Muffled conversation and some scuffling, as if people were moving around.

Hawk hadn't touched base in a while so we couldn't be certain, but I suspected the omegas were all loaded into the truck, awaiting transport.

I led my team down the right side of the truck while Knox led his down the other. There were a pair of guards positioned at the far end. We moved in tandem to take them out—Knox a little more efficiently than me.

I stepped up to the back of the truck. The doors were metal and bolted shut in the middle. A heavy padlock held the bolt in place.

I grimaced. Shifter strength wouldn't be enough to break a lock like that and I didn't think the bolt cutters we'd brought would either.

I tapped Dad's arm. "Get Nathaniel."

Dad turned and motioned Nathaniel forward. I moved out of the way, but as I was turning to address Knox, a bright light burst into existence a short distance away. I cringed at the intensity and blinked as my eyes struggled to adjust.

When my vision cleared, my gut plummeted to the soles of my boots.

A ring of men surrounded us.

Each was armed, and the guns looked military-grade.

In the center stood a well-dressed man, and slumped against him, with an arm that looked like it had gone through a wood chipper and a gun to his head, was Hawk.

FORTY-FOUR

R*EID*

"It's taking too long," I whispered, peering through the front windshield, trying to see something—*anything*—in the dark. Unfortunately, I had useless human eyes, not cool shifter eyes, and they couldn't make out a godsdamn thing.

My nerves were on edge and every noise in the dark made me flinch, certain that the warlocks from my coven had caught up with us. The others seemed to think we'd gotten away from them—at least for now—but it felt too easy to me.

"They said they might have to search for the omegas and that it could take some time," Melinda reminded me, but I could tell from the wobble of her voice that she was worried too.

"It's been nearly thirty minutes," I hissed. "Their stealth spells will wear off soon. Something must have gone wrong."

She grimaced. "I can't hear anything from inside the car. Maybe if we open the door, I'll be able to."

"Are you sure that's a good idea?"

"The ward isn't affected by opening or closing the doors and windows," she reminded me, and eased it open. For a long moment, she didn't say anything and I slumped. So much for that idea. But then she tensed and cocked her head, her eyes flashing gold in the darkness.

I dug my fingernails into my palms to stop myself from demanding to know what she could hear. Rushing her wouldn't do anything good and might stop her from hearing something important, so I stuck my tongue into the side of my cheek and forced myself to wait.

"The traffickers have—" Something slammed into us from behind and rocked the entire vehicle.

I lurched forward, wrapping my arms around my belly just before I slammed into the front seat. Unfortunately, Melinda wasn't so lucky and she tumbled from the car and hit the ground with a thud.

I spun, looking over my shoulder, searching for whoever was attacking us. I hadn't sensed anyone approaching but I was tired and my magic was depleted. Perhaps I'd missed something.

The car rocked again, and through narrowed eyes, I made out a solid male form in the darkness. They attacked again, and my breath stuttered as I realized they hadn't physically moved.

This wasn't one of the traffickers. It was a warlock.

Melinda scrambled up, a growl rumbling deep in her throat.

"Get in the car," I urged.

The wards were still holding firm. If we stayed here, he might not be able to get to us—especially if the others returned soon. She threw herself inside, bumping into me as she landed.

The warlock stopped attacking and cocked his head. He stood, motionless, as seconds ticked by. I stared into

Melinda's frightened brown eyes, uncertain of what to do.

Then, all of a sudden, the wards vanished.

My blood ran cold. The warlock stepped closer, sparks crackling around his fingertips.

"What happened?" Melinda asked.

"The wards are down." I swallowed. "Nathaniel..."

Gods, I hoped this didn't mean he was dead. That I'd gotten him killed by insisting on this raid after he'd survived decades as part of the PBI.

Melinda leaned closer and spoke softly. "I need you to run. On the count of three."

I tensed, wondering how on earth she thought a pair of omegas—one of them pregnant—were going to outrun someone who could fight with magic.

"Three," she murmured, her eyes glued on the man outside. "Two. Go!"

She sprang from the backseat with the spryness of a much younger woman, and for an awful moment, I thought she was going to run and leave me there. But then she shifted, her clothes tearing as a huge bear replaced the matronly woman.

She roared and I was frozen in place until her golden eyes met mine.

Run, they seemed to say.

So I did.

I scrambled out of the car and tore down the road, my legs burning and my lungs struggling to drag in air.

The ground at my feet exploded, spraying dirt and gravel everywhere. I stumbled but managed to keep going.

Another roar sounded behind me.

Was Melinda okay?

What the hell was she doing?

My foot landed in a pothole and I winced as my ankle

rolled, but I caught myself before I tripped and focused on the road.

Melinda could turn into a grizzly. She'd be all right, wouldn't she?

I veered to the left, ready to dart into the fields to hide, but another figure appeared from the darkness. I considered dropping to the ground and praying that they hadn't seen me, but then I chanced a glance over my shoulder and jerked in surprise at the sight of a hulking silhouette bounding along behind me.

Melinda.

Thank fuck. She was alive.

Some kind of magic tendril thing came out of nowhere and tried to wrap around my ankle, but Melinda grabbed me and yanked me free. I expected the warlock to try again, but no strike came.

A third warlock appeared ahead of us as he drew level with the driveway, forcing us to turn.

A chill ran through me. Why did it feel almost like they were herding us somewhere?

I ran over to the nearest shipping container and flattened myself against the back of it. Melinda followed, keeping low to the ground and making almost no noise.

We circled around the end of the shipping container and my heart nearly stopped. The traffickers had surrounded our people and had weapons trained on them.

My feet glued me in place. I glanced at Melinda, wondering what on earth we were supposed to do now. We were coming here for reinforcements, not to *act* as reinforcements ourselves.

I was a magically depleted, pregnant omega and Melinda was a middle-aged housewife who could turn into a massive bear. What good could we do against a team of career criminals?

At the forefront was a tall, heavyset, bald man who had positioned a bloodied Hawk in front of himself like a living shield.

I gestured to the trees, silently asking her if we should go back and risk running into the warlocks. I still didn't know why they hadn't caught up to us. They should have been right behind us. She motioned—I think for me to stay put, but it was hard to tell—and crept closer.

None of the traffickers had noticed us yet.

Zander glanced up and his gaze caught on mine. His eyes widened before he smoothed his expression over, trying to hide his reaction to our presence. I could still see the silent plea in them though. He wanted us to turn around and leave them here.

A stick cracked behind us.

I looked over my shoulder and bit my lip so hard I tasted blood. The first warlock was staggering out of the trees, clearly injured but hellbent on getting to us.

We were trapped between him and the others, and despite his injuries, he might still have the capacity to hurt us.

I felt inside myself, searching for any remnants of power. I didn't want to use magic when I'd been warned not to, but if these guys caught us, I might lose my baby and everyone I'd come to care about.

Sensing the familiar buzz of magic within me— including the magic that belonged to my baby, I relaxed a little. My supplies were diminished but not nonexistent, and my baby was fine. Carefully, I summoned as much energy as I had to spare and channeled it into two bolts of blue sparks. Nathaniel had been teaching me to improve my accuracy and I gave my entire focus over to ensuring that the bolts were aimed exactly where I wanted them to go.

Then I released them.

One flew toward the warlock and the other at the bald man.

Both bolts struck true. The warlock dropped as if his strings were cut and the bald man collapsed, his hold on Hawk loosening. Hawk weakly pushed him away.

Caught off guard, the traffickers reacted more slowly than I expected. I dashed behind the corner of the container as they spun to see who'd attacked.

Meanwhile, Melinda did the opposite of what I'd thought she would and charged at them. She leapt on the bald man and tore his throat out. I gagged and forced myself to swallow the bitter taste of bile on my tongue.

One of the traffickers had the wherewithal to shoot Hawk. He slumped to the ground, limp and unmoving.

Carnage broke out.

Our Grizzly Ridge companions launched themselves at the traffickers, many making contact before shots were fired.

I silently debated whether to stay hidden or run over to Hawk. Now that Melinda had taken out the bald man, she was trying to help him but had gotten caught up in the fight and couldn't give him the attention he needed.

I looked around. All was quiet, sound muffled by the frantic hammering of my heartbeat, the scene unfolding before me in terrible clarity, teeth and claws and blood spattering the ground.

Hawk's head lolled back, exposing the blood that was slowly pumping from a wound on the upper left side of his torso.

Realization dawned, swift and sharp. For him to survive, someone needed to put compression on the wound. The fighting was vicious and Melinda was too busy protecting him to give first aid.

I checked to make sure that no one was paying me attention, raced to Hawk, and maneuvered him into a seated position, wrapping my arms around him from behind. Bit by bit, I dragged him toward the container.

If we could hide, they might forget about us.

Melinda struck down a coyote shifter and prowled alongside us, ready to defend us if necessary.

I got him behind the container and pulled off my jacket, which I folded and pressed against his throat firmly but hopefully not so much that it would cut off his oxygen. I kept an eye on his face to make sure he wasn't struggling for air.

"We need Nathaniel," I told Melinda. "If he's alive. He knows some healing spells. He might be able to stop the bleeding."

She nodded her huge, shaggy head and lumbered around the corner, but stumbled backward a moment later with a tiger shifter bearing down on her.

"Melinda!" I cried.

That's when another man—likely human—leveled a gun at me.

Oh, fuck.

Fuck fuck fuck.

I glanced at Melinda but she couldn't help me now. If we were to get away from this man, it was up to me.

CHAPTER

FORTY-FIVE

R^{EID}

"Let him go and keep your hands where I can see them," the human said, unperturbed by the fact that a massive tiger and a grizzly were engaged in a battle to the death only yards from us.

I reached inside for my magic, but I doubted I'd have enough to knock this man down and I *really* didn't want to hurt my baby.

Were there any spells I could cast to protect myself?

I'd never tried to create a ward that was immune to bullets before. Was it possible?

Wards used less energy than offensive spells so I might be able to pull it off. Slowly, I released Hawk and raised my hands in the air. I stepped away from him slowly, allowing him to slump to the ground so that he was out of the line of fire.

Immediately, I tried to create a ward, but my vision wavered.

I was exhausted, and I'd already used more magic to take down the warlock and the trafficker. I couldn't risk using any more.

"Come over here," he ordered.

I moved as slowly as I could, silently assessing him. I wasn't much over five feet while this guy was closer to six, so there was no chance I'd be able to physically overpower him. I just had to hope that I was worth enough to Ace Amato that he wouldn't hurt me.

He rolled his eyes. "Speed it up. I haven't got all day."

Narrowing my eyes, I scanned the area frantically, searching for Nathaniel. My heart sank when I spotted him standing near Aaron, both of them in cuffs. Aaron was standing guard over Nathaniel's prone body in his human form—the cuffs must be preventing his ability to shift and blocking Nathaniel's magic.

Neither of them could help me.

I tripped, my legs weary, and fell toward the man. He shoved me and I staggered back, spots appearing before my eyes.

He raised the gun and I stared down the barrel.

My life didn't flash before my eyes.

Instead, there was a void.

Just blackness.

And then Melinda roared and swiped the gun from his hand, tearing his arm to shreds. He screamed and fell on his ass, scrambling away from her.

I turned, almost numb and with none of the urgency I should have felt, noting that the tiger was bleeding from a gut wound. Not dead, but temporarily out of action.

Melinda shifted, and my eyes flew to her face because I really didn't want to see her naked. "We need to hunker down and stay very still. Keep up the compression."

I hurried over to Hawk and resumed my post at his side. Melinda grabbed his ankles and dragged him closer to the side of the container, where we were less likely to be seen.

My gut dropped at the sound of footfalls nearby.

I didn't dare look back, but Melinda's wide eyes told me I should worry.

"Hands up," a man ordered.

When I turned, four men had us pinned against the container.

One of them aimed his gun at Melinda and shot with absolutely no forewarning.

I screamed, and a blaze of blue light—so bright it was almost blinding—pulsed from my body. My magic, reacting to intense emotions, trying to protect me even though I'd nearly used it all up.

My vision flickered, darkness creeping into the corners.

My body flopped sideways and I opened my eyes just in time to catch myself as I hit the cold metal of the shipping container.

Everyone was on the ground. All four assailants, but also Melinda and Hawk.

Belatedly, I became aware of an emptiness inside me where my magic should be.

Fuck.

I'd unwittingly attacked someone from Grizzly Ridge and now my magic really was completely gone, leaving me defenseless. Not only that, but without my magic, I couldn't sense my baby's magic. Until now, I'd known they were—at the very least—still alive because I'd been aware of that different magical flavor inside me.

Now, that reassurance was gone. I could only pray that my magic wanted to protect my baby as much as I did.

Sluggishly, I got up and I scrambled over to Melinda, checking her for a bullet wound. I couldn't see one. Maybe I'd somehow destroyed the bullet before it hit her.

Another trafficker, who must have heard people hitting the ground, stumbled around the corner and caught sight of me.

"You're the warlock omega everyone's saying is worth a fortune," he growled, stepping closer before pausing to look at his fallen comrades. With an angry curse, he rushed me. His arms came around my waist and he tossed me over his shoulder like I weighed nothing.

A rhythmic thump-thump-thump sounded somewhere nearby.

I'd heard something like it before but couldn't put my finger on what it was. I turned my head, searching for the source, but the alpha carrying me readjusted his grip and I had to close my eyes against a wave of nausea.

The wind whipped my clothes, but it wasn't natural.

Oh, no.

Suddenly, I knew why the rhythmic thumping was familiar. It was a helicopter. They'd occasionally come and gone from my coven.

I beat my fists against my captor's back but he didn't slow. Metal clanked in front of me and then the world swam as he dropped me onto a hard floor and shoved me until I was pressed up against something firm.

A wall, maybe?

Or the inside of a helicopter?

My captor jumped in behind me, metal clanked again, and then my gut dropped as we began to lift into the air.

FORTY-SIX

*Z*ANDER

My heart threatened to burst from my chest as I sprinted for the helicopter and launched myself into the air, reaching for the skids. I strained as I drew near, desperate to feel my fingers wrap around the metal so I could tear the damn door open and rip Reid from the clutches of those evil bastards.

Why wasn't he safe in the car?

Fuck, I thought I'd never be more scared than when I'd seen him sneaking around the corner of the container, but watching his limp body get thrown into the helicopter had been a hundred times worse.

I couldn't lose him.

If I did, I'd never forgive myself.

My fingers brushed the skid and I lunged, clawing at it with partially shifted hands as I started to fall.

"No!" I shouted, trying to reach just an inch farther.

That was all I'd need. One fucking inch.

But gravity brought me crashing back down to earth.

I leaped again, but the helicopter was still rising and this time, I didn't get anywhere near it.

"I'm sorry."

I spun, claws extended, but came up short when it was only Momma standing behind me.

"I tried to protect him, but he knocked us all down," she added, watching the helicopter lift above the buildings, putting more distance between us with every passing second.

"Why are you even out here?" I demanded, my shoulders heaving as I battled for control.

"A warlock attacked us and the wards failed."

"Shit." I kicked the ground. "They caught Hawk so they knew we were coming. That's how they trapped us. The first thing they did was disable Nathaniel's magic."

Scanning Momma, I grimaced. She was battered from fighting, her body raked with claw marks and a few bites too. A chunk had been torn from her shoulder but was thankfully not bleeding heavily. Omegas healed more slowly than alphas but still faster than the average human.

Save mate, my bear insisted.

Save him.

Yeah, but how was I supposed to do that?

My legs ate up the distance around the end of the container.

"Nathaniel!" I shouted, searching for the warlock. He was in the process of having his cuffs unlocked by Knox and they both looked up at my shout. "Can you bring that helicopter down?"

Nathaniel rolled his wrists and reached toward the helicopter, his lips moving quickly as he voiced the words of a spell. Yellowish bands of magic stretched from him to the helicopter and encircled the skids. He gave a slight tug and the helicopter dipped dangerously on one side.

"Careful!" My voice broke. "Reid is on board."

Reid, and the baby I'd come to think of as mine.

With a growl, Nathaniel tried again, but with similar results. He shook his head. "I can hold it steady so that it can't get any higher, but I don't know how to bring it down safely without a team. Usually I have backup for this sort of thing."

Over the roar of the helicopter, another noise intruded. The crunch of tires over gravel.

I spun around just as a pair of armored off-road vehicles tore onto the property. They screeched to a halt near the floodlight, sending stones and debris flying.

Fuck, the traffickers had backup.

My throat threatened to close over and I debated how to address this new threat. A figure jumped out of the nearest vehicle and held out her hands, palms out.

"We're here to help."

What the hell?

Knox echoed my thought aloud.

"No time for explanations," she said, and then more people spilled from the vehicles. They surrounded Nathaniel, their chanting joining his, and new threads of magic secured the helicopter on all sides.

"Tug!" the woman cried.

They all yanked on their magic, drawing the helicopter lower to the ground.

"Again."

They repeated the motion over and over until the helicopter hung only a foot above the earth, the blades whizzing as it struggled to pull away from the intangible ropes now holding it in place.

"Who the fuck are these people?" Garrick asked, approaching Knox and me.

Unfortunately, before any of us could figure out what was going on, the helicopter door opened and a bulky man appeared in the frame.

No, wait.

It was *two* men.

The guy who'd grabbed Reid earlier was holding the little warlock in front of himself as a human shield. Reid hung limply from his grasp, his eyes closed, his skin almost white in the artificial light.

I moved forward, my hand on my weapon. "Let him go. Don't give me a reason to shoot you."

I planned to shoot the fucker regardless, but saying so wouldn't bring Reid back to me safely.

People were moving around me and I was vaguely aware that my friends and family were rounding up the surviving traffickers and subduing them.

"If I let him go, I'm dead," the trafficker shouted back. "Tell the warlocks to let go of the helicopter or I'll cut his throat."

My vision sharpened as an involuntary shift ripped through me, shredding my clothes. I stared at Reid, unable to take my eyes off him. I barely even processed what I should have done much earlier.

It was *warlocks* helping us.

The same warlocks we'd run from earlier?

That didn't matter right now. The most important thing was that man could not be allowed to harm my mate.

"Why don't you pass him out to me and then I'll get them to release you," Garrick said, bargaining in my stead since it was all I could do not to charge him immediately. If I did and I messed up the timing, Reid would be gone.

That's when I noticed something.

Reid's eyes were closed and his head dangled as if he was a puppet on a string but his heartbeat was fast. Too fast for him to be unconscious.

He was playing dead.

Perhaps that meant that together we could get him out of this predicament.

Stay calm, I willed him. *We'll save you somehow.*

But as I watched, the helicopter dropped an inch and both men swayed, almost thrown clear.

Holy shit.

I roared at the warlocks. How dare they play games when Reid's life hung in the balance?

"Calm down." Knox grabbed my shoulder. "Shift back. He needs you in your other form."

I forced the shift, every part of my body protesting, but the cry that came from me when I noticed the thread of red dripping down my mate's neck was purely animalistic.

That asshole had cut him.

He had to die.

FORTY-SEVEN

Z *ANDER*

"Enough of this," the dead man in the helicopter snapped, his knife sinking deeper. "The only way the warlock goes free is if you release the chopper."

A whine tore from the back of my throat. I couldn't get to the man without risking Reid.

Why wasn't someone else doing something?

"Nathaniel," I growled. "Stop holding the helicopter and save him."

"I can't risk a spell hitting Reid," he replied, not taking his eyes from them.

"You have three seconds," the man announced. "Three—"

He cut off when Reid surged into action, breaking his hold and throwing himself out of the helicopter.

I lunged forward, catching him before he hit the ground. The metallic scent of his blood filled my nostrils and I whined again as I cradled him in my arms and frantically checked him over.

The neckline of his shirt was drenched with blood and

he was limp, but the cut didn't look too deep. Just as well, since warlocks didn't heal as quickly as shifters.

As it was, the cut might scar.

He clung to me, and buried his face in my chest, wriggling closer like he wanted to bind himself to me and never let go. I peppered the top of his head with kisses and closed my eyes, breathing him in, trying to draw comfort from his familiar scent and from the warmth of his body despite the fact that I could still smell his blood and fear.

I breathed deeper, relieved when I still detected that hint of honeysuckle beneath the overpowering ozone.

"I knew you'd catch me," he whispered, the words muffled against my skin. I'd torn my shirt when I shifted earlier, and now it was nothing more than scraps in the dirt. "Part of me thought it was stupid to take a chance like that, but I trusted you to catch me before I hit the ground."

My heart squeezed. "Always." I raised my head, growling when I spotted the man pinned to the ground, subdued by Dad and Everett.

I turned to Knox, who was hovering nearby and thrust Reid's shaking form into his arms. "Take him."

"What?" he asked, taken aback.

As soon as Reid's weight had transferred, I lunged at the man who'd hurt my mate. My fangs descended and my claws tore through the ends of my fingers, ready to sink into his soft belly.

"Whoa!" Suddenly, Garrick blocked my path. "You can't do that."

"Like hell, I can't." I pushed him aside. He might be next in line to become the Clan Alpha, but I was bigger and my claws were just as sharp.

"Zander, stand down."

I froze, my hand in the air between Everett and me. Growling, I struggled, trying to push forward.

"Stop this," Dad insisted, injecting even more Alpha authority into his voice.

He was implacable.

With our bond as clan members, and his authority over us all, I was helpless to fight him.

A terrified scream cut through the air.

Reid's.

Turning away from the man on the ground, I raced back to him, enveloping him in my arms as I looked around for what had scared him so badly.

"Reid! You've been much harder to get my hands on than I expected," Hephaestes, the High Priest of the Havlock Coven, drawled as he removed his hat and strolled toward us.

I stiffened. Oh, shit. In the moment, I hadn't paused to consider why warlocks might be helping us, but now we had to deal with them when we were worn out from fighting and they were energized and ready to go.

Hephaestes smirked and spun until he faced Dad. "Look, I think we've shown that we could just take Reid if we wanted to, but I'd prefer not to make any new enemies. I will, if I have to, but I've done your clan a great service today, so perhaps we can come to an arrangement."

I bared my teeth. "Fuck off."

"What do you want?" Dad demanded, his arms crossed over his broad chest and his face set in a dangerous scowl. He might be getting older, with more salt than pepper in his hair, but he still cut an imposing figure and I was glad to have him beside me.

High Priest Hephaestes grinned like a man who knew he held a winning hand. "We saved the lives of your clan members tonight. As a sign of your gratitude, we'd like you to return our beloved Reid, who we've missed sorely since he left."

Reid wrapped his arms around my waist so tightly that it was difficult to drag out a full breath. Tremors wracked his petite frame and his tears trickled down my chest and abs.

My bear surfaced, glaring at Hephaestes through my eyes. How dare this man steal my sassy mate's courage and blunt his usually sharp tongue? How dare he act as if he had a claim to him when all he'd ever done was abuse him?

"We didn't ask for help," I rasped out, my voice hardly human. "And we won't be paying any price, let alone the life of my mate. Besides, you were going to kidnap him. You didn't do this out of the goodness of your heart."

The asshole had the audacity to laugh. "As I said before, I don't sense a bond, and I rarely do anything out of the goodness of my heart. I saw an opportunity to avoid further conflict and took it."

Reid whimpered and his fingernails pierced the skin of my back. But then something changed. He stilled and began to breathe slowly and rhythmically. I hoped like hell that was an improvement and not a sign he was becoming catatonic.

Hephaestes addressed Dad. "Be reasonable, Alpha Blackwood."

Dad stared at him for a long moment, his eyes golden and bestial. "You're right that we owe you a debt for your assistance."

"But—" I started to protest.

Dad held up his hand. "But my son is also right. We didn't request your help and while we may be inclined to have goodwill toward you because of it, we're not in the habit of forcing people to go places they don't want to. Unless Reid says he wants to go with you, then he's staying with us."

Reid peeled himself away from my chest. With a

strength that stunned me, he turned to Hephaestes, raised his chin, and glared. "I don't want to go anywhere with him."

"Thank you for being clear about your wishes, son." Dad splayed out his hands. "You heard him."

Hephaestes sighed and ran his hand through his long, stringy hair. "Very well. If you insist on being difficult, then I'll give my team the signal to free the gentlemen who look like they want to rip you apart and we'll take Reid by force. You can't beat us, Alpha."

As if he'd given a silent signal, the warlocks who'd been our temporary allies only minutes earlier rounded on us.

Wary, the assembled shifters squared off against them.

I held Reid close with one arm and extended my claws with the other, ready to fight to defend my mate.

The drone of another chopper filled the night and it appeared from the dark behind the other, which had settled on the ground and been turned off by someone—Gods only knew who.

Suddenly, figures in black swarmed the property, spilling in from all sides.

My heart sank. Was this yet more coven reinforcements?

We really did stand no chance of winning.

FORTY-EIGHT

R*EID*

At first, I thought the newcomers were mercenaries hired by Hephaestes, but as the warlocks spun around and took up defensive poses, I realized they were as surprised by this interruption as we were.

"PBI!" a voice called above the roar of the chopper blades. "Lay down your weapons."

A little of the tension eased from Zander's massive body. "Unless you want to be questioned about how you treat your own, you'd better back off," he muttered to Hephaestes.

Hephaestes glared and I stiffened, wishing I had access to my magic so I could defend Zander from him. Shifters were strong, but Hephaestes was powerful and sneaky.

"This isn't over," Hephaestes shot back, then shouted, "Disperse!"

The members of the coven melted into the shadows as if they'd never been there.

"Stop!" The PBI agent's voice rose, as if perhaps we hadn't heard him and that's why people were vanishing into the ether. "No one is to leave the site until we have your statements."

Yeah, that didn't stop the coven.

They were gone and I doubted there would be any way the PBI could trace them.

I tilted my face up to peer at Zander. The underside of his chin was heavily shadowed but his features were illuminated by whatever light source the traffickers had set up. Blood flecked his cheeks and forehead, and there was a trace of it at the corner of his mouth, as if he'd either bitten something or had his lip split.

The pink of healing cuts laced his torso and he had a puckered wound in one shoulder. Had someone shot him?

"I'm sorry," I whispered, tears stinging my eyes. "I feel like this is my fault for insisting that you guys break the PBI's rules and come for the omegas. I put everyone at risk."

"Hey, now. None of that." Zander kissed my forehead. "We all wanted to save them."

I tilted my face up, pleased when he brushed a kiss over my lips. I lingered, relishing the contact. He was warm, comforting, and most importantly, alive.

"You're bleeding." He bent to check my neck and his eyes glinted gold. "I don't think it's bad, but we need to get you seen to."

I swayed, suddenly exhausted. "Hawk's injury is more urgent."

"Yes, but Dr. Black isn't the only healer here." He scanned the area and waved a slim Asian man over. "Reid, this is Li. He's a witch and a healer."

Li dropped to his knees beside us and pulled an alcohol wipe out of his first aid kit. He stood and reached toward me. "Sorry, this will sting."

I gritted my teeth as he cleaned the cut on my throat

and then spread some kind of poultice over it before adding a bandage to hold everything in place.

"Can you tell if my baby is okay?" I asked, my stomach plummeting to my shoes when he shook his head.

Zander knelt in front of me. "I can smell them." He pressed his ear to my abdomen and a slow smile spread across his face. "And I can hear a heartbeat."

My breath caught. "You can?"

He rose and pulled me into his arms. "It's incredible."

Relief swamped me and I allowed myself to draw strength from Zander and revel in how safe I felt when I was surrounded by him.

I trusted him, completely and utterly, but that wasn't all I felt for him. There was so much more.

The truth was terrifying and astonishing and wonderful all at once. It made my heart beat fast and slow, made it swell until it felt ten times its size, and cut through the barbed wire I'd fenced the organ off with as if it was made of tissue paper.

I was too scared to voice the words, but I would soon.

"I was so scared when I saw those men surrounding you," I whispered. "I didn't want to leave you there even though I knew that's what you'd asked me to do. I tried to be sensible, for you and my baby. But the thought of you in danger... it wrecks me."

Zander gazed down at me as if I'd offered him the moon. He squeezed his eyes shut for a moment and then brushed his lips softly—ever so softly—over my temple.

"I feel the same way about you." His eyelashes fluttered open and his eyes flashed the most beautiful shade of gold I'd ever seen—like burnished antique jewelry. "I know you might not be ready, and I'll wait for as long as you need, but I love you too, Reid. More than you could ever imagine."

Our gazes locked and I wondered if he might kiss me

again. My lips parted and I leaned closer, going onto my tiptoes. His cheeks were lightly stubbled, his lips plush, and his naked chest was firm beneath my palms.

My head spun and it had nothing to do with any injury.

"Sheriff Blackwood?"

Zander dropped his head back and groaned. "What?" he snapped at the black-clad man who'd approached us.

I tucked my face into Zander's chest and breathed in his scent—sweaty alpha, pine, and bergamot.

"I'm SSA Rainier," the man said, and from Zander's response, that meant something to him. "Please tell me I didn't interrupt you in the progress of carrying out vigilante justice."

Zander's arms encircled me more fully and he rested his chin on the top of my head. "There's nothing vigilante about a local police department searching a site of interest for a local investigation."

SSA Rainier snorted. "You aren't the sheriff *here*, Blackwood. You're lucky that I understand why you did it. I appreciate you notifying us before you moved in. We finished with our other operation early so we hustled over. It's just a shame that we've been left with loose ends like Ace Amato. I assume he's not here?"

I cocked my head. Zander hadn't said anything about notifying the PBI. My poor mate hated to break the rules. I'd bet guilt had eaten away at him until he'd sent the message.

"Not as far as I can tell," Zander replied, his voice rumbling from deep within him, perfectly delicious.

Rainier grunted. "Hopefully the prisoners will have useful information to share."

My gut churned. There were so many things they weren't saying. Using phrases such as "loose ends" when the truth was that there could be dozens of omegas out there who'd been trafficked by these bastards or their colleagues.

Omegas just like me, who'd made a foolish mistake or trusted the wrong person and paid the ultimate price.

"We'll find them, won't we?" I asked against Zander's skin. "We won't give up on them?"

"We won't," he agreed.

"On that subject." A third man had joined us. Aaron, I thought, but I wasn't ready to stop hugging Zander to check. "Nathaniel has gotten the truck open. The omegas are inside but they're huddled in the back corner, scared out of their minds, except for one that's hissing threats like an angry cat. Reid, will you come and speak to them for us? They might react more favorably to another omega."

My fingers instinctively tightened on Zander.

"You don't have to," he murmured, as if sensing my nerves. "Momma can do it, but if they sense she's a predatory shifter, she might still unnerve them."

I pulled a face. I understood. As a warlock—and currently one without any magic—I was the least intimidating person present.

"We usually have omegas on staff who are trained for this type of situation, but they're all busy elsewhere tonight," SSA Rainier added.

Summoning strength I didn't know I had, I pulled away from Zander and nodded. "Okay. I'll help."

Zander gave my hand a quick squeeze. "You've got this, little warlock."

"Thank you, son," Aaron said, and the word settled somewhere deep in my soul.

Son.

He'd called me *son.* Not because I was valuable to him but because he cared for his family. My throat tightened. Was I actually ready to become part of Zander's family?

"We'll need statements from everyone present, so be sure you've all spoken to one of my agents before you leave," SSA Rainier said. "Good luck, Reid."

As Zander and I began to follow Aaron, he paused and called over his shoulder, "You might want to investigate the Havlock Coven. They were here tonight, and we've got reason to believe they mistreat children in their care."

Drawing in a deep breath, I added, "I can tell you everything. But not yet."

FORTY-NINE

REID

As we approached the enormous truck, my stomach dipped and churned. If Danny hadn't been kidnapped and the Grizzly Ridge pack hadn't come for him, I'd never have been saved and this could eventually have been my fate if Trent had run out of use for me.

As if sensing my thoughts, Zander took my hand. "I'm not going to let anything happen to you. Not now, not ever."

Perhaps once I'd have taken his words as an indication that he didn't think I was capable of looking after myself, or as evidence that yet another alpha viewed omegas as lesser beings, but I'd seen how panicked he was when he'd thought I was in danger earlier and it made things clear.

He didn't want to protect me because he thought I was weak, but rather because he loved me and that was how he showed it.

My heart warmed and I gripped his big hand more firmly. "I know."

Nathaniel and a handful of federal agents were blocking the open door on the back of the truck. To my surprise,

Nathaniel pulled me into a one-armed hug, using the other to wield his cane and remain balanced.

"I'm so glad you're all right," he said, releasing me after a moment. "Did Aaron tell you what we need?"

I shrugged then winced. My whole body ached. "Someone unthreatening to help calm them."

Nathaniel nodded. "These guys"—he motioned to the agents—"have cleared the interior and confirmed that there are no threats within. They tried to engage, but the omegas were frightened."

I scoffed because of course they were. The agents were all clad in black and carrying weapons. Anyone would be intimidated by them.

"Do you mind backing away a bit?" I asked, gesturing for them to give me space. "Crowding the door like this probably isn't helping."

The agents backed up. I took a step toward the door but stopped short when Zander entwined his fingers with mine.

"Be safe," he murmured, his gaze fierce and gold.

"I will," I promised, and backtracked to kiss his cheek. "They're just scared omegas. They're probably tired and hungry and dirty. Perhaps someone could arrange cleaning supplies, food, and a change of clothes?"

"Good thinking."

This time, when I pulled away, he let me go.

I planted my foot onto the step and grabbed the doorframe to haul myself up into the truck. It was a bit awkward but not difficult.

The stench of stale sweat and a few other things I'd prefer not to think of filled my nose and I blinked as I waited for my eyes to adjust. In the rear corner, at least a dozen omegas were huddled together, all staring at me as if waiting for attack.

In front of them stood a man as petite as me. In the dark, I couldn't tell exactly what color his hair or eyes were, but he raised his sharp chin with a defiance that impressed me.

"Are you with the police?" Even though his voice rasped like he hadn't drunk water for days, it was strong.

"They're here, but I'm not an officer," I explained, keeping my hands at my sides and remaining still so they knew I didn't mean them any harm.

The petite omega nodded. "Good. But no one will be making statements until we're clean and fed, and if any alpha asshole says or does anything the least bit mean to my friends, I'll bite their face off."

"I understand."

Unfortunately, the word was barely out of my mouth before the door swung farther open behind me and there was a clang as someone large jumped inside.

The omegas in the corner cowered.

I pivoted, ready to defend them from anyone who wouldn't give them the space they deserved.

Garrick stood behind me, his eyes glowing, his features distinctly bearish.

"Mate," he growled.

Well, shit.

I put myself between Garrick and the other omegas. I didn't care which one was his mate. I wouldn't allow him to scare them.

To my utter disbelief, the sharp-chinned omega sauntered closer, one of his hands fisted at his side. Garrick's gaze followed his every movement.

The omega waggled his finger as if telling off a small child. "None of that. I've had enough alpha bullshit for now, thank you. If you want me to be your mate, I expect to be wooed properly later. There will be none of this instant-claiming stuff. For now, go away. I want a bath and a good meal."

Garrick blinked, and after a long, tense moment, his features returned to normal and his eyes stopped glowing. He cleared his throat. "Yes, boss."

The omega smirked. "Good." He snapped his fingers. "I don't want to see any alphas within a hundred yards of this truck. Your omega friend here can bring us food and clothes. You'll also need to arrange alternate transportation because some of us won't be comfortable traveling with an alpha."

"I'll sort it out with the feds," Garrick promised. "Reid, do you have this under control?"

I nodded and he backed out. I stared at the omega, stunned by how easily he was able to stand tall and make demands despite the trauma he'd experienced.

"I'm Reid." I offered a tentative smile. "I'm a warlock, but my magic is bound for a while so you don't need to worry about me doing anything to hurt you."

The omega cocked his head. "I wasn't worried anyway. I can tell you're a decent person. I'm Kit. I'm a fox shifter."

"Besides the obvious, what do you guys want to happen next?" I asked, well and truly out of my element. I had no idea what trafficking victims needed. "Would you like to give me phone numbers for your families so we can call them and arrange for you to go home?"

"Maybe later tonight," Kit replied. "We're all exhausted. More than anything, we want a full belly, clean hair and skin, and a proper night's sleep. Maybe the police could book us into a hotel or something and we can talk more tomorrow?"

"I'll find out for you."

I scrambled down from the truck and relayed what Kit had said to the federal agents. One of them confirmed that there was a hotel in Grayton where they could book a block of rooms and that they'd arrange for security to ensure the omegas were safe.

"Maybe some of them could recuperate in Grizzly Ridge," I suggested. I hadn't wanted to go home after being rescued. Maybe some of the others hadn't had a good life before being abducted either.

They should get a choice about what happened next.

Zander wrapped his arm around me and kissed my temple. "We'll give them that option. Space can be made available for them in Omega House if they need a place to stay."

I relaxed against him. "Thank you."

Another agent approached with a duffel bag of clothes they'd found on the premises and I dragged it over to the truck. Nathaniel lifted it magically because I couldn't handle it in my current state and I knew the omegas would sense if any alphas came closer.

While they were changing clothes, an agent confirmed their accommodation booking and another vehicle arrived, bringing omega reinforcements and—from the smell of it— several different types of takeout.

I returned to the truck, my heart lightening when I saw that the omegas were no longer crowded into the far corner. They were still dirty but the clean clothes had helped.

"The food has arrived," I announced, loud enough for them all to hear. "There are some new omegas too. Federal agents. They're bringing the food over."

Kit jerked his chin. "Thanks for the warning."

The agents approached. One was carrying a stack of pizza boxes, another had brown paper bags, and a third was wielding a huge pot of what looked like steamed vegetables.

I stood guard while they passed the food to Kit, my stomach churning as the omegas fell on it as if they were starving.

They probably were.

Rushing over to Zander, I buried my face in his chest. "What will happen to them? We need to make sure they're treated right."

"I don't think my sharp little fox will accept anything else," Garrick said from behind me, his tone making it sound like he was bursting with pride despite the fact Kit hadn't actually agreed to be his anything yet.

"The agents will take them to the hotel," Zander said, speaking quietly since his mouth was near my ear. "They'll have the chance to wash off and sleep. In the morning, they'll all be asked to give statements. After that, they can choose to return home, go their own way, or come to Grizzly Ridge."

"They need to know they have options." I wouldn't budge on that.

Zander held me tighter. "They will."

I believed him.

Why wouldn't I?

Zander was strong and steady. He'd been there for me every day since we'd met even though he knew I was broken, used, and mourning for a man who'd done nothing but hurt me.

He deserved my heart. He was a worthy mate.

So why was I nervous about what might come next?

CHAPTER

FIFTY

EID

My stomach was in knots as I knocked on Zander's door. I'd spent dozens of hours with him over the past few days, sleeping wrapped around him, unwilling to let go after we'd come so close to losing everything. I'd eagerly soaked up every affectionate kiss and delighted in the strength of his hard body surrounding mine.

Whenever he wasn't working, we'd chatted, sharing stories about ourselves and our lives prior to meeting, then we'd snuggled together, exchanging sweet kisses and getting to know the feel of each other's bodies.

It had taken a while to calm down after the excitement of rescuing those omegas, followed by an intense interview with SSA Rainier, in which I'd told him everything that had happened to me at the hands of my old coven.

But now, I was well-rested, refreshed, and able to think completely clearly. I knew one thing with absolute certainty: I wanted Zander.

And finally, I was ready to claim him.

I knew old issues would crop up, but for now, my entire being practically vibrated with hope for the future.

When Zander opened the door, I almost swallowed my tongue. I was used to him being clean-shaven and put-together but now he wore only sweatpants riding low on his hips and his cheeks and jaw were thickly stubbled.

His chest... Wow, it was a work of art.

He had defined muscles, a light dusting of hair, and plum-colored nipples that were peaked from the cold.

Heat flooded me. My hole instinctively softened and grew damp.

A couple of weeks ago, this response would have frightened me because I knew his senses were keen enough to detect my desire. But I'd become used to reacting this way over the past days, and now, I celebrated my body's resilience.

I'd been through so much, but I was still able to experience desire for an alpha who deserved it. One who was good and decent and trustworthy.

My Zander.

"Can we talk?" I asked, meeting his beautiful brown eyes, full of so much affection I felt like I might choke on it.

He held the door open. "Come in."

I brushed past him, breathing in his comforting scent. He smelled like home.

Zander closed the door. " "I'll join you in the living room in a moment."

I went through to the living room and sat on a huge, squishy sofa. He'd definitely opted for furniture large enough to fit his own big frame and those of his family members.

Zander padded in, his sexy chest now covered by a plain white T-shirt. I grimaced. He probably thought that by covering himself he was making me more comfortable, but my priorities had changed. I enjoyed the view.

"Can I get you a hot drink?" he asked, hovering a few yards in front of me. "Tea? Coffee?"

"No, thank you." If I dragged this out for too long, I might lose my nerve. Or get impatient and jump him.

"Okay then." He started to sit on one of the armchairs, but I patted the seat beside me.

He strode over and sat beside me. "What would you like to talk about?" he asked gently, those steady eyes never wavering from my face.

I bit my lip, the knots in my gut tangling and drawing tighter. I drew in a deep breath and exhaled roughly. "I know I'm not the easiest person to care about."

He flinched and frowned but didn't interrupt.

"But for some reason, you seem to. And I've seen the kind of man you are. I trust you with everything." Forcing myself to be brave, I held his gaze. "If you still want to, I'd like to mate with you."

"You're not difficult to care about," he said fiercely. "Don't ever think that of yourself. You're worth more than the sun and moon combined, and I will wait as long as it takes for you to be ready to mate with me. There's no rush, sweetheart."

I raised my chin. "I love you, and I want to be your mate."

He reached for my hand, then hesitated. I slipped my hand into his, loving how rough and warm it was. How big it felt around mine.

Zander was capable of violence, but he'd never hurt me.

"You love me?"

"Yes," I whispered, suddenly shy.

"Then I'm the luckiest man alive." There wasn't a hint of doubt in his voice. "I love you so much. I've been fighting my instincts every day, trying not to pressure you, but I want to mate with you. I'll never deny that. I love you, and I want you. I'd kill for you, and I'd die for you. But are you sure you're ready?"

I nodded, holding his gaze, and a silken strand of tension drew taut between us, thrumming with unspoken desire. "Please make me yours."

His hand tightened almost imperceptibly on mine. "Tell me if you want me to stop or slow down. The control is yours. Promise me."

I nodded again, feeling shaky and fluttery and tingly inside.

"I need the words, Reid."

"Yes, I promise."

He curved his free hand around the side of my face and cradled the nape of my neck. I shivered and relaxed into him, my body knowing what it needed even if my mind hadn't released the last of its nerves.

The first time I'd been mated by Trent was seared in my memory.

Violent.

Bloody.

Painful.

Trent had torn into my shoulder without sparing a thought for my well-being as he'd taken me.

But this time would be different. I trusted that.

Zander dipped his head and brushed his lips against mine. They were surprisingly soft. I breathed him in—that faint scent of pine I loved so much—and kissed him again.

Sweet.

Chaste.

Tender.

My heart swelled and tears stung my eyes.

"Are you okay?" he murmured, searching my eyes.

"Perfect."

How could I be any other way when he touched me like I was cherished?

He kissed me again and this time, I darted my tongue out to taste his lips. Heat flashed through me and I pressed closer, scrambling onto his lap. I wound my arms around his neck and kissed him deeper, his tongue coming out to meet mine.

We made out like teenagers until we were both panting and breathless. He drew back, his forehead resting against mine, our mouths only a couple of inches apart.

"We don't have to go further. Never doubt that I want you." He groaned and squeezed his eyes briefly shut. "So damn much. But we can kiss and date and work our way up to more."

I nuzzled the underside of his neck where it was warm and smelled of him. "I'm tired of wanting something and not letting myself have it. I want a mate who treats me well. I want a father that my baby can be proud of. And I want a fucking orgasm."

A grin stole across his face and he chuckled. "Well, far be it from me to get between you and an orgasm."

CHAPTER

FIFTY-ONE

REID

I grabbed at the waistband of his sweatpants and tried to pull them down. He lifted his hips and I shoved them over his ass and halfway down his thighs.

Then I stopped, gaping.

He wasn't wearing underwear.

His cock was right there. In front of me. Almost under me. Hot and thick and way bigger than Trent's had been.

"Oh my Gods," I breathed, gulping. My hole clenched reflexively at the thought of taking that massive dick. A wave of panic washed over me before I drew in a deep breath and remembered that this was Zander and he would never hurt me. He'd proven that over and over again.

As I relaxed, slick coated the insides of my thighs.

Zander kicked his sweatpants the rest of the way off, gathered me in his arms, and stood. "All okay?"

"Yes."

"Then let me take you to the bedroom."

I rested my head against his chest, listening to the rhythmic beat of his heart. "Please do."

294

He carried me as if I weighed nothing. His bedroom had a spectacular view of the forest through floor-to-ceiling windows. One wall was painted dark green, the other two off-white. The bed occupied the center of the space and the bedspread matched the green of the wall.

He set me down carefully, as if I was precious, and my breath caught in my throat. He was so good to me. I don't know how I'd ever feared that he might be the same as Trent.

Zander dropped to his knees in front of me, his broad chest heaving, and gazed at me with hooded eyes. A charge passed between us and he pulled my pants down, then bent his head and swallowed my cock.

"Oh, fuck!"

My hips arched instinctively.

He pinned them in place and wrapped his tongue around me. The heat was wet and the suction intense. My eyes rolled back and I grabbed the blankets.

I couldn't come yet, it was too soon, but I'd never experienced anything like this. How was I supposed to resist?

I whimpered and thrust into Zander's mouth, my lips parting on a gasp as he held my gaze.

He pulled off with a pop. "Reid, sweetheart, can I put my fingers in you?"

I nodded frantically.

He grinned wickedly then took me into his mouth again. I tried to stay relaxed, but as one of his fingers probed my slick entrance, I tightened. Before Trent, I'd found pleasure with dildos, but he was the only alpha I'd ever been with and it had been painful.

"Breathe out, little warlock," he murmured around me. "Trust me. I've got you."

I exhaled slowly, the tension easing from me, and his finger popped inside. I started to stiffen again but then he curled it and touched a spot in front of me that lit my nerve endings up in the best possible way.

I groaned and flopped against the mattress, no longer able to hold myself up. He added a second finger and I wriggled, impaled, and felt my face burn at the way they squelched inside me.

I was so wet.

A third finger stuffed me full.

"Unh." My whole body trembled. "Oh, Gods."

Still, it wasn't enough. I wanted Zander to own me. To mate me. To make me his.

"Give me your knot," I rasped, my voice raw and wrecked.

He rose off me and my hips stuttered, instinctively seeking friction. He wiped his mouth on the back of his hand, his eyes burning gold as he stared down at me.

"Are you sure?"

"Yes." I whispered the affirmation like a secret, like a promise, like the only truth that ever mattered.

"Can I strip you?"

I yanked off my shirt, pausing when his gaze locked on my scar-free shoulder. My lips curved shyly. "I'm all yours."

He groaned and nuzzled my skin. "Thank you, sweetheart." His expression was achingly tender as he helped me move up the bed and crawled over me. "Do you want to be on top?"

"Not this time." Maybe when my pregnancy was further along. "I want to see your face and feel you on me."

He caressed the side of my face. "Then that's what you'll get."

He kissed me, then notched the head of his cock at my entrance and pushed in inch by inch. I was too turned on to resist the way I had earlier. I bore down on him, loving the way he stretched me.

"You feel incredible," he moaned, his big frame dwarfing my smaller one. "I can't believe I finally get to have you like this."

"Forever," I swore.

He withdrew his cock and thrust inside me slowly and with iron control. Over and over again, he filled me.

It was completely different from how Trent had taken me. I didn't feel like a possession or demeaned; I felt completed in a way I'd never known was possible.

All the while, I held his gaze, not even slightly taken aback when his bear surfaced.

"My bear," I whispered, my mouth falling open as he worked me toward a peak I'd never shared with anyone else before.

We exchanged breaths and he nipped gently at my lips.

"My warlock," he rasped.

Each word was like a key grating in the rusty lock of a prison cell, finally, finally, setting me free.

I was his mate, but I'd never be his possession. He didn't want that. He wanted to make me stronger until I dared to stand alongside him.

"Bite me," I whispered.

He didn't hesitate. His teeth sank into my neck and his hand wrapped around my cock. Ecstasy rushed through me as our magics combined, and I spilled into his palm.

Flashes of blue and gold swirled around us.

I pressed my fingers to the side of Zander's neck and muttered the spell that would bind us—the one Nathaniel had taught me yesterday, when I'd decided that I wanted this.

I'd never marked Trent.

The bond had formed all the same, but this way it was deeper. It showed that I wanted Zander in return.

Zander stiffened and a groan tore from him. His cock

pulsed inside me and began to thicken at the base, forming a knot. He continued to grind into my ass as he came in spurts, his knot growing until we were locked together and I was so full of him I couldn't tell where he ended and I began.

I smiled up at him, floating on a haze of endorphins. "I love you, mate."

He gathered me close and kissed me. "I love you too, my omega."

CHAPTER

FIFTY-TWO

ZANDER

"Are you nervous?" I asked Reid as we prepared to visit my parents' place for a family meal. After this, we'd attend a clan meeting at which our newest members would be introduced.

Technically, there was no reason for Reid to worry, but my family could be overwhelming and we hadn't all been together under one roof since we'd mated a few days earlier.

Besides, I knew my little warlock tended to stress about everything.

"A little." He bit his lip. "I know that's stupid."

"It's not." I caught his hand and drew him to me. He'd just donned a beanie and with it low over his eyes, his blond curls peeking out from beneath, my heart clenched from how adorable he was. "Want me to take the edge off?"

He frowned. "How?"

Smirking, I sank to my knees in front of him.

"Oh." His eyes widened. "Yes, erm, okay."

I grinned. I couldn't help it. He was just so damn cute. And now, he was mine.

I undid his jeans and pulled them down. His underwear too. I took his cock into my mouth in one smooth, slow motion and grabbed his ass, urging him to rock into me.

His salty taste filled my mouth and the scent of his slick went straight to my groin, plumping my dick.

I groaned around him. He was the perfect mouthful.

Unfortunately, as much as I'd love to draw this out, we needed to leave soon, so I focused on setting a quick rhythm designed to bring him off quickly.

He clutched at my head—although I could tell he was being careful not to hurt me—and gave shallow thrusts, tunneling into my throat.

I sucked harder and he whimpered and rolled his hips, whining about how empty he was. I'd love to fill him up, but that would have to wait for later.

A few minutes later, he came undone, shuddering and gasping for breath as he unloaded onto my tongue. I sucked him through it, nice and gentle, and kept him in my mouth until the aftershocks had stopped.

He slumped, boneless, and I caught him and pushed to my feet, lifting him into my arms. He giggled and tried to grab his jeans but they were too far away. I reluctantly put him down, holding onto his shoulders for long enough to ensure he was stable.

Once he'd put himself to rights, he slipped his hand into mine and sent me a warm, sated smile. "Time to go?"

"Yeah, sweetheart."

His gaze dropped to my crotch. "But what about you?"

"That was just for you." My poor Reid didn't seem to understand that alphas didn't have to get off during every sexual encounter, but I supposed that his experience had taught him that his own needs didn't matter, only what the alpha wanted.

One day, he'd realize that my whole world revolved around him.

"But..." He squirmed and looked at his feet.

I tipped his chin up with two fingers and brushed a kiss over his lips. "If you feel like doing something else later, I'll take my pleasure then. If not, it can wait."

He dipped his head but then nodded and squared his shoulders. "Thank you, Z. That was so good."

"You're very welcome. Now, let's go."

Together, we left our place—I'd invited him to move in when he was ready and he'd done so immediately, which thrilled me more than I could have imagined—and walked the short distance to my parents' place.

As soon as we arrived, Momma enveloped Reid into one of her comforting mom-hugs, congratulated him on our mating, and assured him that he'd done the right thing by speaking with SSA Rainer about his time in the Havlock Coven.

Milo and Danny each hugged him too. The alphas in the family kept more of a distance. Much as he was healing, Reid was understandably wary of alphas and it would take a while for that instinctual fear to dissipate.

We'd already discussed the possibility of arranging therapy for him with a paranormal-friendly therapist. He was open to it as long as I accompanied him to his first session.

Perhaps it was wrong of me, but I loved being used as his safety net.

We shared a delicious meal—Momma and Milo had outdone themselves in the kitchen—and Reid relaxed progressively as conversation flowed. I wasn't sure exactly what he'd feared might happen, but hopefully he'd eventually realize that he was part of our family now and that we took care of our own.

At one point—between dinner and dessert—Knox took Reid aside. I tuned into their muted conversation. I didn't think Knox would say anything to upset Reid but he could be a little rough around the edges.

What I overheard warmed my heart.

"How are you doing?" Knox asked, his voice softer than usual, as if he was doing everything he could to avoid startling Reid.

"I'm really good."

"Not overwhelmed?" Knox hunched a little. "I know the Blackwoods can be a lot, but they have good intentions and they're... well, they're the best family I've ever had."

Across the table, Danny turned slightly toward them, and I suspected that he'd heard the quiet confession as well.

"They're great." Reid sighed. "Much better than my blood family. It's a lot to take in, but I'm glad to have them."

Knox patted him on the back and they rejoined us in time to share hot apple cobbler—fresh from the oven—and ice cream.

By the time the clan members began to arrive and we moved the party to the backyard, I had a full belly, a full heart, and would love nothing more than to cuddle with my mate and share a nap.

Unfortunately, there was business to attend to.

Everett and Garrick lit a fire in the pit to warm those who weren't shifters and therefore naturally immune to the cold. Reid gravitated to it and I hovered behind him—but not in the way because others needed the heat more than I did.

When it came time to introduce the new additions, Dad stood on the deck and raised his voice to gain our attention.

"We have five newcomers to welcome to Grizzly Ridge,"

he called with enough authority in his voice to quiet even the teenagers who'd been tussling on the edge of the woods. "My eldest son, Zander, has been lucky enough to find his fated mate, the warlock Reid Havlock."

Reid huffed. "Blackwood," he muttered. "I don't want that name anymore."

Dad's expression flickered and a grin broke across his face. Reid had spoken quietly but still loud enough to be heard by most shifters. "I stand corrected. Reid Blackwood. We also have four shifter omegas moving into Omega House."

I looked around, wondering if the rescued omegas were present. As soon as I realized that Garrick was fixated on something, I spotted the sassy fox shifter, Kit. He stood with Milo and Danny, but I couldn't see any of the others.

"You'll notice them around town," Dad continued. "They've all suffered an ordeal so please give them grace. Kit is a fox shifter, Olivia and Joy are domestic cat shifters, and Briar is a witch."

"Stop staring," I murmured to Garrick, almost inaudibly. "You've got to get yourself under control. Acting like an alphahole won't get you anywhere with an omega who's been traumatized."

He motioned discreetly toward Kit. "Does he look traumatized? He's fucking magnificent."

"He's been through a lot."

Garrick grunted in acknowledgment.

Dad wrapped up his welcome spiel and those who hadn't shifted started stripping off their clothes to run with the clan in the woods.

Reid turned into my arms and snuggled against me. "You should go."

"I don't want to leave you."

He smiled up at me, his eyes shining brightly in the firelight. "Milo will be with me. We're going to toast marsh-mallows."

My insides turned to mush. "That's good, sweetheart." I loved that he was getting more comfortable with my family. "Are you sure?"

He let me go and ushered me away. "Do your run, Z. I'll be waiting right here."

Milo rounded the firepit and joined him. "We've got this."

They stood side by side, not touching but supporting each other nonetheless.

I kissed my mate. "I love you."

His reply echoed in my ears as I stripped off, changed forms, and bounded into the woods.

I loved my mate, and finally, he loved me too.

EPILOGUE - 4 MONTHS LATER

REID

I reached for a plate on the upper shelves in our kitchen, searching for the last one with my fingertips. I knew there was an extra one somewhere. The others were all in the dishwasher.

Just as I grabbed onto the edge of it, a sharp pain pulsed through my lower back. I instinctively curled in on myself and the plate slipped off the edge of the shelf and smashed on the kitchen floor, breaking into several pieces.

I clutched my belly and whimpered as another pulse stole my breath.

Fuck. I'd known I could go into labor at any time, but I'd been doing my best not to think about what that would actually mean.

I'd have to push a baby out of my body.

Godsdamn, this was going to hurt.

Gritting my teeth through another contraction, I counted how long it lasted and glanced at the clock.

The baby was coming quickly. Faster than I'd expected. Although, in hindsight, I'd had an achy back all morning. I'd put it down to the strain of carrying extra weight, but perhaps I'd been having low-grade contractions and hadn't even realized it.

Zander, I called through the mental connection we'd developed in the months since we'd mated.

Yes, sweetheart?

The smooth tone of his voice in my mind calmed me and I forced myself to straighten and waddle to the bedroom to collect our go bag.

The baby is coming.

As I picked up the duffel bag, an uncomfortable rippling sensation tore through my lower half and I bent over.

Reid? Fortunately, he sounded calm, although it could have been an act for my benefit. *I'll be there soon.*

I tried to drag the duffel bag to the door, but it was too damn awkward so I gave up and looked around for my phone. I might be able to communicate telepathically with Zander, but I didn't have that same connection with the other members of our family.

Where had I put it?

Water soaked my pant leg and I froze. I knew I hadn't peed myself so that must be...

Holy shit. My water just broke.

The front door crashed open and Zander thumped into the house. As he entered the bedroom, his eyes were completely gold, with none of their humanity remaining.

Despite that, he scanned me up and down and—though his nostrils flared as he scented me—he didn't seem too distracted by the more primal side of himself.

He strode over and took the bag from me. "I've got that, sweetheart. Let's get you into the car. What else do you need?"

"My phone." I hated how plaintive I sounded but he just nodded, sniffed, and disappeared from the room, taking the duffel bag with him.

A couple of minutes later, he returned.

"Your phone and the bag are both in the car." He approached me tentatively. "How are you?"

"I'm okay. I—" I cut off as pain throbbed deep inside me. "The baby is in a hurry."

A muscle ticked in Zander's jaw—no doubt his alpha instincts wanting to protect me when there was little he could do other than getting me to the doctor.

He closed the distance between us and scooped me into his arms as if I weighed no more than the duffel bag.

"How far apart are the contractions?" he asked as he carried me through the house and out the front door.

"A couple of minutes, maybe."

Was that bad?

I thought maybe it was.

"It's happening!" someone shouted from across the street. I didn't pay them any attention. It was probably one of the Blackwoods, and I was sure the whole family would be gathered at the medical center soon enough.

Zander set me down carefully in the passenger seat of his car and rushed around the front inhumanly fast, practically throwing himself behind the wheel and screeching away from the curb.

We arrived at the medical center only minutes later, and he zipped around, undid my belt, and raced me into the clinic so quickly that I scarcely had time to breathe.

Either Zander had called ahead or whoever had seen us earlier must have notified Dr. Black because he met us in the small reception area.

"We're taking him to the same room he stayed in last time," Dr. Black said, and Zander nodded and carried me past him and into the small space.

We'd discussed where the birth would happen. I'd been

worried that doing it here might bring back memories from when I'd previously been held in the clinic.

Fortunately, Dr. Black had allowed Nurse Allison to help me redecorate the space with plush toys and pictures of baby animals so that it no longer resembled the makeshift prison ward it had been.

Zander lowered me onto the bed and I clung to his shoulders and stole a kiss before he released me.

"Thank you," I whispered. "Stay with me?"

He pulled up a chair beside me and took my hand. "I'll be right beside you the whole time."

Dr. Black joined us and asked Zander to remove my pants so that he could check my dilation. Meanwhile, he peppered me with questions about how I'd felt all day, when contractions had started, and assured me that no matter how quickly the labor might be progressing, nothing seemed out of the ordinary.

Some shifter births simply happened fast.

Contractions continued to roll through me, closer and closer together. Dr. Black asked me to hold off on pushing so I clenched my teeth, fisted the sheets, and concentrated on breathing until it was time.

When the birth happened, it was over quickly.

All of a sudden, I couldn't resist the urge to push for any longer and an almost unbearable pressure made it both painful to push and to resist. There was nothing I could do to escape the pain but Zander stayed beside me as I sobbed and cursed and brought our baby into the world.

"He's out," Dr. Black told us.

I gasped and flopped against the mattress, aching everywhere but weak with the relief that it was finally over. Dr. Black showed Zander how to cut the umbilical cord and then he tied it off while Nurse Allison cleaned up the baby.

"Is he okay?" I asked, pushing my exhausted body up

onto my elbows. Why wasn't he crying?

"Your little boy is just fine, Daddy," Nurse Allison said, bringing over a pink-faced bundle wrapped tightly in a swaddle.

The baby blinked at me with blue eyes. It was impossible to tell if they'd remain blue or later change to match that of the alpha who'd donated his DNA.

My face crumpled and a tear leaked out as I reached for him. "He's perfect." I turned to Zander, suddenly conscious of the fact that this wasn't actually *his* biological child, as much as we would raise him that way. "Isn't he?"

If I'd worried about Zander rejecting him, then I needn't have. He was staring at the baby as if he was the most incredible thing he'd ever seen.

"I love him already," he rasped, his voice tight with emotion. "Can I hold him?"

Nurse Allison passed him to Zander. "We'll give you two a moment alone."

She and Dr. Black disappeared, but I hardly noticed, too preoccupied with my mate and our son.

"Is he a wolf?" I asked, mesmerized by the tiny hand that reached for Zander. We'd known he had magic, but I hadn't been certain he'd also possess the ability to shift.

"Yes." Zander inhaled and his eyes—which had returned to normal at some point–flashed gold again. "And he smells of magic."

"A warlock wolf shifter."

Zander nuzzled the baby, breathing him in, his chest swelling with alpha pride. "Where do you think the rumors of shamans started?"

"Huh."

Zander came closer and I shuffled as far across the bed as I could go. "Do you think you can support his weight?"

I tested my limbs. They were weary but there was some

life left in them. "Yes."

Cautiously, he settled the baby onto my chest. I wrapped my arms around him and snuggled him close. He was little and big-eyed and the most beautiful thing I'd ever seen.

He made a sound and I tilted his chin up. "What was that, baby?"

He rubbed his lips together and gurgled.

My heart filled to bursting. "Do we still like Luca as a name?"

"He looks like a Luca to me," Zander said. "What do you think?"

I considered it and nodded. "Definitely a Luca. Hi, little Luca. Welcome to the family. Your Papa will get the others so we can introduce you."

Zander went to fetch the others and I made myself comfortable. As the Blackwoods filtered into the room—Melinda and Aaron, Danny and Knox, Milo and Everett, with Garrick taking up the rear—I couldn't stop one last tear from rolling down my cheek.

Growing up, I'd never had the family I wanted. Instead, the people who should have protected me allowed me to be used and abused for the sake of power.

Now, I had all the family I could ever want, and they would never leave me.

"I love you all," I said, gazing down at Luca so I wouldn't have to meet their eyes.

A warm hand landed on my shoulder and the familiar scent of my mate blanketed me. "We love you too, sweetheart."

And all around the room, others echoed his words.

Because finally, I was home.

THE END

310

About the Author

A.J. Cane is a neurospicy, queer author who writes LGBTQIA+ paranormal romance with love interests who will make you swoon. Her special interests include reading, writing, and eating way too much chocolate.